Shadow Ball

SHADOW BALL

A Novel of Baseball and Chicago

by Peter M. Rutkoff

McFarland & Company, Inc., Publishers   *Jefferson, North Carolina, and London*

Shadow Ball is a work of fiction. Names, characters, places, and incidents are the product of the author's imagination or are used fictitiously. Any resemblance to actual events, locales, or persons, living or dead, is purely coincidental.

Library of Congress Cataloguing-in-Publication Data

Rutkoff, Peter M., 1942–
  Shadow ball : a novel of baseball and Chicago / by Peter M. Rutkoff.
      p.   cm
    ISBN 0-7864-0981-9 (softcover : 50# alkaline paper) ∞
    1. Chicago White Sox (Baseball team)—Fiction.   2. African American baseball players—Fiction.   3. Foster, Andrew, 1879–1930—Fiction.   4. Memphis Minnie, 1896–1973—Fiction.   5. Comiskey, Charles A.—Fiction.   6. Baseball players—Fiction.   7. Blues musicians—Fiction.   8. Baseball teams—Fiction.   9. Chicago (Ill.)—Fiction.   10. Riots—Fiction.   I. Title.
  PS3618.U78 S53 2001
  813'.54—dc21   2001020239

British Library cataloguing data are available

Manufactured in the United States of America

Cover images ©2001 Art Today and PhotoSpin

McFarland & Company, Inc., Publishers
  Box 611, Jefferson, North Carolina 28640
    www.mcfarlandpub.com

For D.E.

ACKNOWLEDGMENTS

With appreciation for the works of William Tuttle, Robert Peterson, and Eliot Asinof; for the understanding and critical reading of Jerry Kelly; for the encouragement of Jim Gates and Tim Wiles and the staff of the National Baseball Hall of Fame and Museum; and for the stimulation and friendship of my colleagues at the Cooperstown Symposium on Baseball and American Culture, Pete Peterson, George Grella and Al Hall.

PROLOGUE

The office is small, its leather chairs and sofa as dark as the wood on the desk. And as scarred. Three men huddle together on Chicago's South Side in the summer of 1919. They have been partners for almost three years, yet this is the first time they actually have sat in the same room. Cigar smoke curls from each, hovering in the air just above their heads, a fog whose redolence matches the heat and humidity of mid–July. Despite the sweltering temperatures, the three men wear wool business suits, white shirts, starched collars, and cravats. Each sports a gold ring whose glimmering stone, surrounded by a dozen diamond fragments, tells the world that he is prosperous and successful.

Despite their "sartorial" uniformity (Comiskey loves using big words, Sam remembers) each speaks a different dialect, vernacular representatives of the city's South Side.

"Are you really sure that he'll take the fucking offer?" Comiskey nods toward Rube but never takes his eyes off Sam.

"Sure. As long as you divest yourself of the appropriate emoluments," Rube Foster chuckles.

Time to up the ante, Sam thinks. "What if the other guys don't go along with it?"

"Don't worry about 'em. I'll take care of them, they ain't got crap to play with."

"Big talk," injects Foster, sensing that Comiskey doesn't quite understand. "You know this ain't never been done before, least since that asshole Anson opened his yap."

"Look," Sam says, "I know how you feel. But that was more than thirty years ago. Everything's changed. And once Mr. Comiskey here does it everyone else will be lining up to get theirs. And where will they go? To you, Rube, to you."

"I donno. It still worries me. If this doesn't work we're really in the wilderness. My boys'll never get to play in the majors, and we'll be back barnstorming from one shit-hole tank town to the next, and playing in your old joint. Not that I ain't grateful."

Sam jumps in. He doesn't want Comiskey to answer, not yet.

"I say we gotta take the chance. The time's ripe, the war is over, the world is safe for democracy, we kicked the Kaiser's ass, and Chicago's going to show the majors that this is the way to the future."

Foster throws up his hands, looks at Comiskey. "Okay. Okay. Charlie, how much?"

"Not sure yet, Rube. Whadda ya think, Sam? How much do we pay the first colored guy to sign? How much is it gonna cost me to buy the pennant and be a frigging social revolutionary at the same time? How much, you Jew bastard?"

"Oh, about as much as the salmon mousse you put out for the scribes. Maybe less."

"It better work. If not, we're gonna have a riot on our hands."

1

THE STREET

The sun beat down hard, red. Its glare made the black shadow gliding along the pavement even blacker.

Sam walked silently through the white summer light, his suit coat already limp with the sweat of exertion and anticipation. Not yet noon and still two more stops to make, one on 39th and the other near the Depot. Two miles apart, but the distance seemed like two hundred. The paper in his pocket, the one that Comiskey and Rube signed, just a few sentences. Outrageous and, still, maybe, just maybe possible. In his heart of hearts Sam saw the irony of each. One thing for sure, there would be no easy solution, only tsoris, trouble.

Sam also knew that he was starving. Bad enough it was so damn hot, but the appetizing store he patronized on Western had just raised its prices again. Seventy-five cents for a corned beef sandwich, for god sakes. Just a year earlier the same thing — with mustard on rye with a dill pickle and a blessing from Rabbi Cohen tossed in for good measure — fifty cents. Sam suddenly shifted his gait, hopping to the left just in time to avoid the mound of steaming horse manure. Hard to believe in the twentieth century that horses still pulled wagons down Chicago's streets.

But it was also hard to believe that only forty years earlier the same streets had been rivers of mud, wet and swampy, their filth hardly an improvement over the expanding — no, exploding — slaughterhouses that some polite magnate and his accomplice in the press called the Stock Yards. Sam remembered his parents telling him that they used to cross Halsted Street, just below Maxwell, on wood planks, raised just high enough to clear the gunk of mud and excrement that lined Chicago's streets. It was barely distinguishable, they laughed, though they never would have used that word, from the street they had left in their shtetl in search of the gold paving stones some shyster had assured them awaited their presence in America. Even then Chicago had already mushroomed out of control. Now, in the first year after the war, it was the same, only three times as big, three times as dangerous.

Noon. The summer sun sent trickles of sweat down the front and back of his shirt, and the stench of the streets and the yards drove the hunger from his mind. Sam reached his hand into his jacket pocket and fingered the scrap of paper that Foster and Comiskey had given him an hour earlier. He quickened his pace, his sweat no longer just a trickle, his shirt wet to his skin, as he made his way across 35th Street walking west from Comiskey's office on Federal. For a moment he caught the taste of the breeze that had been blowing in from the lake, from the newly opened beaches between 35th and 39th streets, but all too suddenly Chicago's sodden humid weight overtook him again. No wonder that hundreds of workers from the Yards—Irish, Italians, Lithuanians, Litvaks, Hungarians, Galizianos—had skipped work that day, even risking a week's wages to hiring retaliation by the packing and slaughtering supervisors. No wonder even that the Negro workers from the Belt, some so newly arrived in Chicago that they still lived in the hallways and back stairs of their kin, no wonder that these men, who often only worked when whites didn't or wouldn't show up, walked east to the relief of the beaches instead of west to the shimmering hell of the yards.

It was, he reflected, the kind of day that disorder ruled, when no one played by the rules. It was too hot, the city too charged, for anyone to pretend that one could do business as usual. Besides, who the hell knew what usual was anymore. The world seemed like a blur, always changing, never sure. The city around him, its peoples and its landmarks, in constant motion. Buildings appeared overnight, thrown up in a frenzy of human activity as if the frames of a movie show had been speeded up by some large invisible hand. Prairie became residential suburb almost as quickly as a once vibrant street became a pest hole of tenements and garbage. There was nothing to do but keep on walking.

Following his early meeting with Comiskey and Foster, Sam doubled back to spend the rest of the morning with Rube, who did his usual song and dance trying, and truth be told succeeding, to convince them both that their plan could work. As usual Sam found himself in agreement, and as usual, as soon as he left he found that strange combination of guilt and doubt creeping into his guts. How in the world were they going to pull it off, he wondered, now that they had convinced the old man that the only way to glory, to riches beyond their dreams, was to sign the veteran, Pop Lloyd they called him, to a White Sox contract.

Foster had hardly stirred when Sam reappeared. "Got any danish?" he said, grinning. No matter that they had broken bread discreetly for the past three years and had come to know each other's habits and tastes almost as well as they knew their own. Rube's sweet potato pie and Texas chili was no less tasty than Sam's kishka and mandlebrot. They were even about the same age, had come to Chicago at the turn of the century, and had struggled with the weight of their Southern heritage. "South Poland to South Chicago," Sam had quipped. But there the resemblance ended. Sam knew he was fated to remain short and wiry despite his appetite for the delicacies of his culture, but Foster was as formidable a giant of a man — tall, broad, and strong as an ox — as Sam had ever met.

His neck as wide as his jaw, Rube Foster wore a dark suit, the coat so tightly stretched across his chest that it appeared two sizes too small despite its custom fit. He loved elegance, but his athletic body betrayed him — the tubes of his arms and legs fit with their joints as if they had been assembled. A white starched shirt and cravat over a gold collar pin emphasized the massive musculature of his shoulders as they sloped to the back of his head and neck. A matching handkerchief and a tan golf hat added to his incongruous yet clearly prosperous image. "You are the cat's pyjamas," he smiled to himself that morning as he stuffed the pearl-handled revolver into his waistband. At age 32 Rube Foster knew he had become one of the wealthiest and most respected Negroes in Chicago. And now he dreamed of something more.

Foster's office on 39th and Wentworth, just across from the band box of a ball park that Charlie Comiskey had abandoned, sat smack in the middle of the Black Belt, the strip of Negro residences extending South from 26th between Wentworth and Cottage Grove. Negroes, as Foster knew only too well, had been coming to Chicago for half a century, but during the war more than 50,000 had arrived from the fields and tenant farms of Mississippi, Alabama, and Louisiana. And now they dwelled, and Rube like the way "dwelled" sounded so biblical, in row after row of narrow and mean wood frame houses whose three stories and alley fire escapes held as many families as there were rooms and landings. The massive influx of Southern Negroes had already combined with the greed of real estate speculators to drive the neighborhood's Jewish immigrants out and send the rents skyrocketing. Even Foster's spacious apartment on 55th Street had once been servants' quarters for some hoity-toity family. Within a decade the Black Belt had been carefully extended just far enough south to house and then contain and finally exploit the new migrants who arrived without jobs, without money, without savvy.

Charles Comiskey, whose nickname "the Old Roman" derived from the slope of his generous nose and not from any sense whatsoever of Republican virtue, thought he had carefully gauged the demographic tides of Chicago's South Side. But not carefully enough, no sir, not carefully enough, Foster thought. Comiskey's White Stockings, or White Sox, had played for years on 39th off Wentworth, just within the boundaries of white working-class Chicago. Then, as the Black Belt expanded south Comiskey moved, actually he ran 'bout fast as he could, north and east to 35th and Federal, building his new park and reestablishing his team in a clearly white neighborhood on the other side of the newly constructed, elevated tracks. That Comiskey always knew the bottom line. Hell, he'd once been a player for the classic White Sox of Spaulding and Cap Anson, the "asshole" who had instigated the whole process of baseball Jim Crow. Now he made more money and paid his players less than any other owner in the American League. More than once Rube had overheard the Irish and Polish working men, who managed to watch the Sox on Saturday afternoons before taking their passions to the saloons on Saturday evenings, saying that Comiskey was one of their own. It was, Foster knew, a grudging admiration, a combination of local pride and intense class resentment, with which they held "fucking Comiskey." For they knew far better than anyone that the owner of the White Sox, who told his field manager to deny the team's best pitcher, the doe-eyed Eddie Cicotte, a final start in 1918 in order to prevent him from winning his 30th game and the bonus promised in his contract, was no different from the lords of Packingtown. No, the Stock Yard barons, the half-dozen owners of the companies that made up Packingtown, in whose dingy and drafty company houses the workers lived "back of the yards" along Ashland and Western avenues, had become wealthy beyond all imagination because they knew that to really screw their workers they had to cooperate.

And cooperate they did. Wages magically remained fixed in the yards. So did prices and hours. Armour never bid more for a man's labor than did Swift. And Comiskey, who willingly paid exorbitant sums for his players' contracts, never paid them more than McGraw of the Giants. Even that hick Joe Jackson, who could barely sign his name even if he did hit over .400 his first year in the majors, barely made more than an accountant at Sears and Roebuck. Jackson and Cicotte, Comiskey's two biggest stars, appealed to the men who lived "back of the yards" who worked their balls off packing and butchering for Armour and Swift. As much as he resented their privilege, Foster also granted them the admiration they were due. "Never turn your back on the white folks," his father, E.F., had told him long ago. "They got lots to teach you."

But the Old Roman had outsmarted himself. "I tell you, Sam," Foster said one day, "he's too smart for his own self. Greedy like a fox, I'd say." By the war's end the influx of Negroes from the South had become a mass movement, and Comiskey Park now occupied a neutral zone between the Black Belt and the Back of the Yards, between the white and black working class neighborhoods that defined Chicago's South Side. Bridgeport and Hamburg, home to Irish and German workers and their vibrant political clubs and taverns, was less than a twenty minute walk to Bronzeville, newly centered at 35th and State just east of Comiskey's new park.

So, less than ten years after building his South Side palace, Comiskey stood at the crossroads of working class Chicago. He had managed to fit his grand stadium into the rhythm of the city's grid. Its symmetry was a function of the block on which it stood. Perhaps Comiskey took his Roman nickname seriously when he commissioned the park's architects. He had them build a park that took something from the Loop's style. Its glass and brick windows encased in arches that Louis Sullivan might have endorsed gave the ball park its architectural distinctiveness, or as Comiskey once told Sam, its "fucking class."

Sam paused briefly in front of the brick ticket kiosks that guarded the glass and concrete entrance to Comiskey's park and office. The Sox were off that day — they were on their way back from St. Louis, due at the Central Station by mid-afternoon, and despite the heat, he had a moment to savor the grandeur of the ball grounds. Imagine, he mused to himself, less than a decade ago this place had been, literally, a garbage pit, a heap, a dump on the South Side where vermin and children from the Belt vied with each other for scraps. And now, just last week in fact, as Swede Risberg pawed the infield with his left spike, shouting, "Okay Eddie, stick it in his fucking ear," the bantam shortstop suddenly called time. And to the bewilderment of the umpire behind the plate, he bent down to exhume a blue enameled coffee pot. It had been buried, or rather had somehow risen from the bowels of the earth to just beneath the surface of the infield skin, there for the Swede to discover it like some valuable artifact, a treasure of a ruined civilization. Flecked with white, the cobalt blue pot glinted in the afternoon sun for a moment before Swede gave it a kick, sending it toward the White Sox dugout.

Afterward the players commented that the pot revealed everything one needed to know about Comiskey. Not only, they snickered, did the old man come running out of the not-so-secret office behind the left field stands to claim the pot, but he had turned around and sold it to some pasty-faced Jew bastard for three hundred dollars. Sam knew all about the story. He was the Jew bastard who had bought the pot. When he told Foster about it afterward, Rube just looked at him and smiled before he rolled his eyes. Foster had, in his time, paid more to Comiskey, and received far less.

Of course, when Swede, who had lost his salary campaign in January when Comiskey had refused to give him a two percent raise that would have made him the next-to-worst paid player on the team, heard about the sale of the pot he quickly realized that "his" find would have more than made up for the raise Comiskey didn't give him. At the time, just before spring training, Comiskey had smiled benignly at Swede, puffing on one of his cigars, and said, "Of course if you don't want to accept the contract I can always find another team — in the minors, say in South Dakota, that will be glad to avail themselves of your services." Swede, hardly college material, not like that snotty overeducated Collins, got Comiskey's drift. Working guys like him were screwed. Play the game and keep your trap shut, or else it's out the door.

Sam had wandered over to Maxwell Street, shaking his head to himself as Swede's vulnerability sank in, to locate Louie, a fence with whom he had once done business. A part-time bookie, amateur pawn broker, and full time gonoff, Louie was short, chomped unlit cigars, and wore his grey pants below the overhang of his belly. He had grey hairs sprouting from all the openings of his head, never smiled, and had the pallor of a long-term prison inmate — which he had been for more than a decade. Louie now devoted himself to helping others. Sam asked only the three hundred he had invested, saying something inane like, "It's a genuine antique, you know, the kind my mother, bless her soul, had on the stove." Louie spoke directly at Sam's shoes. "Yea, and she pissed in it too. Every night. Twenty-five bucks." It took about three more passes for Sam to Jew him up to fifty. Louie peeled five tens off the roll he kept in his left pants pocket and let them fall into Sam's outstretched hand, like cards from a sliced deck.

Sam knew full well that the damn pot might fetch double that in the black market alleys Louie commanded, but he also figured that one day Comiskey would compensate him for his loss. It was, he reflected, a kind of investment, one laced with humiliation, but an investment nevertheless. He and Foster had been playing that game with Comiskey for a decade. And it was difficult to know who was better at it, the black man or the Jew. Time, he thought, for payback.

Sam's footfalls echoed through the deserted walkways as he made his way from the main entrance of the park, just behind home plate, around the infield, past third base to the hidden doorway, just past the "Gents" room, whose staircase lead to Comiskey's secret office above left field. He thought briefly about taking a leak but the idea of using the open troughs made him laugh — too much like feed containers at Packingtown. He knew that Comiskey's private john was so luxurious that the toilet practically wiped your tochus for you. He also knew the gold-gilt fixtures that held the towels cost Comiskey more than the raise that the Old Roman couldn't bring himself to grant to Swede.

Comiskey once bragged to Sam that he had built his park in 1910 to reflect not only the social aspirations of his paying customers, but to remind them that his was a palace for the rich and a carnival for everyone else. His concrete and steel grandstand curved gracefully around the infield, its covered upper deck protecting his classy clientele from the ravages of the elements. Beyond first and third base the grandstand leveled to a single deck and then emptied, in fair territory, into 7,000 wooden bleacher seats which Comiskey sold to the faithful for two bits a crack. Remarkable, Sam admitted. The whole damn thing had taken barely five months to build, from ceremonial shovel to opening day. Comiskey Park seated 32,000 fans, Chicagoans who walked east from their neighborhoods on the old South Side, from Bridgeport and Back of the Yards. Less than a mile away, the White Sox's old place, South Side Park with its rickety seating that accommodated 15,000 Negroes on a sunny Sunday, now served as home to Foster's team, the Chicago American Giants. And that, mused Sam, that was the rub.

He pushed the steel door in. The hallway smelled like Comiskey's aftershave, rich and astringent at the same time, a relief from the residue of popcorn and sausage that wafted through the entire park, riding the summer humidity like a riff, unmistakable and pungent. Comiskey's office was one flight up and Sam negotiated the stairs slowly, careful to put his suit jacket back on, not sure, as always, how he'd find the old man. He half expected him to say, "Well, if it isn't my messenger boy. What you got for me kid?"

And he half expected to find that Comiskey, in just a few hours, decided to renege on the plan. "I'm thinking, Sam. I'm thinking that this Pop Lloyd. What do we know about him. Nuttin. Cut him loose. We'll win anyway."

Comiskey exercised power with great relish. Bristling and pompous one minute, generous the next, Comiskey, in either costume, always let Sam know he was the boss. To step on his prerogatives, to presume to know, think, or advise, was to invite the most politely worded "fuck off" that Sam had ever heard. Those who would traffic with the Old Roman could only hope to do so within the limits of the rules that Comiskey set, amended, and validated. Daily. Sam's modest success derived from his immigrant's ability to trust his gut, to read Comiskey's state of mind from the sound of his voice or the lift of his eyebrow.

His gut, however, didn't prepare Sam for the grunts and howls that greeted him when he walked into Comiskey's outer office. The generous room, all leather and polished brass, smelling of cigars and aftershave, lay deserted. The dark green carpet, plush and worn at the same time, was the loudest thing in the room. On the polished mahogany desk, where Comiskey's secretary usually sat fielding her boss's requests, barked with the command of a general late for tea, one of Louis Tiffany's lamps, its red and blue leaded glass glowing softly, set the stage. Sam thought he recognized all the signs. Invitation, even seduction. He also knew full well that Comiskey had not prepared the table for him. Another guest had been invited, and Sam smelled her perfume in the wake of her muffled cries.

Downtown, at the Loop, Sam found it impossible, simply impossible to cross State Street at noon. The crowds of commuters, laborers, merchants, lifters, fitters, and tourists, competing with trolleys, trams, wagons, cars, carts, trucks, and omnibus, were loud enough to raise the dead — and the iron squealing of the el could drown 'em all out. Sparks fell like shooting stars on the throngs that pressed in and around Sam's shoulders. Cobblestoned streets clamored with the roars of combustion engines, the hollow echo of horses' hooves, and the cursing, panting agitation of the city's humanity. Hundreds of thousands of passengers a day, Italians from Cicero, Germans from Division Street, Irish from Belmont, Lithuanians from Marquette Park, Poles from Halstead

Street, Jews from Maxwell Street, businessmen from Riverside and Hyde Park, and shop girls from north of Fullerton, descended on the Loop. Organized bedlam, orchestrated chaos, ruled Chicago that red hot summer of 1919.

Money, commerce, trade, energy, and competition converged downtown, the accompaniment of masses of Chicagoans who swelled the city's arteries, pumping the streets up with sweat and desire.

Sam knew full well that Chicago, and State Street, had become the center of the nation's commercial and industrial explosion. The older, magnificent and graceful buildings, the Rookery, Monadnock, and even Adler and Sullivan's elegant Auditorium, now seemed quaint, precious, next to the commercial emporiums of plate glass and steel that stretched along the avenue. Gothic arches, rough hewn blocks of brownstone and art deco appointments had given way to functional spaces and unadorned sand and limestone facades. Awnings sprouted to shield the huge display windows from the glare of too much light lest the shopping matrons from the suburbs of Oak Park and Evanston or even the near South Side be distracted from their tasks. Sam wondered, as he reached down into his pocket to make sure that the paper was still there, if anyone in Chicago was really concerned about the amount of sun that, no doubt accidentally, filtered down into the Loop. Between the sidewalk-hugging buildings, which singly or together simply massed themselves along an entire avenue, and the el, there was precious little room for sunlight. Yes, Michigan Avenue, its cultural and artistic face turned east to the lake, from the entrance of the Chicago River south toward the new lake front beaches near Jackson Park, stood in the clear. But the dozen train tracks, freight and passenger, of the Santa Fe and Rock Island lines still barricaded the avenue from the lake, making it a part of the hurly burly of the Loop and not yet the glittering entry way to the pleasure of the shoreline. Light remained a precious commodity for downtown Chicago, a commercial city teeming with all the polyglot nervousness of men and women in a hurry, on the prowl, eager to work, ready to make a buck.

Intersections, like the ones at State and Madison or Dearborn and Randolph, proved especially impassable during rush hour. Trolleys and lumber wagons, horse drawn carts and chauffeured cars competed with pedestrians for space, inch by agonizing inch, cutting off Sam from his destination. Vehicles slowed but never halted the unremitting river of congestion which during rush hour concentrated almost a million souls in an area less than a mile square. The Boston Store at State, Madison and Dearborn, just up from Marshall Field's, and Carson, Pirie Scott added seventeen stories of vast commercial space in 1915 to an intersection which was already regarded as the most crowded in the world. Holabird and Roach, who had designed the elegant and pro-portioned Rookery twenty years earlier, now forsook all attempts to blend the commercialism of the Chicago style with the traditions of decorative ornamentalism and created a massive structure whose function was its form. It was as if they had shorn Adler's Carson, Pirie Scott of its organic, curving, and decorous entry in favor of a few more feet of well-planned, rationally plotted selling space. By 1915 those who built the Boston Store would have found the Grecian columns in front of the main entrance at Marshall Field's an unspeakable extrav-agance. And Field's, where Sam ducked in briefly before resuming his search for John Henry Lloyd, had only been a State Street landmark since 1902.

2

RIDING THE RAILS

What few Chicagoans knew or realized during that swarming and steamy summer of 1919 was that their city, its central Loop as dense as any city could ever hope to be, actually sat atop a subterranean world whose buried and invisible existence allowed even the creepingly slow activity on the surface above. Forty odd feet beneath the grid of the Loop lay a parallel world belonging to the Chicago Tunnel Company.

The Tunnel System, where Lloyd labored, was a honeycombed light rail network that delivered packages to the commercial world above. The System transported excavation materials from building sites, and dumped mountains of ash and garbage at four reviving depots beyond the fringe of the Loop. With sixty miles of two-foot-gauge electric lines, the underground city had a force of 40,000 teamsters who labored in tunnels barely high enough to stand in. Daily, the invisible work force underground fed the insatiable demand for goods and services, for commerce and consumption on the streets above. Good unionists, the Polish and Italian teamsters who manned the tunnel's 117 miniature locomotives that hauled three thousand open wooden carts, belonged to the American Federation of Labor, the AF of L, whose trade-unionism was both resourceful and careful in the first year of the post-war economy.

As Chicago's commerce radiated along State Street's command of the Loop, the els screaming above, and the freight trains gliding silently below, testified to the compression of energy and people that made the city so tough and uncontrollable.

The war had been good to both social layers of the Loop. The grizzly mutilation of millions in Europe had set American industry in furious motion. Chicago's factories poured out the steel casings and tinned meat, the uniforms and artillery shells consumed by war. Massive devastation four thousand miles away meant more jobs, higher wages, longer hours. Chicago grew heavy with the profits of war. White collar above ground and blue in the parallel city below found themselves bound by an invisible commonality, the ever expanding commerce of Chicago's extraordinary wartime production. For those below, moreover, the combination of industrial explosion and the draft meant an ever increasing shortage of skilled and semi-skilled workers.

Once only regarded as strike-breakers, the new Negro migrants to Chicago's South Side found, often for the first time, real work during the war. Some discovered that the lords of Packingtown would hire them to work in Negro units, as carters or slaughterers; others, like Pop Lloyd, worked beneath the loop.

The carts and engines that clattered over the narrow gauge tracks of Chicago's underground city served as the arteries of commerce, opening the passage between the retail emporia on the surface and their wholesale distributors on the outskirts of the Loop. Three massive warehouse depots and a huge cache of coal for heating stood just beyond the confines of the Loop, small cities in themselves, comprising long and narrow buildings whose side walls opened along motorized tracks, like those on the side of a cattle car, to empty their never depleted stocks of goods into the delivery carts which swarmed in and out of the mechanized openings. This process of feeding and replenishing went on around the clock, so gargantuan was the commercial appetite of the city. The small wagons and lifts that sped from warehouse to the miniature subway loading docks produced a continual racket of two-cylinder engine noise and exhaust whose din could be heard for a mile in any direction. When added to the smoke and soot and clanks and whistles of the never-ending Illinois Central, Rock Island and Santa Fe freights that hourly brought in goods from the four corners of the continent, the cacophony that rose from Chicago's four depots numbed the mind, blinded the senses.

Men grunted and cursed in the summer heat as they steered, then loaded and finally disgorged the factory made coats and dresses, the mass produced veneer furniture and cast iron wash tubs, the carpets and linoleum that tumbled from the rows of skids that lined each of the hundreds of warehouses. Each depot looked like a vast army encampment, its neat rows of storage buildings forming streets and alleys, surrounded by barbed wire, cornered by three story watchtowers.

Of the four great depots, in fact, one belonged to the United States Army, the Chicago Quartermaster Headquarters, which the government designated USGHQ-ChIll, the "Chilli." The men like Lloyd who worked there, the drivers and loaders, the civilian employees who moved the goods from train to shed and from shed to the honeycombed underground net beneath the Loop's streets, simply called it the "shit-hole." Located south of the Loop, along the rectangle which commenced at 22nd and Western, the shit-hole was subterranean Packingtown, a world unto itself.

And if the Reileys and Murphys who made up its uniformed force of staff sergeants and quartermaster supply officers had only to hop the trolley from their homes in Bridgeport, the civilian workers, almost all Negro, had but a short walk from their kitchenettes and tenements that dotted the northern fringes of the Black Belt.

In the summer of 1919, almost a year after the end of the Great War, the U.S. Army Quartermaster Depot in Chicago was so crammed full of surplus gear, greatcoats and gas masks, puttees and tin helmets, khaki undershorts and unstamped dog tags that it was bursting at the seams. Such was the momentum of American production that eight months after the Armistice the nation's factories continued to send out material in record quantity.

John Henry Lloyd could hardly stand the heat. The only respite, he knew, was the cool of the subterranean tunnels which awaited his tram when he finished unloading the flat-backed jerry rigged truck filled with woolen blankets that some wise-assed and white-faced sergeant had told him to send to the soup kitchen up on the northwest side. Just what they need, mused Lloyd, some new Negroes just off the train from Clarksdale and Memphis, with no jobs, no places to live — it bein' the hottest day of the year. And we give 'em surplus puke green blankets.

The sweat trickled down his forehead, droplets running past the barrier of the bandana he had just wrung out and into his eye. Lloyd cursed at no one in particular, looked up at the noon sun, and said, "Fuck. I'm thirty-four years old. Doin' this. Doin' it for money. Not playin' ball. Fuck."

His name, John Henry, had been bestowed by his parents, sharecroppers in Mississippi, themselves born slaves, in honor of the fabled spike driver. Imagine, Lloyd thought, people sing about my namesake. About work, and love, and death. More sweat, and another idea interrupted. Several years back, Lloyd had managed to put away enough money to go home to Clarksdale and visit his family in the Delta. One evening they had taken him to a backwoods juke joint, its clapboards green with mildew and kudzu, where local folks gathered to sip and listen in the summer evening. Lloyd remembered it like yesterday. A young skinny fellow, all sinew and elbows, his skin dark chocolate and his eyes deep with sorrow, began playing a song he called "Spike Driver Blues."

John Hurt played the Delta blues, so he fit the story "John Henry was a steel drivin' man" into its pattern, rhyming and repeating, 'til the tale was told. His voice husky with the sounds of rolled cigarettes and gin, Mississippi John played his ancient guitar with a pulse that seemed to come from way inside him. As his voice slid though the words, "Kaint kill me, kaint kill me," Hurt moved the three fingers on his right hand with exquisite economy. His thumb kept the beat, alternating between the two top thick stings, while his first and second fingers danced the melody into the steady pulse of the thumb. To John Henry Lloyd, it was like two hands playing at the same time, jumping, making him want to tap his feet and his hand, "Honey 'til I'm home, honey 'til I'm home."

John Henry Lloyd wiped the midday sweat again from his eyes. It had been a marvel to him at the time that someone like John Hurt sang about someone with his name. John Henry was flattered that night at the juke joint, and whenever he found himself working so hard that he wasn't sure he could continue, like now, he thought about the song that bore his name. The blues and work, the blues and the South, the blues and death. John Henry, carrying and sweating that hot and humid day in Chicago in 1919, was a damn far way from home.

One of the sergeants, a red faced string bean of a fellow named O'Hare, took off his flat brimmed hat and looked at John Henry. They were both standing in the shadows at the entrance to the building where the blankets stood folded, hundreds each square yard, from floor to ceiling.

"Lloyd," the sergeant said.

"Yes."

"I want you to take off the next half hour and go bring us back a case of River Beer. Casey's got the stuff chilled in the walk in. Take a couple of bottles, like usual, before you bring it over to the hut."

O'Hare had always been this way with John Henry. Treated him decent but always made it clear who was boss and why. Lloyd had become used to O'Hare's style. For a white man he wasn't all bad. It amazed him, when he thought about it, that such a skinny kid of a man, all ruddy and bones, a man at least ten years younger than he, could exercise such power over black folks. Yet, unmistakably Lloyd acknowledged that the man's very white–Irishness bred in him a furious combination of envy and resentment that translated itself into deference. O'Hare commanded and Lloyd, for the price of a couple of bottles of beer, did his bidding. "Yessir," he always said, careful not to let his feelings show. Sure, the war and the chance to make some real money had something to do with it. Regular work, regular pay, some overtime made it possible to move out of his old South Side tumble-down frame house into a newer apartment building on 37th and Indiana. Couple of rooms, a good stove, real furniture, these all signified to Lloyd that he had made something of himself. But he sure missed the team, even missed Foster.

Three blocks from the depot Lloyd knocked on the back door of the tavern. It pushed open easily and the puff of rancid air, a mixture of stale beer, cigarette smoke and a dash of urine, greeted Lloyd. "Hey Pop. The case is here, got it out for you. I'll keep your two inside for later. By the way, a fellow inside wants to talk with you. Come in, you can sit in the back." Not at the bar, John Henry thought. Clancy, like O'Hare, wasn't a bad fellow, but he sure wasn't about to challenge Chicago custom. The thing is, Lloyd realized, that the rules which governed who could live, work, eat, drink, and fuck allowed him and the white bosses, sergeants, barkeeps, and women to dance without actually touching. Their codes—down South they had 'em too—and Lloyd was under no illusion as to who made them and who upheld them, preserved the power and prerogatives of whites and only the illusion of dignity of Negroes. Of course he knew that underneath, the women and men whose lack of wealth might have bound them together existed on a volcano of fear and resentment.

Silently screaming, "Fuck you, motherfucker," Lloyd responded, "Okay. I can take a couple of minutes to talk with the guy," and followed Clancy into the back of the bar. Next to the hole in the floor that served as urinal and drain, John Henry "Pop" Lloyd, civilian teamster for the United States Army Quartermaster Corps in Chicago, pulled up a chair and sharply drew closed the curtain that transformed the john into Clancy's back room.

Lloyd had been at these meetings before. Some guy wanted him to do, get, trade, fence, inform, something or someone. He thought of saying, "Get your own damn hemp," but usually he complied, politely.

Sam entered the toilet room at Clancy's less in fear than in trepidation. After all his dealing with Foster it was neither a mystery nor a source of discomfort to be with Negroes. And, goodness knows, Pop Lloyd, well he was something special. Had been playing for the Chicago American Giants since 1914 when Foster had lured him from New York to play shortstop and hit cleanup in a lineup that included Oscar Charleston, Bingo DeMoss, and Bruce Petway. Lloyd had earned about four grand a year with the Chicago Americans, almost as much as Comiskey's gang, and a lot more than black and white workers in Packingtown.

Lloyd had, Sam realized, the kind of open and amiable face that made whites relax. His smile, large and genuine, lit up his broad face, and his eyes, even when considering, as he did now, the unfathomable, seemed alert and friendly. To encounter him in the back urinal of Clancy's was to meet a warm and convivial man who was also baseball's, at least Negro baseball's, premier line drive hitter and the fiercest competition this side of Ty Cobb. But unlike the Georgia bigot, Lloyd left his fire on the field, holding his own inner counsel to himself. Sam had seen Lloyd play on numerous occasions, most of the last season for Foster's team in fact, and marveled at Lloyd's ability to transform himself in a split second from a relaxed and conversational fellow into a man burning with the desire to win. A left-handed batter, Lloyd, who wore his dark stockings long from ankle to knee, would stand at the plate, the picture of nonchalance, the bat cradled, almost lovingly, in the crook of his left elbow. Then, as the ball spun and dove toward the plate Lloyd uncoiled and wiped his bat, flat and hard, driving the offending ball back through the pitcher.

Even in his thirties, a time when lesser players had already begun to slow, Lloyd hit the cover off the ball.

"You shoulda seen him," Foster had told Sam, "a regular Achilles, he played for me, on three champeenship teams, no, four, '14, '15, '16 and '17. And you know what," and Foster pushed his finger into Sam's chest, "you know what, mister big shot lawyer. He hit .350," Foster paused, "once, in 1915. The other years he did better."

Remarkably, Lloyd's greatness stemmed not from his hitting, but from his extraordinary ability in the field. One day at one of Comiskey's famous spreads, which the Old Roman regularly fixed for visiting owners and member of the press, Sam overheard the new owner of the Philadelphia team extol Lloyd's praises. The owner-manager of the Phils, a lanky Irishman with the unlikely name of Cornelius McGillicuddy, whom everyone called Connie Mack, was as tight as Comiskey with the salaries of his players, and as generous as Foster with his words. In between munches of cold roast beef and salmon, as Comiskey obsequiously filled Mack's champagne glass anew, the Phillies' owner offered his opinion of major league shortstops, and stopped with Honus Wagner, the preeminent player of the century. But then he paused and said, "You could put Wagner and Lloyd in a bag together, and which ever one you pulled out you couldn't go wrong." When Wagner, on the eve of retirement, heard of the comparison, he said with his own brand of generosity, "I am honored to have John

Lloyd called the Black Wagner. It is a privilege to have been compared with him."

Wagner, Sam knew, had hit over .300 for the Pirates every season between 1900 and 1914, and even in 1917 was still going strong. And like Lloyd, the Flying Dutchman had gained his real fame for his prowess in the field. With hands as big as hamhocks, Wagner's strength was unsurpassed. Sam knew that Lloyd was no less impressive as a shortstop. Like almost all of Foster's ball players, Lloyd played in the Cuban leagues every winter, and the adoring fans of that Caribbean island had bestowed on him the nickname "El Cuchara" — the shovel — in respect for his ability to dig hard-hit balls out of the notoriously difficult Cuban infields. The dirt in Ponce and San Juan, the players reported, was so thick with gravel and debris that Lloyd had to toss a handful of the stuff along with the ball to the first baseman. In 1918, however, when Wagner began his first summer in retirement, John Henry Lloyd decided to continue working for the Army, underground, beneath the surface of Chicago. It paid better than Foster, and Lloyd need the bread, bad.

Lloyd's smile hid his unease, Sam realized, as the two men looked at each other across the wooden barrel that served as the table in Clancy's back room. Even Sam, who crossed Chicago's racial divide more easily than most, perhaps because he really didn't fit in with either, understood that Lloyd's grin only masked suspicion.

"How are you, Pop?" he inquired.

"Not so bad," Lloyd replied, "not so bad, 'cept I miss playing. For Rube, for the Side, for myself."

"Well, that's just what I came to talk with you about, that's just what I wanted to discuss."

Sam took the paper from his pocket and put it between them.

"Comiskey wants you to play for the Sox this year."

"What Sox is that?"

"You know, the White Sox."

"Listen, mister. Don't be bullshitting me. I been at this too long. It's too important to me."

"Mr. Lloyd, I'd really appreciate if you'd think this over. Take some time if you wish. But, Rube Foster thinks it's a great opportunity. For you. For us. For your people."

Lloyd looked deep into Sam's eyes, as if to say, who is this white man who calls me Mr. Lloyd. "Well, I don't know 'bout my people. But if Rube's behind this, I believe I'll give it some thought. Yes I will."

With that he took the paper and disappeared. Felt as if Lloyd just sucked it into that big palm of his, Sam told Foster later.

On the edge of Lake Michigan, on Park Row, just east of 11th, the largest of Chicago's four railroad terminals, the Central Station of the Illinois Central reached its protective arms over the flood of new arrivals who disembarked daily. Central Station stood at the hub of Chicago's interconnected spokes of steam rail, elevated, trolley, horse, and cable car lines that crisscrossed the city and the county. Completed in 1892, the station, its clock tower a sentinel to the power of standardization and industry, commanded the shore of Lake Michigan. Massive and monumental, the Central housed the offices, the bureaucracy, of the city's most important rail link. The Central lacked the charm of the Chicago and North Western Depot to the west, along Kinzie Street, whose gingerbread turrets and gables made it look like a transplanted Bavarian relic. The Central Station depot, in fact, housed four tenants, including the New York Central lines that connected Chicago to the East. In mid-winter, as the ice formed and cracked on the lake, shipping came to a frozen halt. The vapor of the massive steam engines which crawled and howled in and out of the black roofed train shed seemed to freeze even as they bellowed from the churning and straining pistons.

But the Central Station belonged to the South. Illinois Central trains daily disgorged hundreds of passengers who had commenced their journeys northward in a hundred cities along the Mississippi. From New Orleans and Muscle Shoals, from Memphis and St. Louis, from Clarksdale and Natchez, Negroes plunked down their dollars, in paper and silver, for the long ride to the city, to new jobs, to new opportunities. Copies of the Chicago *Defender* tucked under their arms, the new migrants, many recruited by the organized Pullman and Sleeping Car Porters of A. Philip Randolph, emerged at Central Station half expecting that they had arrived in Canaan. In 1917 the *Defender* had proclaimed, "Northern Invasion Will Start in Spring—Bound for the Promised Land." In overalls and calico, carrying burlap sacks and live chickens, the grandchildren of slaves arrived in Chicago during the first year of America's entry in the Great War.

On the same day that Sam and Pop Lloyd began their discussion of Foster's great scheme, the Chicago White Sox, variously called the White Stockings or the Black Sox (the latter in homage to Comiskey's refusal to launder their home uniforms with anything close to the regularity with which he proffered roast beef and sparkling wine), arrived at Central Station on the Limited from St. Louis.

During the last weekend in July 1919, the most powerful team in organized baseball had demolished the hapless St. Louis Browns in three straight games at Sportsman's Park. Even with the wins, most players on the White Sox found that games in St. Louis were depressing affairs. The Browns averaged barely 2,000 fans a game in 1919, and the humidity of mid-summer provided little enticement, even with the league-leading Sox in town, to enlarge that number. Notorious for its Jim Crow seating, as baseball's Southern-most city, St. Louis—along with Washington, D.C.—allowed colored patrons only in the bleachers and outfield pavilion, not in the grandstand. Half a day's ride on the IC to the north, Chicago's municipal ordinances would have never tolerated the distinctions of legal segregation. In fact, of course, the city was no less divided.

The City of New Orleans chugged and screeched slowly to a halt at Central Station. The six-hour ride from St. Louis, Negroes in the trailing coach cars and the White Sox, their admirers, the "working press," and assorted hangers on in the leading Pullman and club cars, had taken the City of New Orleans straight up the Mississippi and then sharply east to the city. The IC rails cut into Chicago at 38th Street and crossed the Chicago River's west branch at Grand Avenue before merging with the Atchison, Topeka, and Santa Fe line at Pittsburgh Avenue. As the train moved steadily east and north toward the depot downtown, the players could see the outline of their, well, Comiskey's park, to the right before pulling into the station precisely eleven minutes later.

Sam stood on the platform waiting. It was mid-afternoon. Lloyd had returned to work without giving him an answer, and now it was his job to make sure that all the players had actually made the trip from St. Louis. He watched from the shade of the overhang of the station roof as the train crept slowly into its berth, its own momentum slowed by the enormous weight of the string of deep red cars, their gold-gilt letters proclaiming, "Illinois Central." Porters in black suits and red caps scurried, pushing, pulling their wooden baggage carts on iodized greenish wheels along the knobbed concrete station platform. Even before the train stopped, a parade of uniformed conductors, as if one, opened the doors at the ends of each railway car and tossed out, precisely four feet ahead of their positions, small black footstools which landed exactly where the door would be when the train came to a halt.

Railway car windows snapped open and men and women let their belongings clatter to the ground, each an accompaniment to the symphony of sounds from entire platoons of porters and conductors. It was, Sam mused, a wonderfully and carefully unrehearsed ritual, one whose patterns and parts each of the players knew at some level just below consciousness.

As was his habit, and according to Comiskey's orders, "Kid" Gleason, a weathered man in his early 50s, hopped down from the Sox's club car first. Like his players, Gleason, a short man with a grey crop of very closely cut hair, had dressed for the season. He wore his pants cinched up high on his waist, and his shirt, long-sleeved and striped, blue with a touch of tan, stuck to his back, a souvenir of the hot train ride. The rest of the Sox followed, and as usual, Sam could see the two groups. Second baseman Eddie Collins, Columbia-educated and one of the highest paid men in the American League, led what Sam called to himself the North Siders. It wasn't that they actually lived north of the Loop, but their very standing — proper, prosperous, clean-living — led Sam to associate them with Chicago's middling classes. Men in their late twenties and early thirties, the North Siders kept to themselves, hobnobbed with the press and avoided the "shady" characters who had attached themselves to professional baseball since the game's inception.

In contrast, Risberg, Cicotte, Joe Jackson, and a half-dozen others led by Chick Gandil were distinctly South Side. Rough and snarly, these working-class men labored under the limits of inadequate education, bad debts, and Comiskey's unerring instinct for making the most of their weaknesses. They might just as well have been, Sam mused, the South Side Joes who came to Sox games on the weekends fresh (ha, Sam smiled at his own ironic inner speech) from their jobs in the Yards. Tough characters, these South Siders hated Comiskey with a vengeance, resenting his ostentation and his tight-fistedness. They were, Sam thought, ready to explode. And he wondered how in the world they would react to his plan.

Leaning against one of the iron pillars that stood midway between the twin tracks that shared the station's middle platform, Sam remained in the shadows. If any of the players noticed him they didn't acknowledge his presence. Sam preferred it that way. Oh, the Sox knew that he had some kind of business relationship with Comiskey. But with the exception of third baseman Buck Weaver — who often greeted him with a friendly "How's it hangin'?" — none of players seemed to know that Sam was someone with a name and a place that he called home. Most, if they thought of him at all, thought of him as "that Jew bastard."

As the players filed by in twos and threes, arguing over how hard Joe Jackson had hit his home run the night before, or arranging to share a cab back to their hotels and homes along the near South Side, Sam wondered how they managed to play together. Second baseman Collins never spoke with his infield teammates, Risberg, the shortstop, or with Gandil at first. Never. Some kind of bad blood that derived from Collins' lucrative contract. It was, Sam figured, a kind of social resentment, one which Comiskey fomented by pitting his players against each other — something he knew how to do all too well. Even Joe Jackson, as sweet and simple man as one could hope to find, even Joe Jackson who could barely sign his name, seemed to seethe with resentment. How, Sam wondered rhetorically, could the best pure hitter in baseball be angry at anyone or anything? Then he remembered Lloyd.

The players disappeared into Central Station's waiting room and Sam lifted his head, seeing now, not just observing, the train's other passengers as they walked down the platform toward the station. Chester Wilkins, the head Red Cap, a man Sam had come to know well over the years, sauntered up. Wilkins spoke slowly, nodding toward the stream of men and women in overalls and house dresses, "See, they don't even know where they are going." A member of the board of directors of Chicago's Urban League, Wilkins, a middle-aged Negro who had worked at Central Station since its opening almost thirty years earlier, always took it on himself to pick out the most disoriented looking person on each train. He could spot them in an instant.

"Your boss," Wilkins spoke softly to Sam, "tells me he be needin' some lil' gal to hold his trays. Maybe I'll tell Mz. Binga 'bout that one."

Sam followed Wilkins' gaze down the platform. In the wake of the White Sox's sauntering vitality, scores of Negroes, the latest transport, walked slowly toward the waiting room. They struggled with cardboard valises and assorted bundles of food and bedding, arms bulging at the elbow as they tried to carry their lives with them in a single haul. Many huddled in small groups, families Sam was sure, with young children tugging at already occupied parents' hands, their faces open with a combination of wonder and fear.

Sam saw her a split second after Wilkins. He watched as Wilkins straightened his back, shifting his weight away from the pillar he had shared with Sam. Sam was still taking her in as Wilkins moved toward the young woman, hand out, and mouth open, saying, "Say, there, you look lost."

∾ ∾

Lizzie Douglas looked up. She felt incredibly tired. As tired as the day was long, she told herself. And it bein' mid-summer. Wearily she hoisted to her shoulder the large burlap bag, its worn red and blue lettering, "iscut Company," barely legible. Then she sagged and felt her eyes glaze over. The fatigue numbed her finger tips. With all her effort she reached her other hand down and picked up the scarred black cardboard case which she had leaned against her leg. "Oh, my," she said to herself. "My oh, my. How'm I ever gonna do this." Unlike the sack, the box had a makeshift handle, a rope which she had knotted and twisted in Helena to make it easier to carry. Lizzie, who everyone at home called Kid, felt herself hobble from one side to the next, shifting the weight of her burdens from hip to hip as she struggled to make headway up the platform.

She hitched the waist of the flowery house dress, its white background dull with the grime of soot, whose red and pink figures almost matched her red high heels, and sighed again.

Down the platform she could see two men, one white and the other Negro, who looked just like those city slickers she had run away from in Memphis. But when they returned her sad smile she thought, "But I ain't got no money. But that man, that white one, he's got the kindest smile I ever did see." Kid stopped. The sweat poured off her brow, and she couldn't even see the waiting room. Then she stopped again, looked up at the two men. When she opened her mouth she found that she didn't know what to say.

She was so tall and slender. Her dress too loose to establish the outlines of her body, the girl looked as if she had worked long and hard in the South, in whatever saw mill or cotton town she had come from. Just as she reached Sam and Wilkins, and even before Wilkins had launched his words of greeting, she paused and slowly let her burden down, as if she had decided to cast her bags into Chicago's waters. Testing the temperature, Sam thought, just seeing how the city feels. Like everyone else on the station platform the girl was covered in sweat, the beads of perspiration forming on her upper lip and along her forehead. And it was then that Sam noted her most remarkable feature. Her eyes. Behind the fatigue and the wonder Sam was sure he saw a flash — of what, he wondered, not knowing exactly how to answer his own question.

Wilkins interrupted Sam's rumination. "Say there, you look lost. You got anywhere to go?" Wilkins had asked in such a kindly way that it would have been impossible to misinterpret his intent. The girl looked up, sad, weary, but not frightened. "Well, I could use some help."

"What's your name, child?"

"Lizzie Douglas, but my family calls me 'Kid.' Kid Douglas."

Wilkins and Sam, who was introduced as Mr. Sam, soon learned that Kid Douglas (and Sam laughed at the coincidence of two Kids on the same train), born to a sharecropping family from Walls, Mississippi, just down the river from Memphis, had come to Chicago to find her fame and fortune. Actually, she told them, she hated farming, loved singing, and had run away from home. She didn't have the faintest

idea what to do in Chicago, didn't know a soul, and hadn't had anything to eat in two days. As she talked she took the scarf, more correctly Sam thought, the cotton schmatte, off her head and shook out
her hair. It tumbled in waves to her shoulders, and Sam realized it
had been processed, probably for the first time, for the trip north. Someone must have told her to do it to make an impression in the big
city. Her face changed before his eyes. Sam was startled. The girl was
striking; her arched eyebrows, wide smile, and soft long face made
her look different. Her eyes glimmered as she used her scarf to wipe
her brow. She reminded him of… "If you come with me," Wilkins
interrupted softly, "I'll introduce you to someone, Mrs. Binga. She'll
help you find a job and someplace to live. You willin' to do domestic
work?"

South of the Loop, in the first year after the Great War, State Street
opened as spacious and airy there as it was cramped and overcrowded
downtown. Within a mile of the Loop in the years after the great
fire of 1871, Chicago's wealthy families built their mansions along
Prairie Avenue. Anchored by the Pullman mansion, by 1900 the Near
South Side turned into the city's first Gold Coast. Neoclassical facades
attached to balloon frame construction marked the elegantly spacious
homes. Ironically, the new South Side, which existed as a social buffer
between the commercial empire of the Loop and the segregated city of
Bronzeville, also lay adjacent to the city's Levee District, home to
Chicago's whores, pimps, gamblers, numbers runners, and racketeers.

Chicago's wealthy found themselves surrounded on three sides by
the crass commercialism of downtown, by the teeming tenements of
Bronzeville, and the honky-tonk of the ever-expanding tenderloin.
Matrons might sneer at the plight of Chicago's polite classes, but the
more astute of the city's business elite knew that wherever misery
existed there was money to be made. And none knew this better than
Charlie Comiskey, whose fine Italianate home on 21st and State, just
north of the Armour Institute, took up almost as much property as his
ball park just a mile to the south.

Comiskey rarely came home in the evenings before 11. He lived alone — Rube had once said, "Who in the hell would have him? Would you?" Sam only smiled at the question. But Comiskey's vast house still required a staff of a half-dozen, not including the chauffeur and gardener, to keep the joint going. Comiskey was, if nothing else, regular. His hours were as steady as the left hand of the stride piano player who held forth at Harold's, a club on Clark Street that Comiskey occasionally ducked into when he felt that his life and world had become, even for him, too predictable.

Despite the hour Comiskey remained dressed in his business suit, his collar, and tie. He always said that it was important for him to look like a member of the Century Club, like a merchant prince or at least a captain of industry. Baseball, he often proclaimed to Sam, was more than a sport and a business, it was the American way of life. And those who, like him, were its leaders deserved the acclaim that the public normally reserved for gentlemen. Comiskey knew damn well that most of his colleagues were bookies, numbers runners, beer barons, and stock manipulators. He also knew that they resented his real affiliation with the game, one which extended back forty years to his mediocre playing days with Spaulding and Anson. "Whatever you say about him, darlin'," Foster proclaimed, "you gotta give him this. He loves the game. Almost as much as I do."

But, if Comiskey hoped to challenge the aristocratic Cubs for the hearts and wallets of Chicago's fans, he needed both respect and success. He also understood that these two qualities did not always complement the other. His team had won the pennant and series in 1917, dipped in 1918, and was again driving to baseball dominance in 1919. The trouble was, as he observed, two-fold. The dreaded Cubs, the other great team, in addition to the New York Giants of the National League, had been victorious in 1918, and his players, ones like Collins and Jackson, were getting old. His team had remained static for almost five seasons, and new American League stars, like that young upstart pitcher Ruth in Boston, threatened to surpass his aging team. He needed to do something by the end of this season. Even if Kid Gleason could guide the Sox to the pennant, as he was sure to do, Comiskey calculated, the time for dramatic change was close.

Sam knew that it wasn't, at 11 P.M., the best time to visit Comiskey — but he didn't want to give the old man time to reconsider the plan they had hammered out. In fact Sam realized that if they were going to convince Pop, they would have to make a dramatic offer, one that Lloyd couldn't turn down.

He entered Comiskey's home using the key that the Old Roman had given him. It wasn't that Sam was a special confidante of the old bastard, but Comiskey had said, "For all the fucking money I'm paying you I want you here when I want you here. Take the key." Sam entered and realized that Comiskey had already gone upstairs, and decided to wait for a spell before ringing the private bell that would signal his arrival. Without turning on the light, Sam slipped into the parlor, made his way over to Comiskey's bar, and poured himself a shot of malt whiskey. My parents would probably faint if they saw me now, he mused. Sabbath wine and nothing else, nothing more. That was the rule in his Old World household. Papa's beard, Mama's kugel, that's what his life had been about until he had, although he had never put it quite that way before, run away from home. Be an American, he had told himself twenty years earlier. You can't be a shtetl Jew, not here, not now. Tell them, he said with an inner anger that surprised him, as his eyes darted to the paintings of the Armours, McCormicks, and Wards that Comiskey had presumptuously set on his brocade walls. Tell them.

As Sam leaned into the high backed armchair and sipped his whiskey, he gradually discovered that the house was neither as dark or as quiet as he had imagined. From beyond the dining room he caught first the faintest glint of light, and then the sound of a voice. He put down his glass and treaded silently across the carpet through the chandeliered dining room and halted. Down a long hall he could now see a sliver of light coming through an almost closed door. The light reached down the hall, as if it had been squeezed through the eye of a needle, until it almost touched his feet. And then he heard more clearly a woman's voice.

Transfixed, Sam held his breath. The door slid noiselessly open a few inches to reveal the young black woman, head down, sitting on the side of her bed. She held an old guitar, the one she had carried off the train which she played softly. It's the girl from that town in the Delta, he realized. Wilkins must have gotten her this job.

Then he was quiet inside his head and he listened.

Honey chile, honey chile,
    come on home to me
Honey chile, honey chile,
    come on home to me.
You got the sweetest honey
That I ever did see.

Even as she played softly Sam thought Kid Douglas handled the guitar with great authority, her slender fingers picking the melody as her thumb provided the rhythm of her song. From music Sam didn't know much, but he did know the blues and this kid from Mississippi, she played the blues, played them as she must already have lived them. Her passion — unmistakable even to Sam — and her power jumped from her voice into the silent and empty house. Here this country girl, thought Sam, right in Comiskey's damn house, just down the hall from the paintings of those dead rich goyim, is singing about sex and lust. Amazing.

Saw my honey chile this mornin'
    At the chime of four
Saw my honey chile this mornin'
    At the chime of four.
I tole him baby
Bring that honey in my door.

3

SAM'S SONG

"In the old days the streets, even Maxwell Street, was lined with dreck. Wall to wall, Sammie. Wall to wall." Max Weiss liked to tell his son what life was like in the old days. Horses clattered up and down Maxwell but the noise and the odor had become so much a part of life in the tenements that the residents hardly noticed. Besides, it wasn't so different from the muddy villages Max had left behind in the "old country." Old country was a wonderfully vague description for the impoverished peasant lands that had spawned the waves of Russian and Polish Jews who, beginning in 1881, had fled some tsar's or emperor's or archduke's army. Traveling by foot, literally walking north to Hamburg or Stetten, the young Jewish men of the decaying empires of Eastern Europe hoped — for better, for freedom, for a good living. "Don't worry," they said to their wives and sweethearts, "I'll write, send money, tickets, for you and tante Etta and Zeta." Maybe.

When Max Weiss was fourteen, he told Sam, he woke up one morning to find his mother leaning over the straw pallet that stuck to the mud floor in the corner of the family hut. She had been cooking the usual grey mush in the black kettle suspended over the fire in the opposite corner, but now she looked him in the face. Her eyes dull with fatigue, her hair only as long as the stubble on his father's chin, she reached into the pocket of her smock, pulled out a cigarette, lit a match on the stone next to Max's pallet, and inserted the tube in her son's mouth. "Here," she said softly, "here. It's all I have." And she put a small pouch into his hand, kissed him on the forehead and said, "Just go north. It's all on the paper here."

Three hours later, 8 A.M. Cossack time, Max felt as though his kid- neys would burst as he sat, his tochus hurdling up and down against the wagon on the road to Minsk. Max had never been to the capital before — sure, it was the capital of nothing except the scattered towns which made up the Pale of Settlement in what he called White Russia — but he clutched to his chest the handbill that he had picked up in his village a week earlier. Written in Yiddish, the notice promised "good jobs, good housing" in America. All the bearer had to do was present himself to the agent of the German-American steamship line in Hamburg by the end of August, 1891.

No small print, no nothing, just a promise, and Max knew that he had to keep the appointment. He had two months to make his way from Minsk through Poland, and then north to Germany. At least that's what the man who had sold his mother the handbill for ten rubles had told her.

In the telling, Sam's father had made the journey into a parable of Jewish survival, by his wits. Max loved to recount stories of malevolent Polish peasants, wild forest beasts, and rag-tag gangs of thieves. In fact, he made his way out of Europe by walking fifty kilometers a day, stealing shoes and food from farmers' houses, and drawing on his physical strength, which allowed him to lift and wash and bale when he needed a few kopeks. At the end he found himself in a kind of informal army of Jewish dreamers and draft dodgers who proclaimed their mutual solidarity and then, a day's march from Hamburg, set about to steal whatever they could from each other. Each spoke in the language of their locale, Russian, Polish, Ukranian, Lithuanian, and then German, but Yiddish remained their common tongue — their medium of exchange. Max, who read Yiddish and Hebrew, could speak Russian and Polish and write in numbers.

"Lemme see that," the agent commanded when Max thrust the threadbare piece of paper at him. But the agent addressed him in German, and while Max got the gist of the question, he felt for the first, but hardly the last time, that he existed in a fog. Physically full grown, Max at eighteen stood barely over five and half feet tall, had a full head of black curly hair, and deep blue eyes that he passed on to his son. To call him stocky would have been to minimize his barrel chest and incredibly strong arms. What was remarkable, however, about his features were his long and delicate fingers. Long and slender, like reeds, Sam remembered. His father's fingers were his tools. He had a broad back, a quick brain, and nimble fingers. The agent immediately sized him up and took him for all he was worth — in material terms virtually nothing. "Sign here," he ordered.

Max grabbed the pen and made his mark, an X, a kickle in Yiddish, and the agent called him, this time in English, a dumb kike. Max smiled and followed the agent's finger toward the gangway of the boat that loomed behind them. What he didn't know, and this was true even in the retelling, was that he had just agreed to trade his passage for a seven year apprenticeship with a jeweler in a city he had never heard of.

Two weeks later, Max retched over the side of the *Bloomgarten*, which had become a twice daily ritual, just as the ship steamed past the new and still copper-colored Statue of Liberty in New York harbor. He had passed a fortnight in complete misery, made only the acquaintance of a young Czech typesetter with whom he shared his plank bed ("You take it from noon, I got it from midnight," the older man ordered in Yiddish) and missed his family so much that he considered taking the next boat back. He knew, of course, that he had neither the gelt nor guts do to that, and so he suffered his hellish passage in steerage and waited for the boat to stop.

The Statue of Liberty offered no stirring thrill to Max, and the sight of Manhattan, its bristling wharves, the unfinished Gothic piers of the Brooklyn Bridge, the city's compactly dense warren of buildings, factories, and warehouses made little impression. He watched more intently as the ferry chugged and gurgled its way into the narrow channel cut into Ellis Island. New York, the Battery, and Customs House stood in the distance, across the expanse of choppy water that separated the immigrants from their port. With the chill of autumn already in the air, the grey clouds of October hung down over the Hudson as Max huddled on deck, his arms draped over the railing, waiting.

Suddenly Max found himself caught in a human river. Along with hundreds of passengers who had been transferred from the ship to the ferry at the dock in New York, he was swept in a current that began moving, mysteriously, down the stairs and gangways of the boat toward land. It was as if he could see himself from above, caught in the torrent. There, he felt his feet touch the mud and gravel path that led to the main pavilion. Max pulled the collar of his grey coat up around his ears, tucked his small packet of belongings under his arm, and set foot in the New World.

It took two days to be processed. Max passed through corridors commanded by cross-eyed matrons, walked silently in and out of white tiled examination rooms that reeked from camphor and excrement, had his anus, nose, and eyeballs pried open with rusting iron implements, ate slop from huge black buckets, slept on rancid mats, and showered with a hundred others. When the process was finished they pinned a yellowed piece of paper to the left breast pocket of his jacket. It identified him as a healthy Jewish male. Finally he found himself standing in a cavernous room, its ceiling four stories high, at the end of one of a half dozen lines of non-tubercular immigrants seeking official entry into the United States. Six hours later Max arrived at the head of the line, standing before a simple wooden table behind which sat an enormous, and Irish, immigration official whose large red hands almost covered the ledger in front of him. "Name," he barked.

"*Meine namen ist Max Weissenheimer,*" he said, proud that he understood the question. "Max Weiss," the officer recited. "Max Weiss, that's your name now, lad," and he wrote the letters in ink as black as midnight. Max felt himself shiver, felt something change, irrevocably, within him. Not the new name, but the utter incomprehensibility of what had transpired. He was a new person in a new land and there would be no going home.

Max never saw his European family again. His parents and younger brother chose to remain in Russia. Some in his family were swallowed up by the revolution, on one side or the other, Sam learned from letters that arrived in what they called the Red Summer of 1919.

And that, Sam knew, was how his father, Max Weiss, had come to America. By 1894, the year that Max and Sarah Weiss gave birth to their son Samuel, the family had moved from the labyrinth of Manhattan's lower East Side, from the notorious Bandit's Roost on Mulberry Street, to Chicago.

But, first Max had worked in New York as a jeweler, fourteen hours a day, six days a week. "You got Saturdays off, keep the Sabbath and your nose clean," his boss, Misha Kronberg, a huge bear of a Silesian coal miner turned sweat shop operator, told him on the first day. First Max sized rings and then graduated to pouring gold into lead molds. By the time he was twenty his eyes had become permanently focused on his hands, he literally couldn't see beyond his bench, and his fingers were scarred with burns and hundreds of tiny lacerations. Nights he struggled to an alley rooming house, to a room which he shared with six other greenhorns, Jews who had all arrived the same year, clutching the same precious piece of paper which delivered them to the same laboring fate. They all worked for Kronberg, slept in Kronberg's rooms, ate his food, and made his wages. When the room and board were deducted their pockets were empty.

Only the energy of their youth led the seven young men to discover that if the streets of New York were not paved with gold, they were covered by tons of horse manure — in desperate need of cleaning. Dutifully, every morning, including the Sabbath, at 4 A.M., the seven rose from their thin and somehow still lumpy mattresses and spent the next three hours shoveling horse shit from the streets into the "limey," a large three axle wagon that hauled excrement and dumped it into the East River. For their enterprise they collected a single dollar every week. For some the money went to schnapps and young girls with pink cheeks and soiled ribbons in their hair. Max hated drinking and saved most of the rest of his money.

Sam's mother, Sarah, had been sent from Poland to New York to stay with relatives when she was six. Tenement life taught her to serve the men in her life whatever they needed for nourishment, and little else. Skinny as a broom, Sarah looked old by the time she was twenty, the year she bore Sam in Chicago in 1894. Many years later Max told his son, in the only intimate conversation that Sam could ever recall, that he had never seen his wife without her clothes on. Sam summoned his courage and asked how he had come into being and flinched only momentarily when his father told him about the hole in the sheet that Sarah had sewn closed the next day.

Sam's childhood memories of his mother remained fixed in the family kitchen on Maxwell Street. Sarah commanded the kitchen, issued orders, summoned and stored provisions, and maintained control. All else — but what was there? Sam asked himself on reflection — she ceded to Max. Sam thought that his mother wore the same dress, a kind of grey-beige print whose pattern had long since been scrubbed illegible, for his entire childhood. Its most distinct feature, a strip of buttons running up the front from hem to plain neck, had been replaced a dozen times. The randomness of their size and color, for Woolworth's on Halstead didn't carry the same buttons for the entire life of Sarah's dress, gave her a style, a dash of accidental panache, that contradicted her weary and somber plainness.

Sarah cooked. A different meal for each member of the family. "Uncle Benny's coming for dinner tonight," she might announce, "go to the butcher and get some chop meat (never chopped, only chop), you know how he likes it." A large mound of something that looked like a cross between meatloaf and muskrat greeted Uncle Benny, a Chicago garbage man, that night. And as Max sucked his boiled chicken from the bone, Sam, or Samileh as his parents called him nasally, quietly ate his helping of cabbage soup and flanken. If Sarah ever ate no one knew. She certainly didn't do so in public. She simply stood at the stove and doled out the appropriate dish for each participant. Hardly a democrat, Sarah intuitively knew what each of her charges liked, and once decided, she fixed their menus for life. As a kid Sam never brought a friend home for a second visit. Never.

Sarah and Max had come to Chicago because Uncle Benny had conned them. Or, rather Uncle Benny had conned Max. One dandy New York spring morning in 1893 as Max quietly ("Who could sing?" he explained at a family dinner thirty years later) shoveled his burden into the sanitation wagon on Mott Street, the city worker, who turned out to be Benny, slid down from his driver's perch and looked at Max. "Hey, you tired of shoveling shit, yet?" Max was simply tired, and when he nodded, Benny introduced himself and told the younger man about a scheme he had to get rich, very rich, quick. "See, they breed like fucking rabbits. All we gotta do is get 'em, stick 'em in a cage, and before you know it we got more pelts than the Tsar."

The next day, after work, Benny took his new friend Max to a small stall on Avenue C. There, among the welter of carts whose aproned owners announced their wares in voices loud enough to raise the dead—"Cash for Clothes" and "Mending and Fixing"—they found Benny's target. The evening crowds swelled and jostled for space, elbows insuring that even a small seam between shoppers could become wide enough to pass through to get a bargainer's glimpse. The two men wedged their way into the circle that stood three deep around a cart filled, overfilled actually, with what looked like wire cages. "See, just like I told yuz," Benny announced proudly. "All we need is just two of 'em. Just two, and we'll be knocking on heaven's gate." With that he looked directly into the eye of the tiny Jewish peddler whose hands fluttered over the cages and announced, "Okay. Here's the guy I told you about. We're ready to buy. How much for the pair."

Benny haggled as Max watched, wondering what in the world he had agreed to. After several exchanges punctuated by untranslatable Yiddishims and a reference to a strange combination of female anatomy and the Master of the Universe, the negotiators reached stasis. "One hundred, that's my final offer," Benny announced, knowing that he had an extra ten to play with, "not one fucking cent more, you gonoff." The peddler turned his back, and without taking a breath asked a heavyset woman just on the other side of the cart, "So, Mrs. Moskowitz, what can I do for you today?" Benny jumped, "One ten. That's it." And that's what they agreed on. One hundred ten dollars, fifty-five each, more than a year's worth of shoveling horse crap, and Max was the half proud owner of a pair of minx. Or was it, he wondered, minks. If Benny were correct within three weeks the two furry animals would have produced four more, and so on for the next three years. They were ranchers, regular city cowboys, and the dozens of breeding and multiplying minks would make them rich. One mink pelt sold directly to Fred the Furrier on 14th Street, just one, would bring five bucks. Max didn't bother to ask if the pelt came with or without the skin attached, and he didn't much care. But as he thought more about it he realized that it would take them more than a year just to recoup their investment.

The other thing that Max didn't realize was that neither he nor Benny knew how to tell a male from a female mink. But six weeks later when the anticipated pregnancy failed to announce itself, they took the two furry beasts to a vet. Well, not exactly a doctor, but to a

Lithuanian abortionist known for his wisdom and intelligence, who lifted the critters up by the tail and pronounced proudly, "It's a boy." By which he meant they were both males.

Naturally when they sought out the mink pushcart the tiny mer-
chant was nowhere to be seen. Max was out his cut. Virtually his life savings. Yes, he still had his apprenticeship at Kronberg's and still could shovel shit every morning for three hours. He jumped when Benny, in a state of utter remorse which when combined with his usual good cheer, produced a never ending stream of new schemes, plans, and daydreams, offered him a new deal. "If you like my sister and, god willing, marry her, I'll give you your money back and see you get a job with a guy I know, a landsman, in Chicago."

Eventually Sam realized that his father had exchanged shoveling shit for taking it. But, in early 1894 the young couple, Sarah just pregnant, found themselves standing on Maxwell Street where they would live in the same apartment for the next forty years, and where Sam and his wife Jeanne visited dutifully each month until they could no longer tolerate boiled chicken and flanken.

Max owned his own cart on Maxwell Street, selling the wedding rings that he learned to make in New York. Sarah cooked, resentful of the strangeness of a new city and a new family, and sat by the window each day watching the world pass by. From his father Sam learned a kind of focused industriousness, a Jewish version of the American dream that placed personal happiness well behind, if not beyond, duty and discipline. From his mother he learned a soft bitterness, an unarticulated rancor which could cut open even the most carefully protected self.

Toward her son Sarah showed only care, so much protective and suffocating concern that Sam imagined he would grant her deepest wish by placing himself in a cotton lined coffin and never leaving. She would never have to remind him to "watch out for" almost any and everything. Even his childhood walks over to Halstead Street, to the reading groups that he attended at Hull House, were cause for concern. "Stay away from the Paddies," she ordered, "and come right home." And, as he was halfway out the door, "Don't forget your hat."

There, on the near West Side, in the generation before the First World War, Sam Weiss became a man and learned to love baseball, his claim on being American. Marked by wood-framed shanties and tenements which stood alongside sturdy, but small, brick row houses, by the turn of the century, Chicago's West Side had become home to fifteen thousand Jewish immigrants from Eastern Europe. Sam knew that within walking distance of his house on Maxwell there were more than forty orthodox synagogues, where men in Russian boots prayed on the Sabbath while their wives listened behind a curtained gallery. Yiddish, Sam's language at home, was also the language of the streets and alleys that the knickered children staked out for themselves. But the weight of tradition found its match in the lure of the new century.

By the time Sam had put his bar mitzvah behind him in 1907, he had begun to expand his world beyond the small rectangle defined by Halstead, Maxwell, Cabrini, and Racine streets. He learned that even Jewish life in Chicago encompassed more than cheder and gefilte fish. Just a couple of blocks north along Maxwell, Wisenfreund's Pavilion Theater beckoned. "If I EVER, and I mean EVER, catch you going to that, that, Galiziano schmendreck place, I'll beat the living stuff out of you, so help me." Pop's bark was always worse than his bite, and Sam knew immediately that the Pav was someplace he wanted, no, needed to go.

The mishmash of vaudeville and minstrelsy that passed for popular entertainment in turn-of-the-century Chicago carried Sam into worlds he never imagined. Jokesters and hoofers made him laugh and stamp his feet while bowdlerized Shakespeare — "What's this I see, a stain on my conscience?" — taught him the rudiments of scheming and revenge. The newest rage, however, the so-called art dance, the classy version of a strip tease that owed more than a little to the astounding success of Little Egypt on the Midway a decade earlier, scorched his blood. Never had Sam seen something so fascinating — and exciting. And when Little Bo Peep or Savannah Sally (and after a while he began to suspect, correctly, that they were all the same not-so-young girls from Back of the Yards) strutted on stage before the flickering waxy footlights and lifted up their skirts, well, he was, at least for a time, in heaven. But Sam had seen nothing like the dancer who called herself simply Miss Ruth.

On a chilly autumn day in 1909 Sam saw Miss Ruth perform Rada on stage. He remembered the date because it was the same day that Alice

Norman told him about one of the bigshot architect Daniel Burnham's famous Chicago Plan to transform the waterfront downtown into a combination of Atlantic City and Washington, D.C. Of course, of Rada Alice knew nothing, but the proprietors of the Pav thought she was really something. One of them had figured out a way to squeeze the infamous Ruth St. Denis onto their program. Sandwiched between a recitation of "Casey at the Bat" and a troupe of Polish plate spinners, Miss Ruth, already recognized as the pioneer mother of modern dance, held Sam in the palm of her hand. Transfixed, Sam sat in the front row while directly before him a woman covered in seven veils danced, shimmied, and stroked her way to ecstasy.

All whirl and light, St. Denis tossed hundreds of rose petals on the stage, their rich scent somehow a complement to the incense burning in the wings, as she moved with a fluidity and grace that mesmerized him. As the music gained in intensity Rada, an exotic bejeweled goddess of the Orient, brought down the house. The men in the audience stood for minutes speechless, clapping, as the dancer on stage quietly bent at the waist to retrieve the admiring flowers that circled her feet, and then, silently she was gone.

To Sam she had been the epitome of sensuous art, hardly the model for his future Presbyterian princess. Feminine, alluring, and erotic, the St. Denis–Rada figure forced him to imagine, no, to think about women as something more than young versions of his mother. Yet, curiously, they remained for him idealizations, figures on stage to be observed, even lusted after, but never pursued. Sam sighed as St. Denis disappeared off stage, walking in slow stately steps befitting her billing as *artiste*. The applause drifted after her, and as she extended her hand to her husband and partner Ted Shawn, Sam couldn't help but notice the question implicit in the gesture. It made him less lonely when he understood.

The Polish plate spinners, to the enormous delight of the contingent from Pilsen, just to the south of Maxwell Street, worked fast and furious. A half dozen young men dressed in flowing white shirts and red tied-around-the-neck kerchiefs, the Wonders from Warsaw (as they were alternatively billed) could spin and balance up to eight white dinner plates (each) all the while dancing to accordion renditions of Galician folk tunes played at breakneck speed. Occasional breakage was simply part of the evening entertainment, and after four minutes both the act and audience had spun themselves into a state of exhaustion.

Sam, almost sixteen, had, however, arrived at a state of relative cynicism when it came to the variety acts at the Pavilion Theater. He loved the girls, true, but the so-called feats of extraordinary acrobatic balance or sleight of hand struck him as ho-hum. He was decidedly unprepared for what he saw next.

As the red velvet curtain closed on the Warsaw Wonders and the last staccato notes receded back into the orchestra pit, Sam noted that a dozen men and women dressed in tuxedos and black velvet bow ties had begun to walk quietly, almost reverentially, from the back of the theater up toward the stage. With the house lights up Sam could see the audience, mostly working-class men, stir in anticipation. The ushers disappeared behind the curtain only to emerge a minute later with a rectangular wood scaffolding on which they quickly fixed an expanse of white material. Slowly the lights went down, and as the audience settled into its seats, the musicians in the orchestra began to play.

From the back of the theater a whirring sound seemed by just a fraction of a second to anticipate the beam of bright and steaming light that jumped onto the screen. The audience clapped with excitement as the musicians stepped into "Take Me Out to the Ball Game." Images of men in white flannel uniforms, knee high socks, and black leather shoes with metal teeth on the soles, flickered before Sam. CHICAGO'S GREAT TEAMS, the title card read, CUBBIES AND WHITE STOCKINGS READY FOR SPRING. Sam watched entranced as the great ball players of his day, Frank Chance, Eddie Collins, and Joe Evers, went through the rituals of spring training. Somewhere in Georgia Chicago's two major league teams had assembled and would spend the next five weeks playing (and drinking) themselves into shape for the coming season. The players tossed baseballs back and forth to each other with uncommon grace, managing to attain a smiling nonchalance before the camera's eye. PEPPER ALWAYS PUTS THE SPICE INTO SPRING, the next card intoned. The black and white script dissolved to reveal the 1908 World's Champion Cubs, vanquishers of the New York Giants, moving a half-dozen balls simultaneously between two rows of players standing ten feet apart, some with bats held halfway up the handle, others with hand-sized leather gloves. As one player tossed a ball his partner half swung, sending the ball back on a line. They struck and retrieved with a languorous speed, shouting silent encouragement fortified by ever present squirts of tobacco juice. Even Sam, slack jawed and wide-eyed in a way that might have made Savannah Sally jealous, could not help but notice the incredible contrast between the physical ease, the youthful innocence, of the players' bodies and the worn and weary looks in their eyes. The camera closed its focus on first baseman Frank Chance to reveal a man of intense seriousness, his face etched with a network of lines, the battle ribbons of a hard life, booze, and constant competition. Take off his uniform, Sam thought, and he's not so different from all the working men drinking nickel beer in the alley between acts. A decade later, as Sam walked over to Comiskey's office, the contract for John Henry Lloyd in his pocket, he remembered the hard man he first saw on the screen at Wisenfreund's on 12th and Halstead.

Baseball had, of course, seduced Sam well before his initiation at the Pav. Kids played some version of city ball on his street all summer, and Sam was no exception. Broom handles, pink rubber balls, "Spaldeens" they called them, and old sneakers as bases created the game down long alleys filled with laundry billowing over mossy cobblestones. Nightly rituals of knickered boys calling out to each other in the language of the game, "Putter right in there," "Good eye, good eye," and "Straighten her out" increasingly replaced their families' observance of the Old World ways. And one late summer evening, when Sam had just passed his tenth birthday, he got the most solid hit of his life — then or ever.

Scrambling down the three flights of stairs that zigzagged up the rear of the tenement, Sam had almost tripped. Afraid that he was already late for the game, he stumbled over his shoelace and only caught himself at the last second by grabbing hold of the wood barrier that stood guard at the landing. Paying no attention to the splinter that had lodged in the palm of his right hand, Sam raced into the alley, breathless, "Hold it fellas. I'm here."

Three other boys, each from a different flat in his building, waited impatiently for him, their hands and feet tangled, sustaining their balance despite the slouches that they affected.

"We wuz gonna start widout yuz, Sammie. But yuz wasn't here. Ya know."

"Funny. Very, very funny. You a comic too."

"Too?"

"Yeah. You know, too. Too dumb to be anything else."

And so it went, as it did every evening. Joking and jostling, the four boys made up teams, with Sam and Horny winning the toss to decide which team could bat first.

Horny, Israel Horowitz, whose Hungarian parents had arrived in Chicago two years after Sam's, hence the Green Horn, shortened to Horny for several reasons that all the boys thought extremely funny, hit first. There was a good reason for that as well. Horny was as large as an ox, "strong as a bull ... no shit" is how they put it, and if he didn't lose the ball on the first swing, then the boys knew that they'd have some time to play. Cause "either he hits it so far its never coming back, or he never hits it," they explained to the occasional, usually female, onlooker who ventured out into "their" alley for an evening divertissement. So, Horny hit first that night and Sam leaned against the rickety wood porch that served as the pitcher's target, home plate, and the batter's box all at the same time.

"Hey, Sammy. Stand back, will ya," the pitcher, a skinny kid named Morrie called. "Stand back. I can't get a bead on the plate wid you standin' so close to Horny."

As the batter rubbed his hands together, friction being the friend of all stick ball hitters on the West Side of Chicago that year, Sammy backed a bit off, well out of reach he thought of even Horny's mammoth swing.

Morrie wound up tight as he could, three pumps, and let the pink ball fly. The pitch arrived belt high and wide. "He'll never even swing, no less hit it," Sam thought as the ball continued to move away from Horny's body, his bat. But, Sam's silent words failed to convince Horny, who pulled back the old broom, its handle taped and sticky, cocking it behind his ear and then, extending his arms, as he tried to reach for the ball still darting away from him, swinging with all his might.

Horny connected, his bat sending a sharp crack echoing down the alley, and he lifted his head to follow the flight of the ball which he just knew would clear the narrow corridor of buildings and, even now, be bounding across Halstead. Instead, the ball caromed off the wood railing neatly back to the pitcher, who held it even as he heard Sam choke and then begin to wail.

The night turned red and orange and yellow all at once, and Sam's reflexes brought his right hand immediately to the place just over his left eye where Horny's bat had opened a gash across his entire eyebrow. With the pitcher yelling, "I told you to stand back. You dumb Kike. I told you," and Horny beginning to sob uncontrollably, Sam somehow remained calm. In truth he didn't know exactly what had happened, and only began to realize the enormity of the wound a moment later when the blood from his head began to run sticky and red down his face, filling his mouth with foam.

He had to wear a patch for the next six months, but, "Thanks God, it could have been worse, much worse," he didn't lose the sight in his left eye. He did, however, lose any chance he ever had of playing ball. Even more than the Pav, Chicago's two professional ball fields were off limits to him. "Go where? And lose an eye. Not now. Not ever," his parents told him, shaking. So, if the staccato images on the screen that day at the Pav seduced Sam to the heroic grace of baseball, the ground had been well prepared. That same year, however, an altogether different encounter led him out of the Jewish Near West Side into the not yet venerable halls of the University of Chicago. His parents, who never spoke, as far as he could tell, with each other, expected that Sam would become, following his high school career, a more successful version of his father. "Go, Semmy. Go to Simka, I've already told him about you. He'll make you into the best jeweler in the city. One day you'll take my cart and turn it into a factory. Imagine." Few things appealed less to Sam than his father's admonition. But he had little sense of what he really loved, except baseball and the follies.

By 1909 the old C. J. Hull mansion at Halstead and Polk, just a short walk from the Pav, had been functioning as a neighborhood settlement house for twenty years. A remnant of pre–1871 days when the Near West Side had been Chicago's first gold coast, Hull House existed in the midst of the city's most densely settled ethnic-immigrant neighborhood. Italians, Germans, Jews, Bohemians and French-Canadians had transformed, in the wake of Mrs. O'Leary's cow, the once wealthy enclave into a teeming crowded working class immigrant district. Poverty, community, disease, and celebration existed side by side, their currents swirling around Hull House making its Italianate red brick and white pillars even more incongruous.

The legendary and remote directors of Hull House, Jane Addams and Ellen Gates Starr, had brought to the tumble of the Near West Side a refuge and a sanctuary. They also hoped to bring the children of the Near West Side the accouterments of polite culture and worked tirelessly to save them from the excess and exploitation of industrial capitalism.

Their feminized progressivism, reform built on the defense of childhood, placed them in alliance with Chicago's trade unionists. It was not uncommon for immigrant children of ten to work thirteen hours a day in the mills, slaughterhouses, and sweatshops of Chicago. But despite reasonable success of the reformers, there was little they or anyone at the time could do to break the cycle of poverty, privation, and powerlessness that chained immigrant families to patterns of child labor at home. Piece work, finger numbing, repetitive piece work — sewing ties, wrapping cigars, making tiny paper flowers — brought the factory system back to the home and hearth and made it the labor of women and children, where it remained unregulated, unmitigated, uncontrollable.

In this respect Sam had been fortunate. For every day that Sarah sat and stared out the window of their tenement, spinning stories of her neighbors' peccadilloes, was a day, Sam thought, that she didn't have to take something in.

Pop insisted, and in this respect she did too, when his father forced him to remain in public school up to the bitter end. "You want to take over my trade. You gonna do it with some good sense in your head," Max insisted whenever Sam fidgeted about his pals Horny and Moe, who at age sixteen had already taken on adult work. "Them bums. You wanna be like them? And do what? Lift bales of newspapers into some Paddy's delivery wagon, or clean the streets in some schwartze neighborhood." It did Sam little good to remind his father of his odorous beginnings in New York. The old man would hear nothing of it. "Or, maybe you'd like to be like your Uncle Benny. A garbage man for life."

Sam, who understood that his was not the bitter lot of immigrant poverty, knew in some part of his consciousness that he aspired to be neither like his father — working with his hands almost a hundred hours a week — or his friends.

"Its all in the execution. Just look at the way Cassatt has suggested the bow of the boat, there, just beyond the gaze of the woman." Sam followed Miss Norman's slim finger which pointed at the painting on the wood paneled wall in front of him. He never quite knew why he so frequently found himself on the fourth, and top, floor of Hull House. It seemed so, well, refined for a guy like him, as if he stepped into another world. And that, he reflected a decade later, was probably how the women intended it.

Alice Norman, all dark hair and deep eyes, had taken an interest in him two years earlier, and like the founders of Hull House was convinced that what these children of immigrants needed was a deep and personal dose of cultural sophistication. Through her intelligence, charm, and care she had systematically introduced Sam to the great works of late nineteenth century American art: the paintings of John Singer Sargent, William Merritt Chase, Winslow Homer, and especially Mary Cassatt, whose luminous murals had graced the Women's Pavilion of the great Columbian Exposition in 1894. Now in her mid–30s, Alice Norman lived in Hull House, loved art, and wanted nothing else than to send Sam to the newly opened University of Chicago. A wonderful convergence, she told him, on the very site of the World's Fair, along the Midway, a great and powerful institution of higher learning. Alice smiled to herself as she walked with Sam along the gallery hallway at Hull House, spinning tales of Cassatt's residence at Barbizon, of her close affinity with the great French impressionists. "You see, Sam, how close she was to Monet. Even the tilt of the woman's head, there, in the boat, reminds us of Monet's figures, the way they look to us and, see, even at us."

Sam had to admit that Alice had something there. But he wondered if the world that these painters had created, a world of quiet Sunday afternoons and straw hats floating in the breeze, even existed.

They paused in the gallery atop Hull House. The sun filtered in through the small windows that ran around the room just below the ceiling, the panes reflecting and refracting the sunset, casting rainbow prisms of light and dark along the oak floor. Alice reached and took Sam's hand with such gentle tenderness that he forgot to pull it back. "Come on, I have something else to show you," she said, and led him to the end of the gallery to a long and deeply polished mahogany table strewn with sheaves of newspapers from all over the world. She let go of his hand and reached down to retrieve a small folded newspaper. The *Defender*, the masthead read. "Did you ever hear of this?" she asked.

Sam, who only read the headlines of whatever paper was held aloft by the knickered kids who hawked them and couldn't tell the *Defender* from the *Tribune*, didn't know whether to confess his ignorance. Hard enough that he didn't really understand the difference between Monet and Cassatt, not to mention the difference between Manet and Monet. He sure didn't want to learn everything there was to know about the complexity of newspaper publishing in Chicago. His father only read the Jewish paper, and then only if someone left him a copy in the bathroom down the hall. So, he shrugged silently to himself, what did he know from newspapers? "Well, I don't think I actually ever read that one," he said quietly. "What can you tell me about it?"

Alice picked up the neatly folded *Defender* and passed it to Sam. She began to speak about the small contingent of Negroes who lived in Chicago, about the politics of financing a newspaper, about how labor laws and unions discriminated. Her words formed a fog in Sam's ear. He heard them all, understood none. It was like reading a book with your eyes, he suddenly thought, without even following one sentence. Suddenly he realized as Alice talked, speaking with her perfectly enunciated vowels, her sentences composed as if she had written them, that he had been looking at the front page of the *Defender* with an intensity that surprised him.

An image of a man stared out at him, underneath a headline that Sam finally read: "Du Bois Galvanizes National Negro Conference." The story described a mass meeting at New York's Cooper Union designed to create biracial organization to defend the rights of Negroes, to work for a unified black and white working class alliance, a sentiment seconded by someone called William English Walling who spoke fervently about the persecution of Russian Jews under the Tsar, but it meant little to Sam. He had few political ideals, understood nothing about Negroes, and only had used the word class to define his place in school. That W.E.B. Du Bois would be among those who would later that year create the National Association for the Advancement of Colored People had, as yet, no significance for Sam.

But the image that so captivated him did. What was it, he wondered, about the face of this black man, his collar white as snow and hard as ice? What was it that seemed so fascinating?

To Sam the face that peered out at him seemed familiar and mysterious all at the same time. Du Bois' skin, its very darkness was equally luminous, his deep-set eyes languid and penetrating. Slowly, Sam took in the whole face, its immaculate goatee and mustache, Du Bois' aquiline nose and high forehead. It was like no other face, no other black face, that he had ever seen.

Sam had observed, yet never spoken with, colored people in Chicago. Downtown at the Loop, Negro men worked as porters and street cleaners. Occasionally on the trolleys that ran along Western and Ashland avenues Sam encountered small groups dressed for work in the slaughterhouses. But in the bristling world of Maxwell Street, of Hull House, and the Near West Side, with its mosaic of European immigrant populations, colored men and women remained invisible.

Slowly Sam allowed his surroundings, and Alice's voice, back into his consciousness. "You see, Sam," she continued with a soft lilt, "these men, colored gentlemen and, there, a Jewish man, they want to ensure that what happened to those people in Springfield last year never happens again." Sam had not the slightest idea what she was talking about, and again hid his ignorance in assent. "The awful race riot, it was one thing when they killed all those people in Atlanta, but to think here, in the north, in Lincoln's own state, in our state capital, I just couldn't believe it." Alice's voice rose with a passion that Sam had never experienced, and slowly he took in her words.

It was almost too much. The beneficence of Hull House, the sweet patronage of Alice, the beauty of Cassatt, the passion of this fellow Du Bois. Sam hardly knew what to make of it all, save that, somehow, he had to find a way to master this world, the uncharted territory, beyond Chicago's West Side. He just couldn't, for the life of him, figure how.

It took Sam a decade. At least insofar as that was possible for the son of Jewish immigrants to master the intricacies of Chicago. Hull House, Alice pulling the strings of German Jews who put up money for the children of their less fortunate Eastern brethren, found him enough scholarship money to attend the University of Chicago where Sam studied a field — "What kind of business is that, sounds like a disease if you ask me," snorted Max when Sam announced his major in sociology — that put him out into the streets of the South Side as an "investigator."

By the time he graduated Sam knew how to gauge the rents landlords might charge in a given apartment by studying the ratio between floor space and the average number of years that the immigrant population in question had been in the city. He knew about red-lining, about urban politics, payoffs, payouts, and patronage. In short he learned how to understood who was being screwed and by whom.

It also took Sam only two more years to study the law and pass the bar, but when he graduated in 1915 he discovered that few firms and even fewer business wanted another Jew lawyer on their payrolls. Sure, he could have a position at the Rosenwalds', but, he reasoned, did he really want a career defending Sears Roebuck against the suits of dissatisfied customers in Cedar Rapids?

The start of the war in Europe had virtually no impact on Sam's life and career. The United States was, after all, neutral, and Chicago stood to profit, and then some, by the huge demand created by the conflagration. That was then Sam met Comiskey, and through Comiskey he began to work with Rube Foster.

"So, kid, watcha want? When you pass the bar, know what I mean?"

"I'm not sure, Mr. Comiskey," Sam said softly. "I'm not really sure. My pop says I gotta get a job right away in case Wilson drags us into the war. I keep telling him that Wilson's one hundred percent against the war, that we'll never enter..."

Comiskey brought the flute of champagne up to his mouth, cocked his eye, balanced his cigar between the first two fingers of the hand holding the glass, and glared disapprovingly. He waved his other hand, the left, "Look kid, that's politics. That crap got nothing to do with us, unnerstand? Not a fucking thing. What I need to figure out is how to win the pennant with a team of drunks and has-beens. Now, are you sure you want to work for me?"

Sam tried to fan the cigar smoke away from his eyes without drawing attention to his distress. The scar had faded but it still ached when he was anxious. Sam was aware of the dozens of sportswriters, city pols, saloon keepers and what his mother would have called "shady characters" who filled the reception room at Comiskey's, a multi-colored human kaleidoscope, always in motion, their chatter clinging no less disconcertingly than the smoke that September evening. Sam tried to get his bearings, to fathom what the charmingly smarmy man before him was really trying to say. Was he actually offering him a job?

All through college and law school Sam had forsaken the girlie shows at the Pav and devoted himself, at least once a week, to his city's two major league teams — the White Sox and Cubs. A fan of both, in his heart of hearts, he favored the Sox, and in the early fall of 1915 he had reason. Joe Jackson, who since 1911 had literally terrorized the American League with his astonishing bat, hitting over four hundred as a rookie with Cleveland and in 1913 pounding a ball over and then out of the right-field grandstand at the Polo Grounds in New York, Joe Jackson, in August of 1915, was "sold" by the cash-poor Indians to Comiskey for three players and $31,500. It was, Sam knew, the largest cash transaction in the history of baseball, and he wondered how someone like Comiskey could be so extravagantly wealthy and yet so remarkably cheap. It didn't take very long to find out.

One of Sam's law school pals, Cyrus Spalding, one of the few who deigned to befriend a Jew, had been as well connected as his name, and had simply sent one of his father's business cards over to Comiskey asking the owner to speak to Sam about future employment with the Sox. The next day Sam's invitation arrived and a week later he was standing in front of Comiskey fanning the cigar smoke and wondering what the old guy had in mind. "Come to the office tomorrow. I'll tell you what I want ya t'do," Comiskey said as he turned from Sam, stuck out his hand and slammed an unsuspecting grey-suited sportswriter on the back. "How ya doin' tonight, Ring? Got enough to eat? Take a load off. Something I gotta talk to ya about."

Sam didn't get a job with the White Sox. By the time he finished his "interview" with Comiskey it was clear that the team owner had something somewhat different in mind. "Here's what I'm gonna do. Now listen, and if ya can't keep your yap shut tell me now, or I'm gonna find out anyway."

Sam, who wanted the job, whatever the job, more than anything he could possibly remember — even Miss Ruth in her various incarnations — simply nodded, his eyes filled with a combination of intimidation and reverence. "What I need, ya see," continued Comiskey, looking up from his desk at Sam standing, hat in hand before him, "what I need is a smart Jew-lawyer, ya know a regular shyster, who can do certain things for me."

Sam gathered his wits. "What things, Mr. Comiskey? Cy Spalding told me there might be a job in the front office. With the Sox."

"If Spalding had real balls he'd be standing here now instead of you. He's just some rich kid showin' off. You want a job with me or not? It's all the same to me." Comiskey leaned forward, lowering his voice, and finally motioned Sam into a chair across his desk. "Look. I'm gonna make the Sox into the best ball club in the world again. The Federal League is shaking the trees. The players, and we already got Joe Jackson as you damn well know, are ripe for the picking. I got the dough, the connections, and a couple of other things up my sleeve. But there's some stuff I can't do. And I need someone to do 'em for me. Got it?"

Sam grasped for that curious combination of comprehension and approval. "You mean you want me to work for you. Personally, I mean."

"That's it kid. For me. Doing things. Talkin' to people, making contracts, being where I can't, delivering the goods." Comiskey's blend of bluff and charm, attributes for which he had become legendary, settled over Sam, flattered him, and soothed whatever ethical misgivings he might have conjured up had he more time to reflect. "I'll pay you three grand a year, and more if what I ask you to do works." And then his voice got hard. "And if you fuck with me, if you even think about it…"

And that was how Sam got to know the fences, pimps, bookies, backroom politicians, union bosses, tavern owners, and anyone else whose sweat and guile made Chicago work. Comiskey kept the McCormicks, the Armours, the Wards, the Spaldings, the governor, and the other owners to himself. They came to grand soirees at his mansion, entered his office without knocking, shook their heads and said, "Good old Charlie, can't put one by him." But Sam soon realized that the Old Roman's charm and polish were just that, no different from the finely tailored suits and cravats that he wore each day. His prominent friends, his champagne, his manners were put on and taken off each day. At bottom Charlie Comiskey was an old ball player with an insatiable appetite for power. And at bottom he was an old ball player from Chicago determined, no less than any party boss, to have the best, most dominant machine he could possibly assemble.

And Joe Jackson was just the first piece. Comiskey knew that this humble sounding and illiterate appearing man was a flawed and needy human being just like anyone else, and he, Comiskey, played Jackson for all he was worth. In some sense the two men, Jackson and Comiskey, were each other's mirror image — but only Comiskey had any glimmer of that fact. The South Carolinian, who sported a hundred pairs of shoes and insisted in living and dressing in a hotel just up the street from Comiskey Park, also carried rusty iron pins— for good luck — in the back pocket of his uniform. Uncomfortable with his image as "Shoeless Joe," a bumpkin from the sticks, Jackson could be a canny business operative, who thanks to his wife made wise and sound investments in his hometown.

But the contradictions between his incredible ability as a player, and many concurred with the judgment of rookie Red Sox pitcher George Ruth that Jackson was the best natural hitter in the history of the game, and the humiliation of his illiteracy left him vulnerable to the manipulations of others. Comiskey soon learned that it was easy to flatter Jackson about those things which he was most insecure —"Great tie you got there kid, really swell. Tell you what, why don'tya go down to my tailor and have him make up a new shirt to go with it." And at the same time the owner could take Jackson to the cleaners over his contract. "You see right here," he once pointed out, "you signed this deal, just down there on the dotted line, and that means that you promised to work for the Sox every year. Every one. No holding out, no long term deals. You work for me, and don't you forget it." Comiskey regularly bragged to "his" sportswriters that he paid Jackson the princely and almost unheard of salary of $10,000. In fact, Jackson received $6,000 from the Sox and more than once overheard Comiskey laugh, "Yeah, and I think he spends half what I give him on shoes."

Jackson, who constantly struggled against the mockery of his teammates, writers, and most of all Comiskey, could only hang his head and mutter. It was, finally, no different from all the moments on the dining cars to St. Louis, Philadelphia, or New York when he would study the breakfast menu and announce to the Negro Pullman waiter standing deferentially to the side of the swaying table, "I guess I'll have that too." Always the last to order, Joe Jackson, who could whip his forty-eight ounce black bat with the suppleness of a conductor's baton, found himself reduced, daily, to complete social impotence. Not only did the discrepancy drive him crazy, but increasingly he discovered that he held Comiskey responsible for his despair. In fact, it was Jackson who first figured out that Comiskey had more in mind than restoring the Sox to the championship when he also signed the great Philadelphia Athletics second baseman, Eddie Collins, to a contract.

When Sam first reported to work he found Comiskey leaning over his desk, his voice conspiratorially low yet harsh. "Now look, you son-of-a-bitch, I need the money now. Not tomorrow, not next week but now. Mack is ready to deal and I need the cash." He whacked the receiver into the cradle and looked up. "Well. You came at the right moment. I got a job for you. Sit.

"I got a partner. No one knows about him but me, see. Name's Foster. He's over at the old ball park, on Wentworth, and I want you to go see him. Just take the package and bring it back. Don't ask no questions. Just do what I tell ya."

"Okay, Mr. Comiskey."

"Good kid. That's just what I like."

"Um. When should I go over there?"

"Now. Right now. And if he offers you a shot, just say no thanks, you'll take coffee. Coffee means business, a shot means he's out to scam us, 'cause he don't drink. He's my partner, but he's a nigger."

4

RUBE

The wind howled through the clapboards of the small boarding house. It blew strong enough to scrub the paint clear off, except the previous ten threadbare years had already done their work and the skin of the house gleamed bone-grey. Andrew Foster lay absolutely still in his narrow, sagging bed, listening to the wind compete against the snores and low groans of the other occupants of his room. It was impossible to sleep amidst the howling of the Lord's wrath outside and even more difficult against the grunts of sin within, and Andrew knew that fornication was sinful.

As the hint of grey light seeped its way into the room Foster allowed his eyes to play along the ceiling, reading the map of its cracked plaster, remembering how the parched earth, as dry as the outside of the boarding house, sent its fissures radiating out in all directions. Foster blinked, clearing his eyes and his brain, remembering that he was now in Waco, Texas, feigning sleep as he waited for another day, and another game to begin.

Waco may not have seemed the asshole of the world to some-one like Foster, who had been born and raised in the dust and scrub of southeastern Texas, but to almost anyone else it was. And Miss Grundy's boarding house, where the team roomed when the Yellow Jackets played at home, sat smack in the center of town. In the center of dark-town, that is, where Negroes, the older ones born in slavery, lived. Foster rubbed his eyes, scratched his crotch, stretched his long and muscled arms into the still air, and began to plan, as he always did, his day.

Stretching his arms, he caught a glimpse of the red Texas sun that slanted through the cracks in the bare walls. Rube raised his head, resting it on his hand as he turned over on his side. He thought of the others who shared his room in Mrs. Grundy's and wished they would go away. Hard enough, he thought, to do the Lord's work all by himself, no need to have these fallen brothers drinking and whoring all night long. He reached under the greying pillow just below the crook in his arm and was comforted by the series of tiny smooth bumps that almost tickled the pads of his fingers. Still there, he thought, and he sighed quietly as he cradled the white bone handle of the revolver.

"Son, you take this piece. And anyone whomsoever messes with you, you show him what I taught you out back behind the shop, you hear." Yessir, Andrew Foster had replied to his father's going away present, yes, he understood. The gun was for peace, for protection, for privacy, and it was the Lord's way, or so his father had taught him, in a heathen and sinful world. Now, three months later, in the early summer of 1896, Andrew Foster had already become the starting left fielder and occasional hurler for the Waco Yellow Jackets, the "toughest and winningest" team of Ethiopians this "side of the border" (so the yellow and black flyers proclaimed).

In Calvert where Foster had grown up, just south of Waco along the Brazos River, black folks had talked of only two things—the right Reverend Ebenezer Foster, who also was the town's wealthiest Negro man and the proprietor of Foster's Barbershop and Tonsorial in Rio Brazos, and the weather.

Ebenezer Foster had, he always reminded his children, been born free. "Free as the behind of a newborn is smooth," he proudly said before tipping the brim of his black hat in respect to whoever happened to be listening. "And don't you ever forget it. No one can ever take it from you. No white folks, and no colored either." And then he would look about the room, his eyes finding and locking onto the face of his wife Linda, who nodded her assent. "Yep, EF," she always called him that, and was the only one in the family to use his "professional" name, as in "I'm goin' to EF to get me a haircut. Best damn barber in the whole damn state, black or white, ain't that right?" Yep, she said, seconding his assertion, we are a free family, never been slaves either to the white folk or to the cotton gin.

Whether that assertion had any generational validity was a complete mystery to Andrew and his brothers and sisters. Townfolk just reported that one day, just after the Jubilee, this long and lean black man rode into town and proclaimed himself the newly appointed minister and put down twenty dollars in cash to buy the storefront that he rapidly made into his barber shop.

Ebenezer Foster dominated the town from that day forward. His stern demeanor, his serious gaze, and his love of color made him a figure of great command. As a preacher in Calvert's newly opened (by him, after a whirlwind fundraising drive when people often heard, "if you don't give you will go straight to hell and never ever get a good haircut") Baptist church, EF wore the customary black. But when he wandered across the back street to his parlor (he also pulled teeth, the only moment that he tolerated anything remotely related to alcohol) he slowly peeled off that long black morning coat, removed his wide brimmed black hat, loosened his starched white collar, and carefully draped over his shoulders his newly laundered, crisp white jacket which he snapped together using the two hooks that fastened the collar tight up to his chin.

It was EF's specialty that he cut the hair of anyone who wandered in. His church was black, and he was proud of it, but his shop was open to all. "It's the only way white folks gonna see that we ain't a bunch of cotton pickin' big-eyed good for nothings," he proclaimed more that once to his assembled morning audience. For, despite the integrated nature of his barber shop, his best parishioners always showed up first thing to hear EF's latest opinion on the events of the day. And rarely were they disappointed.

EF, in fact, never ever quit sermonizing. Give him a moment and he would praise the Lord and tell folks what he thought. As his oldest child, Andrew never had the slightest doubt about what was right and what was not. His father, the holder of the word, God's ordained minister on Earth, and the most important black person in Calvert, Texas, told him: "Never, never ever drink. It's against God's will and moreover it's the way that white folks have of trying to enslave us. And we

Fosters, we are free. Have I ever told you that? Free as a baby's ass is smooth. And don't you ever forget it."

Remarkably, Andrew, son of a Negro Baptist minister, never put a drop of the stuff to his mouth. Not a drop. Not in training in Arkansas when he met the great Irish pioneers of white baseball, Mack and McCarthy, not in Chicago with Frank Leland or even in the back room of Comiskey's estate. Not a drop. He knew that someone powerful, and he didn't mean the Lord, would strike him dead on the spot if he ever broke his father's commandment.

By the time Andrew found himself in Waco at eighteen playing for the Yellow Jackets, he had reached his full adult height of six feet four inches, and weighed more than two hundred pounds. But big and strong as he was, his father still scared the devil out of him. And, later in life, when he still had the clarity to think about it, before the pains robbed him, Foster understood why.

In early June, 1887, when Andrew was eleven, he sat in his father's parlor, knees up to his chin, just next to the door at the rear of the cutting room with its leather barber chair, wood cabinets and wall-sized mirror in whose wrinkled glass he could see reflected the faces of The Reverend's early morning customers and callers. It was a Saturday, unusual for its high clear sky, deep blue, almost lapis, and its fragrance, a mixture of pine and hibiscus. Andrew's job, for which he would be paid two bits, was to sweep as unobtrusively as possible the cuttings that collected at his father's feet and to remain silent. He knew the routine, he had been "working" at the shop on Saturdays for the past three years and had learned how to listen and remain in the corner, invisible.

The early morning men, all Negro, all parishioners, all talk and no haircut, shared their opinions on almost anything. But this particularly fragrant and gracious late spring morning they came to EF worried and scared. What, they wondered, would they do if the drought that threatened to plague all of East Texas made it impossible for them to bring in the crops? These quarter mule tenant croppers, most of whom had been slaves on the very land they now wrestled with against the challenges of season and price, knew with the same instinct that enabled them to gauge the next storm by just a glance at the sky, that a dry season meant trouble for black folks in Texas. No one needed explain that hard times, no cash, and meager yields meant that they and their white neighbors, some of whom would be jangling into EF's Tonsorial Parlor within the hour, would have to scuffle even harder to make ends meet. And they also knew that when push came to shove, when they had to pay back the Bradys and Longstreths for their allotment of seed, fertilizer, and silage, and then add interest, these families who owned practically all the land that both black and white farmers cropped, the financial burden, that is to say, the "axe" would fall on them. As one of the men said just loud enough for Andrew to hear, "That's right. When Prince Albert up there in Waco come for his share and no one got any, not us and not them peckerwoods neither, ain't no doubt who gonna carry the freight." The congregation murmured its assent, and EF looked up and said, "Okay. You are correct. Right. So, what we do about it?"

And so began a debate that lasted through the summer, through the worst drought that East Texas would see for the next fifty years, or, more precisely 'til that Monday in May 1934, when the sky turned black with the topsoil of the dust bowl and the day turned into night. By that time only EF, remarkably, of all those assembled in his shop would be alive, in his 90s, talking up his own storm to a young white man from some place in Washington, D.C., who wanted to interview anyone born during slavery — despite EF's protest that he was free, "free as...." But as EF remembered that hot dry angry summer of 1887, while Andrew sat quietly in the corner and recorded it his own way, the debate among his parishioners had prepared them for the storm that would burst on their own time.

Most of EF's congregation believed that life was hell and that the good times would never roll in. Whatever God, nature, and the white folk had in store for them, well, so be it. Forewarned was only that. As one of them said eloquently in mid–August, "Knowing what will happen don't mean shit. Can't do anything about it anyway. Least not when it don't rain and they can still beat up on us." Others murmured their assent. More than twenty years after slavery most of them saw that the world had not really changed. The federal troops, Freedman's Bureau, and long-coated politicians of Reconstruction had come and gone. They knew, these men, that they were stuck on the land out of money and the relatively fluid state of race relations (though none of them would have used those precise words) was as temporary as the pimple on the Reverend's ass. "Pardon, EF, don't mean any disrespect."

"I still say," EF alone would respond in that way he had of being both exasperated and yet somehow patient, "that we got to be ready for the worst. No counting what'll happen when they can't make their payments neither. They'll come after us, and if we sit here talking they'll just burn us out. You mark my words." "God's will is one thing," he would tell them, "but you sometimes got to take a stand. Even against the white folks."

And everyone in the room understood. EF wasn't telling them what to do — well of course he was — but actually he was announcing what he was going to do. And they also understood that black men who stood up to white jealousy, anger, bigotry, and piss were as liable to be lynched as they were to be hungry after a day's work. Simple justice in the presence of none.

But no one expected that Bud Woods would be the cause of it all. Yet, there he was, on a day in late July, a hot, dusty, dry day when the sun had already been up for hours and the earth parched and cracked for its lack of moisture. Even the wind that day just blew hot and steamy breaths of sweat and sorrow. Woods lived not far out of town, just beyond the Calvert-Waco line of the Texas Central Railroad, where he farmed about twenty acres in cotton and a few more of vegetables just to feed his family during the winter months. A farmer, or as they called him, a half-mule sharecropper, Bud Woods gave a third of his annual yield to the same landlord that many of his Negro neighbors worked for. For the past ten years he, and they, had managed to clear, when all was said and done, about twenty-seven dollars a year. Sometimes a bit more, usually somewhat less.

Sometime in the recent past Woods had married the eldest daughter of his nearest white neighbor, George Gudger, and in return he loaned his father-in-law the use of his mule, free, two weeks a year. Not only did the deal cement their familiar relationship, but it continually reminded Woods that he was not the poorest white man in Calvert. At the advanced age of forty-seven Woods had lost half of his front teeth, most of his hair, and all of his sense of humor. As scrawny and tough as the leather cinch on his mule, Woods was little more than an indestructible bag of bones, his bright green eyes the only feature that gave him a semblance of life and hinted at the intelligence he once possessed before the numbness of Texas farming had taken over three decades earlier.

With his wife and six kids Woods lived in a small rectangular cabin, unpainted, with three bedsteads and a cast-iron stove. Everything else, all clothing, food, implements, and whatever, had its own corner for location and identification. The family relieved themselves outside, wherever they could, and fetched water from the Brazos River, which they could reach by crossing the train tracks that lay, an iron boundary, between their farm and the river. With only the mule as transportation, and at that only for fifty weeks of the year, the Woodses rarely made the four mile walk into Calvert. But Bud was a man of great regularity, and on the third Saturday of each month he and the mule walked to Calvert to buy provisions and, at least twice a year, to visit EF's Tonsorial Parlor for a haircut.

Calvert stretched but one block, its two story wood buildings sheltered the usual rooming house, stable, bank, dry-goods store, saloon, and, of course, EF's barber shop. At either end of the street stood the town's two churches, white churches that is, Baptist and Methodist. The African Baptist Church, Ebenezer Foster, Minister, a small frame building whose gable not only suggested a traditional steeple but was barely twice as wide at its base as the door of the church, lay directly across Calvert's other street, the alley that ran the length of the town behind the barber shop, stable, and dry-goods store.

When Woods started to walk into EF's parlor, kicking the dust from his boots as he stepped up from the street onto the bare boards that served as sidewalk and porch, he lifted his gaze from its usual focus on his shuffling feet and noticed that just about every white man in town, and he knew just about all of 'em, was standing in front of the shop barring his way.

"Hey, Bud," one called out, "how you doin' today?"

Woods barely comprehended the question. It had been rarely asked, least not in the past twenty-five years. He knew no one gave a shit how he was doin'. And he also knew that they knew that how he was doing that day was no different from any other day. So, he looked blankly at his interlocutor and said simply, "Howdie."

"Hey, Bud," another said, "We have to talk to you."

"Gotta go get my hair cut."

"That's what we mean to talk to you about. There's been trouble again in Millican. Had to shoot the son of a bitch."

"What that got to do with me?"

"The niggers up there's all upset. Say he was lynched, that they gonna come down here and make trouble."

Woods stared at the men. "But EF ain't like that."

"No matter, we've decided that no nigger gonna cut a white man's hair in Calvert no more."

"But he always cuts my hair."

"Look Bud, he can't cut white hair and nigger hair, not in the same shop, not at the same time. It ain't right. They can't go into Sally's Saloon 'cept round the back, and we ain't gonna get our hair cut here neither."

Woods' eyes remained uncomprehending. He shrugged his shoulders and started to turn away less in resignation than in bewilderment. This was stuff he couldn't fit in his head. Better to have one of the kids trim him up with a razor anyway.

At that moment, however, EF appeared at the door dressed in his Sunday best, that is black from head to foot, from the top of his broad-brimmed hat to the toes of his boots. The men turned to face him as they heard his voice, strong and firm, say, "Morning Mr. Woods. Glad to see you this fine day. I been waitin' for you. Had a good winter? Chair's all ready for you."

And with that Bud Woods turned on his heels, walked back up to EF's emporium, and made his way to the front door. The twenty or so men gathered in front parted, silently, as Woods passed in front of them and disappeared inside.

Andrew went to bed that night with his skin tingling. The family lived in the few rooms atop his father's shop, and the evening wind seemed to seep the grit of the Texas heat right into his body. When he rose to look out the window, something he often did when he couldn't sleep, he could see the moon hanging yellow just over the dry-goods store across the street. The light cast a soft glow on Calvert's dusty street, making shadows of the storefronts into dark cutouts that stretched almost to the family's door. As they slept Andrew leaned his arms against the window sill, felt the rough and splintery texture against the heel of his palms, and leaned slightly out. Silently Andrew contemplated the nightscape, and hearing nothing, he turned his back to the window before retracing the half-dozen steps to his bed. Suspended between wakefulness and sleep, Andrew felt just the slightest disturbance — some inchoate motion that made him stand completely still, searching with all his senses for some hint as to its meaning.

At first he thought it must be the storm that the whole county had been conjuring to break the drought. It started like that. Just a hint of sound accompanied by a change in the air's weight against the skin of his upper body. Frozen in his steps, Andrew focused all of his sense toward the street, peering, feeling, stretching himself to read the change. And then, little by little, like the dawn at its very earliest appearance, the darkness of his awareness lifted and the movement that had translated itself into an echo became a low, soft, distant rumble. It was, he thought, a summer storm. He could feel the thunder as it marched its way toward town. In relief Andrew let his body sag, he had been holding it with exquisite rigidity, and he turned and walked softly back to the window.

The moon had risen slightly and it stood almost over the town, looking down at Calvert's street, watchful, Andrew thought, as God's eye. The yellow-green light gave the night an eerie glow, pale and iridescent as it played against the edge of the town's shadows. Andrew craned his neck out of the window, leaning to his right, stretching his senses up along the street. As he listened to the storm approaching he thought he could see the dust swirling ahead of the deepening cadence. Caught in the thickening atmosphere of wind and moonlight, the tumbling grains of sand billowed and sped toward the center of town.

Only after he actually saw the men on horseback, the white of their sheets snapping in their own speed, heads pitched forward leaning over the necks of their horses, arms akimbo holding the reins in their fists, did Andrew realize that the storm had become a vision. Men, horses, dust, and, now Andrew realized, the light of a dozen torches filled Calvert's street to overflowing. The red-orange flames shot into the night air and Andrew could see their reflection on the ceiling of his room. Awesome, he remembered thinking later, just like the Apocalypse, the horsemen, he was sure, of death.

The men in the streets wheeled their horses to a standstill, the animals pawed and shuffled their hooves in the dirt as their hooded riders pulled up on their reins, each pair, horse and rider, now making small circles around themselves, whirls of dust and menace.

And then, like the eye of a storm, it was quiet. Deathly, abruptly, and unnaturally quiet. Twenty men in white sheets, the cones of their masks each one slightly off kilter, held their horses still with their left hand as they raised their torches in unison with their right. Andrew shuddered at their threat, and as he struggled to comprehend what was happening below, he finally screamed silently, so loud that the chamber of his head vibrated for minutes afterwards, "Father! What do they want?"

EF appeared below. Andrew could see the round brim of his hat, black as the night, coated orange by the torch light which also glinted off the barrel of the shotgun he cradled in his arms. "Good evening gentlemen," he said softly. "Nice night for a ride, Randall. Oh, and Merlon, how's that new calf coming along?"

One by one EF unmasked his visitors and one by one their bodies sagged in response, the nose flaps of the white masks, the small strips that hung down between their eyes, had become coated with sweat and some stuck to the wrong part of their faces, covering an eye rather than the bridge of their nose, or folding up and sticking to their foreheads. Finally Randall Cummins, a local farmer who came in once a month for a shave and a haircut, broke the silence.

"We just don't want you cuttin' any more nigger hair, EF. That's it. No disrespect intended, just tell us that you'll abide and we'll be off." Cummins' voice was brittle, and it cracked as he spoke.

"Well, you know Randall, I have tended to your hair for 'bout a decade just like I've been cutting most of you," and he swept his gun hand in a circle just at their eye level from left to right, "and I don't see how its possible to remain in business just by cutting white folks' hair, you know what I mean. So, I've been giving this a lot of thought since you and your neighbors decided to pay a call on me, and here's my proposition. I think if you leave now I won't have to shoot any of you, and if you leave now and I don't shoot any of you I'll just forget that you left the comfort of your wives and children for this foolishness, and if I forget that you awakened me in the middle of the night and scared the bejezus out of my wife and kids then I'll cut your hair, each and every one of you, every day after 10 o'clock in the morning. Of course I'll cut my brothers' hair every day before then."

EF's words sliced the Klan's bravado in two. Reverend Foster may have thought, "Now go home and wash your linens before your wife discovers you stole 'em off the bed," but he knew that his Solomonic decision depended on his unbending and utterly self-contained demeanor. "You know," he said afterwards to his wife and to Andrew, "I half expected they would be so angry, so filled with vinegar that they would go dig poor Woods out of his bed and string him up, like a Negro, in front of our church."

Andrew, still shaking from the event, equally awestruck by his father's bravery and scared out of his wits by the Klan's midnight ride, ventured, "Why Father? Why did they do that to us? We've all been friends here, haven't we? Mr. Cummins even tossed me a nickel last time he was in. I mean, I understand they don't really like us, you know on account of our color, but I didn't think they wanted to kill us."

And then EF took his collar off, placing it on the kitchen table. He looked exhausted, his eyes red with pain, and Andrew noticed that his left hand shook just a little bit as he steadied himself against the table, its green oilcloth still streaked from the evening meal. "Here's how I considered the situation," he said, looking at Andrew, perhaps for the first time, as something more than a child. "We've been here ten years. Came just after the Federal troops left, and haven't had any problem with the whites. After all most of them are just like our folks. Poor, honest, scrapping to make ends meet. And then, bad times makes for less to go around, you know."

"But, why do these men who let you cut their hair want to burn you out?"

"The way I see it someone put them up to it."

"What do you mean? Who could want to do that, anyway?"

"You got to understand, Andrew, these cowards who dress up in sheets at night to scare Negroes into doing something we don't want to do, they are just as scared themselves. So, and here's what I'm trying to tell you, and I don't want you to forget it, never. When there isn't enough to go around that's when just poor whites and us, our people, that's when we got something in common. And that's exactly when the rich ones, the landlords in Waco and Fort Worth, the ones who everyone around here works for, that's when they get scared too."

"Scared. How can they get scared? They got all the land, all the money. I'd like to be scared like that." Andrew looked at the floor. It was about the longest sentence he had ever addressed to his father, and EF had never talked with him, Andrew realized, like a grown up either.

"Look at it from this perspective," EF said with uncharacteristic patience. "When times are bad who's got the most to lose? That's right. The rich folks. The rich white folks. Texans. And what they're afraid of more than anything else, you mark my words, is that poor people will get so fed up with having nothing that they'll all get together and just take what they need. So, I figure one of the landlords paid a visit the other day to our neighbors, told them about the lynching up in Millican, riled them up good, and kicked their horses in the haunches for good measure."

The moon had already moved behind the Fosters' house and the street outside grew dark. The two, father and son, grew silent, each encased in their own thoughts. The silence of the night provided relief. It would take Andrew most of the rest of his life to understand fully what had happened that evening. But he couldn't fail to comprehend what his father said to him next. "Look Andrew, you have your own life to lead, and you are still a child, but I want you to have something. Here." And with that EF opened a drawer in the kitchen table and took out a small revolver, and presented it to his son. "I'm going to put it away now. But when you leave home I want you to take it with you. You can never be sure when they will come again."

It rained the next week and the town's people, black and white, seemed content with EF's distinction. The whites thought that it was surely in the spirit of the age, a renunciation of the foolishness of Reconstruction, an acknowledgment that they and the Negroes lived in the same place yet occupied separate spaces. When sometime later the Supreme Court in Washington pronounced its separate-but-equal doctrine in the case of *Plessy v. Ferguson*, the good citizens of Calvert, Texas, smiled to themselves and said, "Old EF, he did that all by his lonesome. And he's one of them."

What none seemed to realize was that EF had reserved the best time, the first hours in the day, the time for drinking coffee and for the community to gather and get its bearings, for his congregation. Whites could wait 'til 10, he knew, and when they came into Ebenezer Foster's Tonsorial and Barber Parlor and Salon the Reverend Foster no longer bothered re-sharpening his scissors. And he surely forgot to strop the long razor he wielded like a baton. "Heck," he said to Andrew just before his son went off to play his first game with the Yellow Jackets, "they don't call these rednecks peckerwoods for nothing."

By that time EF had resigned himself to the fact that Andrew would not be following in his footsteps, that he would take his clippings from the paper in Waco and make his fame and fortune in the world of Negro baseball. "Foster Wins Two," the paper proclaimed on its sports page in June of 1897. And not for the first time, either. Young Andrew Foster was the fastest pitcher, white or black, anyone had ever seen in east Texas. But neither was it the first time that he had made headlines in the Waco newspaper.

The winter following EF's segregation order when Andrew was in the middle of sixth grade at Paul Quinn College, the school his father's church ran in Waco, he and his friends decided to walk to the other side of town. It was sometime after four in the afternoon, a time when the leaden grey clouds of February could bring either a snowstorm or the kind of chill wind that cut right through your back and chest. The children, free of Miss Evelyn's reader and her strictures about penmanship, were oblivious to everything except their freedom.

"Let's go down by the river," one called out. And, as if by universal assent the others fell in line and walked north from school to the banks of the Brazos. They moved silently the mile that separated the outskirts of the town from the meandering bank of the river that flowed, Andrew knew, just a few miles further in the other direction to Calvert. Usually when they went to the river they built a fire, warmed their hands, and told each other stories that they heard their parents tell them. Sometimes, too, they just gossiped about the school, and at other times they fell into serious discussions about recent events, with occasional ruminations about human nature. Marcus, known as Can for his inclination to always volunteer ("I can do that, sure"), was especially fond of speculation. "Where do you think this river goes when it stops?" he might inquire. Or, "If you didn't know the fire was hot would you touch it?" His match, Beverly, whose assertiveness was such that no one ever dared bestow a nickname, would inevitably reply, "That's the dumbest question I ever heard. 'Course not, stupid."

Can and Bev and Andy and a few others comprised the sixth grade at Quinn, which despite its name as a college would send them out into the world two years later, after eighth grade. If anyone had the temerity to challenge the intellectual and racial assumptions embedded in that practice, they would have been rare indeed for that time and place. Black Texans, a generation following the end of slavery and Reconstruction, lived in a world defined by ever-hardening segregation. Their responses to that status were conditioned by practicality. Better to accommodate, to find the proper place for one's self, than risk life, limb, and surely livelihood, in defiance. Only Andrew had the example of his father's resistance, and he had not yet expressed the fierce pride that EF had bequeathed him.

"Do you think them friends of your father will go to jail?" Can looked at Andrew, "Do you?"

"'Course they will stupid. They's arrested, and my mother said that the Sheriff will never allow black folks *not* to go to jail." Beverly, as usual, had cut it.

"But they didn't do nothing bad, did they?"

"Bad and against the laws ain't the same thing, Can. That's how we live all the time. You know that."

Can looked up, his eyes searching the horizon. "I guess. But arrested. That still don't seem right. They just wanted to sit at Stillman's where they been sitting for the past ten years. When the show comes in, there they are, like the sunrise. You know, every month, come rain or shine."

Beverly again, impatiently: "The rules changed. Like they did everywhere, and now we can't sit where we want in the theater, or anywhere else. And the sheriff arrested them when they insisted on taking their old seats. And you know what, Can. There's nothing you or I or anyone else can do 'bout it. Nothing."

"We could always play by our own rules," Andrew said quietly, thinking about EF. "Let them think they are calling the shots. And never let them know what we are really thinking. Or planning. Or dreaming."

And then they fell silent. They weren't used to Andrew taking part in their discussions, and they certainly weren't used to the intellect he had flashed. Andrew was a big, strong, quiet, athletic kid to them, a good pal, not much else, and the path he had just illuminated for them was so clear that their silence became as soft as the evening.

The winter light slanted across the Brazos river bank, almost golden, it cast shimmering shadows of the trees from the dunes, down onto the rocky sand where they stood talking, to the edge of the blackened river. The approach of darkness in the late February afternoon stirred them back to activity, and without speaking, for each knew by rote their appointed tasks, they scattered, scrambling up the dunes into the wooded plateau above them.

A thin layer of fear had descended with the evening on the Brazos river, and as if to compensate for its unspoken presence the children scurried with even more energy than usual, picking up branches, tucking them under their arms, running down the graveled dunes, and depositing their burdens in a large pile. After two such round-trips Can stayed behind to bunch the tangled nest into a proper fire. He stood next to the heap of limbs, now taller than his not very tall head, his hands in his pockets, shivering, suddenly aware that he was alone. Night had closed in on the river, and only random glints of light from the rushing waters disrupted the darkness. Can felt for the matches in his pocket and called out, "Hey. Andy. Bev. Where are you?"

He didn't say he was scared, but the tremble in his voice carried his fear into the cold night air. When he received no response Can opened his eyes even wider, as if to somehow better penetrate the silence, stretched his mouth open and then suddenly closed his jaws in amazement. Beverly and Andrew materialized out of the night right in front of him. Their appearance startled him, but what they carried was even more surprising.

Beverly emerged from the night first, and Can could see that she carried something over her shoulder which she supported with her right hand. At first he couldn't make out what seemed to be pointing right at him, like an arrow. Then, not a foot behind her stood Andrew, his arm and shoulder seeming to imitate Beverly's posture. Can realized they were carrying something, long, round, and, jutting out in front of Beverly's face, sharp. It was as wide at its circumference as his arm, and as he squinted to make out the shape even more clearly, Beverly ordered him to light the fire, "So's we can see what we got."

Within minutes the tangle of branches and twigs was a blaze, sparks flickering up to the dark sky, orange light jumping across their faces and into the sand at their feet. They could see the condensation coming from each other's breath, and slowly Andrew and Beverly lowered their burden to the ground. In the light of the bonfire they could see that it was a pale dirty white, with streaks and yellow and blotches of black scarring its long length. Too curved for a spear, too irregular to have been turned on any machine, the long, cylindrical object was, they soon realized, some kind of tusk, unmistakably ivory. "And you should see," stammered Andrew, "you should see, Can, there's dozens of 'em in the hollow just there, where the inlet goes into the dune."

It was too dark to see where Andrew had pointed, but they all knew the place, a sandy estuary where water flowed from the high ground into the river. There, tucked into the fold between dune and river bank, Andrew had stumbled across the remains of what came to be know later as the Waco Mammoths, a herd of late Pleistocene creatures whose tenure in Texas had come to an end some 10,000 years before his discovery. Scientists concluded that the Waco Mammoths died suddenly in some remarkable traumatic event, and that their remains provided a mirror to their social and family structure — at least that's what one of them wrote to Rube a year later. "Dear Waco Discoverers," the letter began, "Congratulations on your scientific find." The author, a geologist from Houston, explained about the mammoths. "They are matriarchal, with a remarkably close resemblance to their African filum."

When Rube asked Beverly about "filum" she said, "Don't you remember? Part of the classification of the natural world. Don't you listen in school?" Despite her chide, Rube cherished the letter and the story that the newspaper, the Waco *Oxbow*, printed about the entire episode.

Andrew, Can, and Beverly stood next to the fire shivering with excitement. "What do you think it is?" whispered Can, while the other two just stared at the long, curved tusk now nestled at their feet in front of the leaping flames. "It's gotta be some kind of bone, that's what," said Beverly.

"But what kind of animal got a bone like that? It sure don't look like anything we got around here," said Andrew, still full of awe.

"What are we gonna do?" Can asked.

"We better find out what it is," Beverly responded with her usual clear-headedness. "Let's go look at some books. I just know it's some kind of animal bone."

And then Andrew surprised himself and the others. "Look. It feels like a tooth. It's some monster tooth. And I say we put it back before something figures it's missing. That's what I say. We put it back."

And, remarkably, for all of them, the others agreed. Andrew and Beverly carried the tusk back to the cache that had accidentally been opened in the lee of the winter storm that would be upon them the next day. Can carried a lighted log for illumination, and when he stuck the torch in the hollowed out space, the three gasped in recognition.

"Lord," Andrew almost cried, "it's a burial place. Look at all the bones." And there in the cave, three children from the African Baptist church school in Waco, Texas, saw the remains of the Waco Mammoths. Fifteen piles of bone and tusk, bundled where the animals had settled to the ground, lay in a circle around the mud floor. The silence felt full and frightening. Andrew and Beverly gently put their tusk down on the ground next to the nearest stack of bone. Can turned to leave, his flame already at the entrance. As Beverly pivoted to follow, Andrew bent down and picked up a chunk of ivory and slipped it into the pocket of his overalls.

The next day the three met after school and decided to go to the public library in Waco. They were turned away. There was not yet a Negro library in the town, Rube remembered. Years later he looked up "Pleistocene Mammoths" in the *Encyclopedia Britannica* one evening when he walked down to the Loop, and found an article written by the same scientist who had first congratulated him.

The discovery sent his imagination spinning. And for the next five months Andrew went to sleep every night dreaming of the ivory in his pocket, wondering what it had once been. He had heard his father, often enough, speak of giant beasts that had roamed the continent Africa, where, as EF put it, "all our people were once free and from whence we have all come," and Andrew convinced himself that the smooth and shiny white object that he rubbed so soothingly between his thumb and two front fingers had come all the way from the Ivory Coast.

As he fondled the gun that he kept beneath his pillow, the one his father presented to him the day he had left home a few weeks earlier, Andrew Foster smiled. The ivory from the cave by the Brazos River sure looked good fixed to the handle. His father had carved and polished it 'til it shone like moonlight, and Andrew remembered writing in his wrinkled and cracked notebook, "Pop gave me the gun today. The one he gave me the night the Klan tried to shut him down. But he fixed the ivory to it, from the cave. Told me to take it with me, not to drink, and if I had to play then at least be the best ballist there ever was."

It took Andrew Foster five years to become the best colored pitcher of his generation and the most astute baseball mind of his time. In the late 1890s Negroes played baseball in Texas on Jim Crow teams in small, dusty towns, in front of almost anyone who could afford the admission price of five cents. As a barnstormer in East Texas, Andrew Foster relied on the strength of his right arm. Until he was called first to Chicago and then to Philadelphia, he believed that all he had to do to win was to pitch hard, fast, and every day. The opposing players may have called him "fast-ball Foster" behind his back, but they never taunted him to his face. His ivory-handled revolver and his reputation for shooting as straight as he pitched kept them on their toes.

If Andrew Foster's segregated schooling ended in the eighth grade, which was all that Paul Quinn College provided, EF made sure that his education continued. By the time he left home to play for the Waco Yellow Jackets, Andrew Foster had not only read the Old and New testaments from cover to cover, but had plowed his way through Virgil and then Homer, whose poetry he came to love almost as much as his father's sermons. And daily he wrote in his journal — observations on everything from the weather to the cost of a can of beans. As he grew older he peppered his speech and his business letters with his trademark blend of economic acuity, classical allusion, and East Texas Bible thumping. Big, brash, and clever, Andrew Foster brimmed with confidence. But it was not until 1903 that he earned the name that he would forever carry with him, when he also learned that being strong did not necessarily mean being the best.

That spring the Yellow Jackets played a series of games in Hot Springs, Arkansas, the training home of the Philadelphia Athletics. Late March in Hot Springs, coincidental with the arrival of wealthy northerners come to take the waters, brought with it warm breezes and dry sky. The Athletics had just, under owner-manager Connie Mack, finished playing a series of exhibitions against John McGraw's New York Giants, and Mack was furious. Not only had he lost three in a row to a team and a manager whom he regarded as ungentlemanly, for McGraw had emerged as a skilled and manipulative strategist whose teams practiced what he called "inside baseball," a combination of guile, finesse, and skill, but Mack's best pitcher Rube Waddell had missed his turn. That meant that Mack would have to take his team east with Waddell badly in need of game experience before the start of the regular season.

McGraw had already noticed Foster, who pitched one afternoon when the Giants' manager slipped into the stands to watch a Negro contest. McGraw, a massively contradictory character, had in public upheld the exclusion of Negro players from the Major Leagues, and at the same time continued to scout light-skinned blacks whom he imagined he could pass off as Cuban, Filipino, even American Indian. Anything to get a leg up in the highly competitive baseball world he determined to dominate. Foster's heavy fastball, not his deep color, attracted McGraw, who told Mack that he had just the pitcher for the Philadelphia team to match against Waddell.

It proved easy enough for Mack to convince the Yellow Jackets to take on the Phils, to set the contest of Waddell against Foster. Waddell needed the outing and the Yellow Jackets, at best a good semi-pro team, always needed the money. Mack promised a hundred for the team and an extra ten if Foster agreed to pitch. As it turned out it was no contest.

The twenty-four-year-old Foster fired fastball after fastball, his full, windmill windup as furious as his delivery, en route to striking out a dozen Phils in a 5 to 2 victory. To add insult to injury, Foster squeezed in the go-ahead run in the fourth inning. It was a decision he had made on his own by signaling to the Yellow Jacket runner on third with a swipe of his left thumb across the short bill of his cap just before stepping back into the batter's box with a two and two count — and with two out. His audacious bunt would tell onlookers far more about Foster's baseball acuity than his strong right arm. But, that day, even his teammates, normally wary of his intensity and his revolver, stood in awe of his pitching. He had beaten the great Rube Waddell, and for that accomplishment he accepted, and used forevermore, the name of the man he had conquered.

Rube Foster rode the wave of his reputation for the rest of the year. Barnstorming across the Midwest, the Yellow Jackets attracted the attention of owners and booking agents from Chicago, Philadelphia, and New York. Frank Leland, the kingpin of Negro baseball in Chicago and the owner-manager of the appropriately named Leland Giants, wired Foster to join his team. Leland enticed Rube with the promise that his club would play all the good white teams. Foster readily accepted, replying, "If you play the best clubs in the land, as you say, it will be a case of Greek meeting Greek. I fear nobody."

Rube Foster, all windmill and fastball, joined his new team determined to set the Negro baseball world on fire. In his first game with the Leland Giants Foster pitched a shutout, and within a month several of the white clubs in the fiercely competitive Michigan League, which sponsored white and Negro teams, inquired about his services. When a white owner offered him five hundred dollars to leave the Leland Giants, Foster jumped about as fast as he could draw. And that was the real beginning of his education.

In Michigan Foster pitched against the best Negro players of his day. They soon came to regard him as a mercenary, less for his willingness to play with whites, for in some respects that is what many of them wished to do, but for his greed. Shunned by his white teammates, some of whom feared ostracism should they openly associate with him, Rube Foster spent the summer of 1903 in complete isolation. When opposing Negro players first saw his full windup they couldn't believe their eyes. One windy afternoon in Battle Creek, playing against the Page Fence Giants, Foster seemed especially determined to establish the strength of his fastball and ignored his catcher's plea to pitch from the stretch. After six innings Foster struck out ten but gave up three walks, two hit batsmen, and five stolen bases—all on his windup. His white catcher failed to assist Rube, in fact only made matters worse by calling for inside pitches which he knew would be harder for him to gun to second or third to catch aggressive base runners. The barrage of abuse that the opposing black players unleashed fed Rube's fire, and pushed him to abandon his experiment with integrated baseball a month later. From that moment on Rube Foster understood two things: that he would learn to win by the force of his intelligence, and that whites only made the world difficult for black folks. Foster was determined to become a great player, and even more importantly, like his father, he realized that the man he allowed white folks to see would only be a pale version of the real person within. "Pitch with your wits," he would say, "and don't let 'em fuck you in the ass."

As he moved from the Michigan League to Philadelphia where he played for the Cuban X Giants, winning four of his team's five games against the Philadelphia Giants in the "Colored championship" that year, Foster supplemented his journal by keeping a finely crafted "book" on every batter he faced, every pitch he threw in every situation. "1∧K," became his shorthand for a fastball up for a strikeout, followed by "0-2" for no outs with a runner on second. He charted habits of opposing players, noted the strengths of their swings, and even kept a book on his own hitting.

When Foster joined the Philadelphia Giants the next season, he struck out fifteen batters in the opening game and hit .400 in the three game series against his old team. Rube Foster added a stunning curve, one which broke sharply and late, to right-handed batters, to his already powerful fastball. His legend which he happily built on the foundation of his nickname included the following episode as retold by Dave Malarcher, the extraordinary third baseman for the Philadelphia Giants, and later for the Indianapolis ABCs.

One afternoon, Foster made a fool of Cuban X Giants batter Topsy Hartsel. He steamed two called strikes past the batter after he signaled for an intentional walk. But each time Foster had the catcher sneak back behind the plate.

"Rube figured he couldn't fool Hartsel that way the last time. So he goes back to the box and stalls around a little more. He was quite a showman, you know. Then he gets in the box and looks at Hartsel. Hartsel's rarin', because he's got those two strikes on him. Then Rube

calls, 'Look out, ump, he's standin' on the plate.' Hartsel looked down, and as he looked down — right through the middle with it! That was it! O, he was marvelous."

Rube Foster laughed as he trotted back to the dugout. As he sat down on the wood strip that served as a bench, his teammates sauntered over and touched him on the shoulder or on the top of his cap. "Rube, you sure foxed him, you sure did," grinned Charlie Grant, who only the year before had been renamed "Chief Tokohoma" in John McGraw's most outrageously unsuccessful attempt to pass a Negro player off as an American Indian. Foster, for the first time, felt that he belonged to a team, perhaps even a community, and he grinned slowly. Not so self-satisfied that his teammates could accuse him of arrogance, but in a way that said to himself and to the others that he was happy to be one of them. He looked down at his shoes and appeared to adjust the laces. Just then he felt a shadow pass in front of his eyes and he heard the full bass voice of his first baseman. "You all right Foster. You all right."

Foster looked up, pleased. Standing before him was the largest black man he had ever seen. The legend PHILADELPHIA GIANTS seemed lost across the breadth of his chest. Jack Johnson lifted his head to the stands behind Foster and laughed, "Yes sir, Foster, you sure made him look like the fool he his. Tell you what. I'm gonna buy you dinner tonight. You just made my day, yes sir." And with that Johnson took his place on the far end of the bench, pushed the cap down over his eyes, and fell, as he usually did between innings, asleep. Foster finished the game by striking out the side in the last two innings, and as he left Shibe Park, to walk to the boarding house on 21st and Lehigh where he and most of the single players slept, dressed, and took their meals, he heard Johnson: "Hey, pal. See you at Bookbinders tonight. Eight o'clock. Look like you belong there." Foster looked up and saw Johnson's open car careen around the corner, on its way, Foster imagined, to Market Street and the 38th street gym that he knew Johnson liked to hang out at. Foster shook his head to himself, laughed, and, bat still resting on his shoulder, he sauntered his way home.

❧ ❧

Rube Foster, from Calvert, Texas, had never been to a place as grand as Bookbinders, a cavernous seafood emporium that gave new meaning to the American turn of the century indulgence of a lobster palace. Bookbinders served outrageously portioned meals, steak, seafood, and particularly lobster, to well turned out, mutton chopped, prosperous business men and celebrities. Women rarely ventured inside the leather and crystal luxe of places like Bookbinders where waiters in suspenders, bow-ties, and white aprons folded to the waist presided over the excess of food and drink that they carefully balanced on silver trays high over the heads of their patrons. Chinese paper lanterns illuminated Bookbinders that evening, its open terrace set above the lapping waters of the Delaware River. When Foster stepped off the South Street streetcar, he couldn't miss his destination. Among the dozen warehouses and wholesale fish markets that lined the river's edge, only Bookbinders, all light and energy that mild evening in 1903, invited him.

But when Rube arrived at the door to the restaurant, the name Bookbinders embossed in gold over a deep red awning, the maitre d' scowled and told him to report to the rear entrance, the one reserved for "the help." A shiver, a combination of shame and anger, rippled through his neck, and he replied, fists clenched against the side of his pants, "I'm meeting some friends here tonight." And then he paused, taking in the already arched eyebrow not inches away, "I would have thought you knew Mr. Johnson."

The waiter stepped back, lowered his head slightly and said, "Mr. Johnson. Right this way." No apology, no deference, just "Right this way." And with that he gestured, pointing Foster to a table in the rear of the cavernous restaurant at which Jack Johnson, the leading contender for the heavyweight championship of the world and starting first baseman for the Philadelphia Giants, was seated.

Jack Johnson, glass in hand, raised his fingers, snapped them, and called out, "Hey. Foster. Over here! Come on, pull up a piece. This here," he said turning to the other man at the table, "this here is Rube Foster, best damn pitcher in baseball. Black or white. His fastball's so quick it'd make you shit, if you had any inside you." And Johnson tilted his head back and roared, "Which you don't." And then Johnson, white suit, red suspenders, and three gold teeth that gleamed when he smiled, introduced Rube to the first white sportswriter he had ever met. The man Johnson introduced, with a kind of a wink Rube thought, was Wally, or H. Walter Schlichter, scribe for the *Philadelphia Item*, and co-owner, along with Sol White, of the Giants. Foster noted quietly to himself that the white man didn't flinch when Johnson jived him, and he wondered what the evening would present.

With the irrepressible Johnson presiding he didn't have to wait long. In less than three hours he learned more than he ever knew about the business of baseball and almost as much as he wanted to know about race relations. Schlichter was the source of information about the first subject, and Johnson inspired the second. The writer-owner spoke with a kind of formal elegance that Foster had never encountered in East Texas. "Well, Mr. Foster, would you care to share your opinion on the vexing question of wagering on sporting events?" Or, "Rube, would you mind my calling you by your given name? Have you ever wondered about how this glorious game of ours, this wondrous contest, has come to be so enmeshed in the culture of commercial exchange?" What Schlichter soon disclosed was his understanding of the complex web of booking agencies and percentages that governed the shadowy world of Negro baseball. "Just like merchandising anything," he intoned, "it's not what you sell, but how and to whom. And he who controls the distribution of the product, controls the sales, the price, the wage. Everything."

"Does that mean that every time I scuffle to play a game, that every train I take, every town I visit is because some booking agent fixed it?" asked Rube.

"Fixed it and along with it acquired what you might call a piece of the action. He calls it a commission. It's even more pernicious in vaudeville and the minstrel show business," Wally added. "TOBA controls just about every act in the country."

Foster looked blankly at the writer when Johnson suddenly broke in. "What's a matter with you, Rube? Ain't you ever heard of the TOBA, they call it the Theater Owners Booking Agency. To us it means Tough on Black Asses. And the only thing tougher are the white sons a bitches who won't even allow us to get our asses in the damn door. Between the two of 'em, we only got but one choice."

"So," Foster calculated, "is that why we hardly get any real pay?

No disrespect, Mr. Schlichter, but when I look up in the stands on Sunday and see four maybe five thousand people and they each paid a quarter to get in, and I know that I don't get but ten bucks for the game. Well, seems to me that someone's making the gravy. And when we're home, that's like Ulysses come back to Penelope, if you get my drift, and I know he did better than we, I just know it."

"Everyone takes their cut. That's how it's negotiated, young man. I can assure you that I rarely make even as much as you from a contest such as the one you have just outlined. Sol White and I, we really just own the team name. Everything else, even the uniforms, we get from somewhere else. That's how fate, and I see you understand the role of fate, decrees it."

Rube thought for an instant, and decided to keep his own counsel. Instead he said, "Yep, I guess even Achilles would only make a ten spot playing for the Giants."

"The real truth, Ruby," said Johnson, "the real truth is that even if these damn agents didn't have their fingers in the pie, the crackers, the white bigots who simply can't stand it that we black folks play ball, box, even," and he paused to sweep his hand around the restaurant, "eat at a swell joint like this, would keep us out anyway. Lookit. I can't even get a fight no more. Not with anyone white that is. The writers, the matchmakers, the agents, even the police, they're all scared that I'll win. It's the last fucking thing they want."

Johnson's eyes went hard. His voice sounded suddenly weary, and Foster felt the combination of anger and pain reflected back at him. "This is some tough town, Foster. It's okay to play ball against other members of the dusky race. But just try to really fight 'em, just try. No sir, they don't want any uppity niggers in their town. Do you know, they call this place the City of Brotherly Love."

Somehow the three men polished off their dinners, each leaving a pile of orange-red shells and translucent fingers of cartilage next to their plates. As the waiter approached, ready to bring them dessert and coffee, "And three of them Martell," grinned Johnson.

Rube pushed his chair back, tilting his head to the side, and, as if speaking to the room, asked, "Why is it so damn hard to be a black man in this world. It feels like we do the work of Hercules and get treated like lepers. I know that whites are afraid of us, I just don't know why, and sometimes I'm not sure, not at all sure, how to live like a black man here, you know, in the north. Back home once they changed the rules on us at least we knew where we stood, and what to expect."

"Don't tell me brother," interrupted Johnson, his voice filled with passion and irony, "now you gonna ask, what exactly the rules are up here. It's simple. Keep your black ass out of the white folks' business. 'Cept, of course, if you are better than any of 'em. And in that case, don't even think about being in the same room. Okay. You gonna say, what the fuck we doin' here? And now my young friend, my outta Texas fireballer, now you gonna learn something you ain't never gonna forget. But I can't show you 'bout it here. Drink up, let's go."

Fifteen minutes later they knocked on a dark mahogany door of a three story red brick town house uptown, on Pine Street just below 42nd. The street had a natural grace, each building looked just like its neighbor, yet each sported some insignia or detail that marked its individuality. The play of the summer sycamore leaves let light and shadow dance on the pavement as their cab drove off and the three men walked up the half-flight of stairs that led from the street to the main door.

The black man greeted Johnson with a raised eyebrow, "Jack. Another seminar I surmise? Won't you all come in? I'll find something of a refreshment, Jack can show you in, he knows the way. N'est-ce pas?"

"None a that French stuff, W.E.B., us black folks, we done hardly learned this here English yet. Ain't that right, y'all?"

W.E.B. Du Bois returned some minutes later and joined his seated guests. He looked at them with curiosity, the one white and two black men. "Well, Jack. Will you introduce me to your friend? Of course, I already have made Mr. Schlichter's acquaintance."

Johnson introduced Rube to his host, and as he leaned back and stretched his arms out and over the back of the sofa, he added, "I thought Rube here could use a little lesson in survival. He's from Texas, got a hellofa fastball, daddy's a preacher there, and this is his first time in 'de land o' milk and honey'." Du Bois nodded, and stood.

He talked for almost half an hour, about how Negroes had been coming to cities like Philadelphia for almost two hundred years, living and working alongside whites, yet never really part of their city, their social structure, their culture. But unlike the man whom he referred to with great elegance as Mr. Booker T. Washington, Du Bois believed that blacks in the North had a new obligation: to oppose segregation, to fight it hand to hand, neighborhood to neighborhood, and at the same time learn to live within the limits it imposed. "You see, Mr. Foster, this kind of race-hatred is our political enemy, but it is also our cultural and psychological condition. We need to learn to both live in it and to fight against it with all our energy. Did you know, for example, that ten thousand black folks live down near Lombard Street, all crushed into the Seventh Ward, where they are impoverished, ill-housed, and commit more crimes, have more diseases than any other group of people in this fair city?"

Foster looked hard at Du Bois, at the elegance of his head, the fine cut of his goatee, his deep and lustrous skin. It was as if his father, EF, had been reincarnated into a polished academic, his shotgun replaced by an invisible yardstick that could measure the welter of chaos, of appearances, and mark it clearly. Jack Johnson sat, his body steady, a few feet away, and as if in a church service, out of pride and not without a tinge of jealousy, he injected, "That's right brother," and "You sure said it," from time to time while Du Bois continued.

"We are, we black folk, both different from and equal to our European cousins. You know the spiritual, 'Nobody Knows the Trouble I've Seen?'"

"Nobody knows but Jesus," Foster responded.

"Well, Brother Foster, that part of our culture, our blackness, is only part of our heritage here in the New World. We are also participants in the traditions of Shakespeare and Tennyson, of Emerson and Whitman. And that, if I may quote myself, is our curse and our blessing, for we black folk are of two cultures, two warring ideals in one dark body, and it is our inner strength, our courage as a people that keeps us from being split asunder. It is also our mission. We black folk have but one obligation, to maintain our integrity so that we may destroy racism."

Rube Foster pitched and then managed for several Negro teams over the next dozen years. In 1907 he became the booking agent for the Leland Giants, and immediately negotiated a fifty percent share of the gate from the white ball park proprietors on Chicago's South Side. "You want me and my team to play, this week, against the Cubs," he argued, "then it's gonna cost you. Half, and not a penny less." His team lost three of four to Hall of Fame pitcher Mordecai "Three Finger" Brown, but Foster's fifty-fifty policy remained in effect until 1919. In 1909 Foster took over the Leland Giants completely, managing and pitching his team to a season record of 129 and 6. His shortstop that season, John Henry Lloyd, had already earned his famous "Black Wagner" nickname. He hadn't yet earned the reputation for being Foster's match at negotiations––until he held out in 1910, "unless you pay me what I'm worth. I'd rather clean the streets than play this game for less." When Foster tested Lloyd, he learned to take him for his word. Later, Foster always believed that the 1909 Lelands were the best team, black or white in the history of the game.

Two years later Foster owned the team. He forced Leland to relinquish control, changed the name to the Chicago American Giants, and found a silent partner in John M. Schorling, a tavern owner in Bridgeport who had been leasing old White Sox Park on 39th since Comiskey had moved to his new stadium four blocks to the north. Foster insisted on his usual fifty-fifty deal, which the two men sealed with a handshake, and set about building a team which would dominate Negro baseball in America for the rest of the decade. "Darlin'," he would drawl in his sweetest Texas accent, "I play to win, and the only way to win is to attack."

One summer Saturday, the new stands of the old ball park filled to overflowing with more than nine thousand cheering South Siders, some from what they had begun to call the Black Belt and others from the white ethnic enclaves in Bridgeport and Back of the Yards, Foster's Chicago American Giants took on the city's other Negro team, the Chicago Giants. Foster readied his men that afternoon, two hours before game time, with his usual bunting drill. "You don't bunt it into my hat," he ordered, pointing to the cap he had placed midway between the mound and the third base line, "and you don't play. Then, turning to his other star pitcher, Smokey Joe Williams, he said, "And if anyone, I mean any one of them dares to bunt at you, over there by first, you just run right over them. Just like that. Got it?" Williams didn't have to answer the question, he knew it wasn't necessary.

With Williams pitching a two-hitter into the seventh inning, Rube contented himself with sitting on the far end of the bench, smoking his pipe and plotting his victory. He knew Williams had what it took that afternoon, and he knew that his team needed but a single run to win. "How many times do I have to tell you," he yelled to his players during bunting practice, "in most cases the game is won in one rally. That means that when you get the opportunity you'd better win it now."

And now, with a runner on first and but one out, with the score tied at 0-0, Foster judged to be the time. Jelly Gardner, a roly-poly second baseman, kicked his spikes in the on deck circle, glanced over to Foster as he walked, knock-kneed, to the plate and took his stance, left-handed, his bat held high, torqued slightly back over his head toward the pitcher. Foster had decided not to mess with his stance. Gardner was a true slap hitter, with great bat control, and Foster knew not to tinker. "Now's the time," he thought to himself, and sucked on his pipe. As Gardner looked over Foster leaned back and released two smoke rings then took the pipe from his mouth and knocked it against his shoe, and turned his attention to the pitcher. Gardner slammed Harry Buckner's second pitch, an inside fast ball at the belt, over the head of first baseman Sam Strothers, and into the right field corner beyond the lunge of Bobby Winston, who had shaded Jelly to right center. Bruce Peteway, the runner on first, churned his way home even before the right fielder retrieved the ball, and as Gardner rounded second he picked up the signal from the third base coach to hit the deck. Gardner saw the Giants' third baseman, Willy Green, crouched low, glove at his knees, slightly to the left-field side of the bag. As he launched his slide, hooking his right leg out to catch the opposite corner of the base, he felt rather than saw the relay from the second baseman. The ball thudded into the Green's glove waist high and slightly to his right. Green back-handed the ball and swiped his glove down and to the left, his body tumbling into the dirt behind the effort of his arm and hand. But Gardner's hook slide extended the runner's body just far enough away from Green's lunging tag. "Safe," boomed the umpire, who had run most of the way to third from his perch behind the pitcher's mound, "he's safe."

Gardner stood tall on third, dusting himself off, proud that his triple had scored what he too thought would be the winning run.

He wondered if Rube would give him a couple of extra bucks for his effort.

Foster leaned down the bench. "Hey, Smalls," he yelled at Joey Smalls, "you go in and run for Jelly Bean. Now." Gardner grinned as he ran back to the bench anticipating his reward. Foster took the pipe from his mouth, held it up, pointing to the invisible hat between third and the mound, "That will cost you a day's wages, my man. I told you to bunt. You missed the sign." Gardner's face fell as he remembered. Two smoke rings, what the fuck, Foster's secret signs, so secret that Gardner forgot to remember 'em. And now he was getting stacked for hitting a winning triple. "Darlin', you just got to play it my way. It's the only way." Foster's sweetness replaced his disapproval almost instantly and he patted Jelly on the back, turned his attention to the game, and stuck the stem of his pipe firmly into his mouth.

"I dunno," said Malarcher years later, "if Foster was as great a psychologist as he thought he was, but I do know that he was the best baseball manager I ever saw … better than even McGraw or Mack."

5

SPRING 1916

Sam and Rube met the same day in 1916 that Comiskey told Sam about his secret partner. "Get over there, Sammy, and tell Foster that I want him to front for me. You know. That I need him to hold some of my dough while I go after a couple of new players. That Jackson's okay on the field, but I need some real class on this club and I got a terrific idea."

As Sam flipped his straw hat back on his head Comiskey's next words followed him out the door. "And I want you to look his team over. I got an idea. Tell me about Foster's best players," and then he paused, "but don't let on that I asked you."

Sam walked the eight blocks south and east from Comiskey's office to the Chicago American Giants' field. The park was as small and intimate as Comiskey Park was grand and imperial. The new grandstand that Foster had constructed out of concrete and steel contrasted with the chicken wire and knot-holed wood fabrication of the rest of the place. Garbage and papers swirled in the May wind that early afternoon as Sam made his way through almost empty streets. Everyone must, he realized, be working. Nothing like a war in Europe to get the factories cranking. Three story tenements crowded each side of the street as he walked south on Wentworth. Wood frames, creaking porches, windows shielded by dingy curtains, the three-flats, as the apartments of two generations of Irish and Polish workers in the mills and the yards were known, had become prime targets of a new generation of real estate speculators. These men had worked their way around Chicago for the last dozen years, Sam knew, finding new ways to turn a buck on the misery of someone else. Rich folks could bemoan the unethical tactics they employed, and cry loud and long for reform and regulation. But they never cried too loudly, Sam realized, because so many of them were involved in businesses whose practices they wanted to remain, as they called it, discreet.

No sense calling the toll on the realtors if you wanted people to keep their noses out of the mortgage business, or coal delivery, or especially the city government. No, that's not the way Chicago worked. So, Sam remarked, as he walked past block after block of signs that promised the newest answer to the housing shortage in the city, the kitchenette. Take those three-flats, divide each three or four room apartment up into an equal number of units, add the rudiments of a kitchen, a stove, sink, and couple of shelves, and a flat could be made into three or four kitchenettes in no time at all. Figure it up, one of the landlords had told him a year earlier. "I got two buildings, used to bring me twelve bucks a month for the six apartments. Now I get ten a month for everyone of them kitchenettes. That's two hundred forty dollars a month. Waddid I usta make? That's right. Seventy-two. Waddaya think I am, stupid?"

But it wasn't quite so easy. The Irish house painters and teamsters, the German haulers and drapers, and the Polish butchers all understood what a fair rent was supposed to be in the neighborhood. And what they were supposed to get for their money. "Mister," they used to tell Sam, indignation mixed with irony, "you must think we're a bunch of greenhorns. You go rent that trap to the niggers." And that, of course, is exactly what the realtors and building owners did. In dreary offices, grimy with disrepute, a different class of men, fixers and takers, what Upton Sinclair might have called grafters, circled block after block of the South Side, marking their maps with red lines, sealing the fate of the black migrants yet to come. Take just one building, convert it into kitchenettes, move just one Negro family in, and they knew the whole block would turn over within a month. Sam could see it before his eyes, the closer he got to the old ball park, the further south he walked, the more evident the transformation. They even had a new name for it. "Bronzeville," its center now at 35th and State.

Thirty-fifth Street shielded the wealthy of Chicago's near South Side from the Black Belt. Just to the north of 35th the magnates of the packing industry had constructed the Armour Institute at the intersection of 33rd and Federal. There, as Alice taught Sam, in a massive stone building whose Romanesque arches repeated themselves from the limestone base to the gabled roof, Chicago gathered its first generation of professionally trained engineers, while two blocks to the east, on 33rd and Indiana, Adler and Sullivan had designed an equally massive synagogue for the city's oldest Jewish congregation. The wondrous arched entrance to the limestone building seemed to Sam a twin to the cavernous Auditorium building on Michigan Avenue just off the Loop. Not that he had ever been inside the splendid temple. It had been built by and for the city's prosperous German Jews, and the likes of Sam's parents would have never thought to set their worn out schul prayer books inside such a grand structure. Just a few blocks further east on 33rd and Calumet the strangely Tudor-modern Robert Robinson rowhouses designed by Frank Lloyd Wright articulated accurately the class structure of the old South Side. But, directly to the south of 35th, centered at State, the new Negro community of Chicago had begun to lay claim to its share of the city.

There, where two streetcar lines crossed under an umbrella of electric lines illuminated by row after row of black cast-iron street lights, the few prosperous members of the new Negro community had already established themselves. Compared with the Loop, the center of Bronzeville seemed miniature, none of its buildings taller than three stories, almost all of them faced in a dark red, almost brown, brick that made them seem even lower and heavier. Set against the street grid of the city, Bronzeville looked to Sam both spacious and depressing. Many of the neighborhood's avenues, boulevards like Southern Parkway, had been built with park-like islands running down the middle of their divided streets. Grass and park benches filled the new thoroughfares with the accouterments of suburban leisure, while the low building level only made Chicago's remarkable flatness even more open and expansive. Looking south along Prairie Avenue made Sam feel as if he could see out and through the rest of the city, sending his vision and imagination along the red-brown lined avenues all the way to the Indiana border.

On the corner of 36th and State, just a stone's throw from Comiskey's office and park, Sam knew that one of the two or three really wealthy Chicago Negroes, Anthony, called by his friends and enemies — and he had plenty of both — Black Tony, Overton owned his own building. The Chicago *Bee* Building not only housed Overton's newspaper, the city's main rival to the *Defender*, but also the offices of the two small and one large legal and illegal insurance companies that he controlled. Black Tony, whose fortune rested on what he called "makin' good policies, baby," had been a book maker with a remarkable memory, "almost as good as Abracadabra," they said on the street comparing Tony to the legendary Arnold Rothstein, an accountant turned entrepreneur who controlled most of the gambling in New York. Overton turned his penchant for calculating the odds into a thriving back door life insurance business. "You pays a quarter for a whole lot of peace of mind," was the sales pitch he passed on to his network of female policy makers who worked by the building and on commission. "And for a nickel more, we can play the numbers." It was a racket that grew with the neighborhood. And Black Tony, thanks to his newspaper business, where he served as publisher, editor, and feature writer for the *Bee*, had his fingers on Bronzeville's pulse.

By the spring of 1915 Overton had, in fact, calculated that his legal and illegal insurance business would outgrow the space he had available. At that moment he decided to consolidate his holdings into the second largest black-owned company in Chicago and founded Liberty Insurance. Later that summer Overton laid the cornerstone for the Liberty Building, a block-long three story office building along 35th between State and Indiana. The Liberty Building anchored the commercial center of Bronzeville, providing its residents with a downtown, attracting a host of retail establishments, restaurants and coffee shops, tap rooms and laundries, and clothing and barbershops to serve the neighborhood.

Negroes arrived in Bronzeville every day from the South. From Mississippi, the Delta, from Greenwood, and Preston, and Yazoo. They all knew someone in Chicago, a relative, a friend, a townsman from home. And they always were taken to the South Side, the place that white Chicago told them it was all right to live. And if no one met them at the station, or if the men from the Urban League couldn't find them a place to live, they always had access to the "best damn hotel on the South Side," the Negro YMCA, whose doors on 37th and Wabash were always open for "ten cents a night, clean sheets and coffee included."

Sam walked through the neighborhood and glanced at the storefronts that moved past his peripheral vision. Shops that still belonged to Irish, Polish, and German merchants who continued to deliver coal, install hardware, sell dry goods to their new neighbors continued to line the familiar streets the further south he walked.

"Lonnigan and Son's: Painting and Decoration," read the hand lettered sign over the storefront between 37th and 38th streets. "Hey Studs," the proprietor yelled, "be careful where you set that can down, willya."

"Sure Pop," returned the boy, who had reached into his back pocket to find the comb with which to push the stray hair back into place. "Sure. Dontcha worry about nuttin'. I got it all under control." The scrawny fifteen-year-old boy stood now, hands on hips, and lit a cigarette which he allowed to dangle with studied nonchalance from his lower lip.

"And watch them ashes, too. We can't be too careful with that white paint. Don't want to screw up the color. Got that?"

"Sure, Pop," Studs replied as he took a deep drag and flicked the ash into the chalky white paint at his feet. "Sure, Pop, don't worry about a thing."

Minutes later Sam knocked on Foster's door.

"How you doin' Darlin'. I hear Mr. Big's got him a new boy. Well, whatcha lookin' at. Ain't you never seen a black man knew how to dress?"

Sam had hardly poked his head into Foster's incredibly disorganized office when a huge dark hand extended itself and a voice restated, "Whatcha doing there gawkin'? Come right in. Make yourself at home. Just push that stuff out the way. There. Coffee?" And there was Rube Foster, larger than life, dressed to the nines, his voice brimming with good cheer.

Sam felt unaccountably shy, and instead offered, "It's a real pleasure to meet you Mr. Foster. Mr. Comiskey told me I might find you in this time of day."

"Its Rube. You can call him whatever you want. But my friends call me Rube. You want it black?"

Foster's easygoing assertiveness did little to relieve Sam of his discomfort. For all his insider knowledge of the South Side, Sam had little direct experience with Negroes. His awkwardness hardly eased when

he spotted the ivory handled revolver poking out from its leather holster under Foster's open jacket. Foster followed Sam's eyes as they moved up his arm to the gun. He grinned.

"It's a gift from my pappy. He gave it to me when I left home. I always wear it. Only my players don't know it ain't loaded." Foster paused, "usually." The owner-manager-pitcher of the Chicago American Giants glanced over to a clear corner of his desk where EF's photograph stared out at Sam. "That's him. Still alive, still preaching, still cuttin'."

Sam took in the face of a black man, whose dark and luminous skin, fierce eyes, and intensity seemed strangely familiar. "Your father. A preacher and a barber? My old man, he's in the jewelry business. But it's tough, filled with gonoffs, you know."

"Must work down 'round Maxwell Street, right? It's very hamish there. That where you from darlin?"

Sam wasn't prepared to meet a Negro baseball operator who not only knew something about his neighborhood but who laced his Southern vernacular with Yiddish. He smiled slightly, and Foster grinned again. "Yep. Funny. My father always told me that your people were the people of the book, of freedom, that if I ever met any I was to accord them all the respect that they deserved. Besides, when I played in Philadelphia 'bout fifteen years ago I acquired a taste for your cookin'. Not all of it mind you, some o' that meat's stringy enough to mend a chicken coop, but give me some kreplach and kishke anytime. Yes, anytime."

Sam felt his shoulders and neck sag, imperceptibly, in response to Foster's charm. They sat together for the next hour trading stories about their families, their past, their experience in Chicago. Something connected between the son of immigrants and the son of an East Texas preacher — now thrown together improbably in the shadowy world of Chicago baseball.

They compared the best players they had ever seen. "No one, absolutely no one hits the ball better, harder, than Joe Jackson," Sam said softly. "You know how it sounds when a great batter really sticks the ball, its got a crack that's like a rifle shot. Only Joe Jackson hits it like that."

"Lookit. I seen and played with the best colored ball players in the country, and there's half a dozen who Joe Jackson couldn't hold a candle to, nosir. Sure, he's a country hitter. But we're talking ball players, ain't we. Real ball players. Take my shortstop, John Henry Lloyd, even now he's an old man, must be close to forty, even older'n me, we call him Pop. And he can hit circles around Jackson. Why I remember when he hit a ball so hard that the cover came clear off before it drilled a hole in the left field fence." And then Foster wrinkled his nose.

Sam didn't know Lloyd. Not yet. He had, he realized, never been to a Negro team game. But he liked Foster's directness, his understanding of the game, his sense of how to win. "See," said Rube, "you got to out-think and then out-hustle the other team, like Hector did with Achilles, find the weak spot, go slow, then bam, take 'em out."

Sam didn't always agree, but he knew that the other man had acquired such a vast reservoir of experience, as a pitcher and now as a manager, that Sam's casual fandom had nothing to compare with Foster's command. And, it became perfectly clear to Sam that Foster rarely talked simply about baseball.

"It's like this," Rube dropped his voice, simultaneously making it hard as iron, "sometimes you gotta invent new rules while everyone else is playing by ones that don't do what you need 'em to. That's what my father, that preaching barber over there, taught me. And he wasn't talking 'bout baseball, believe you me."

Sam glanced again at the photograph of EF. The skin was so tight, he thought, across the man's skull, it made him look like one of the paintings that Alice Norman had shown him at Hull House when he was a kid. He just couldn't place it, and as Foster talked, showering Sam with information, lore, and lingo about Negro baseball and Negro baseball players, about a virtually invisible world that, "Folks like you, you know what I mean, never even knew existed," Sam continued to turn the image of EF over in his head, running it through his memory. It couldn't have been a painting. He had never seen a black face in one of Alice's paintings. Foster continued, Sam listening intently and still thinking, "What you will never understand my friend is that I got to live in two places. I live in your world, and I live in mine. And they ain't the same place. No sir. Now most of the time it don't cause me no worry. But sometimes, when the peckerwoods, you know darlin' that's Texas talk for crackers, come out of the woods they make it almost impossible to live like a man and a black man at the same time."

Sam dared. "You know Rube, sometimes it's the same for my people. You know, the Jews. Sure in our own neighborhood there isn't much problem, but my parents, they look and talk like foreigners, and the rest of the world treats them either like dumb greenhorns, or some kind of servant of the devil. Like we're going to steal their babies, poison the water."

And he looked into Foster's face for some glint of recognition, some acknowledgment of commonality. Sam didn't even quite know why he needed that from the other man, only that he did. There was, he felt, a common bond, but he wasn't yet sure.

Foster's broad face broke into a grin, one so wide that Sam thought for a moment that he was going to howl, and, after a moment, a suspended silence, he laughed, "You dumb shit. What you think I been talking about all this time. You think I don't know our people keep getting the same short end of the stick from the same motherfuckers? I told you my pappy schooled me right. So, just set down, relax. What we gonna do with that gonoff Comiskey?"

Sam had been so engaged that he had almost forgotten why Comiskey had sent him to see Foster in the first place. He cleared his throat, looked up, and quietly began to speak. "Mr. Comiskey thinks the time is right to reconstitute the Sox, to contend for the pennant, and these are his words, 'to knock them fuckin' Cubs up to Milwaukee.'"

"And what," asked Foster with just a trace of irony, "is new about that news? He's always talking that talk. Ever since I met him and became one of his so called 'silent' partners, running this team to make money off the books for the old horse thief, he's been talking about runnin' the Cubs out of town and winning the Series. I just never knew which was more important to him, do you?"

"He wanted me to give you this package. He said you'd understand. That I was to wait and bring back what he asked for." Sam's voice had changed. He lost his shy inflection, one that ended each sentence with just the hint of a question. Now he was back doing business. Doing what Comiskey had asked, what Comiskey was paying him to do. He looked Foster in the eyes, handed him the package, a small rectangle, the size Sam thought of a book or a box of not so fancy cigars, wrapped in butchers' paper, white and shiny, the ends folded into themselves. "No pickle there," Sam laughed silently to himself, as he watched Foster take the package from his hands and put it in the drawer of his desk, ever so carefully.

Rube moved like a cat, with incredible quickness and remarkable agility. In a blur of action so rapid that he thought that the great Houdini himself had materialized before him, Sam found himself looking at what seemed to be the same package, now extending from Foster's hand. "Tell the old man that's that. Okay?"

Sam acknowledged Foster's instructions with a nod. It had never occurred to him that he would become their bag man, but that's the way Comiskey seemed to play it, and Sam felt obliged to carry out his instructions: at least on the first day. Of course, Rube had already let on that he made money for the old man, so perhaps there was nothing more mysterious going on than a simple banking transaction. Somehow, though, Sam didn't quite believe his own speculations. Another inner voice told him there was more to it. Much more. Still, he and Foster had seemed to hit it off. And as Sam readied himself to leave and report back to Comiskey, he noticed yet again the picture of EF on Foster's desk. And then it hit him. He did know the face, and he blurted out. "You know. Your father looks just like a photograph of a man I saw on a magazine, must have been more than ten years ago. You know. A Negro. Some kind of political leader, who wanted to organize Negroes to, um, defend themselves against attacks. I can't remember his name, but he had several initials…"

Before Sam could finish Rube Foster reached behind him and plucked a copy of *The Crisis* from the shelf behind him. "W.E.B. Du Bois's name, my friend. He's the founder of the NAACP and writes for this paper. I met him in Philadelphia when I played for the Giants there. He changed my life, Du Bois did. And you're right. Not only does he look like my pappy, there's something uncanny about how they look at life the same way."

"You know, I can't quite remember what the paper wrote about him. It was a long time ago, and I hardly had any understanding of the world then. But I remember how he looked, so strong and fierce."

Foster held his breath ever so slightly. Sam thought he was trying to decide whether to tell him something important. Rube exhaled, "I'll never forget what he told me. He said that Negroes had a special burden. Well, hell, I knew that. But he put it in a way I'd never thought about before, even though as soon as he said it, well, it made the same kind of sense my father did when he talked. Anyway, Du Bois told me, and then I read it right here in *The Crisis,* that we, black folks, lived a double life, he called it a double consciousness, part in your, you know, the white world, and part in ours. We are, as a people, he told me, like Sampson, holding two opposing forces, one in each hand, as they pull and struggle to get away from each other. It's the destiny of black folk to be forever torn between these pillars. You might say the struggle makes us the very soul of this country — a white nation that doesn't want us but sure as hell needs us."

Sam continued to shift his gaze between Foster and the photograph. How remarkable, he thought, this is the first real conversation I have ever had with a Negro, and it feels like I can almost read his mind. Suddenly he heard himself speaking. "My father is a small, timid man. He doesn't speak English very well, and mostly stays by himself. He's a jeweler, a damn good one, but he doesn't believe in making waves. But the only really important thing he ever said to me was something like this. Well, you got to understand, his accent is really thick. 'Semmy,' he always calls me Semmy, 'Dats a big voild out dere. And you gots to make do in it. The goyim, vell, you know the goyim. Dey don't like the Jews, believe you me. Better dey shouldn't know you a Jew. But don't you ever forget it. Be a gentile, Semmy, in zee street, wid the goyim, but ven you come home be a mensch. A Jewish mensch.' You know, I think that was the most words he ever spoke to me. I think he meant something very much like what you just said about Du Bois."

Foster looked at Sam. He started to speak, thought better of it. Then he tightened his eyes. "Sons of Israel, sons of Ham. We got lots in common. But, listen carefully, there's a big difference between us. You can hide on the street. No one's gotta know who you are when you are walking down State Street. And everyone knows, or thinks they know who I am. You can be Sam, your skin's white, you got a passport to any joint in the city. Me, they show me to the back door, or they roll their eyes, put me behind a pillar, sell me rancid meat, and ask me to sing a spiritual. Anyone ever ask you to sing a spiritual?

"Look. I know they call you Hebe, and Kike and Sheeney. And I know that the Raglan Colts'd just as well kick your ass as look at you. I know about anti–Semitism. And I know you can't get in their country clubs. But, what you don't know is how it feels to be thought of as an animal. Most white folks would just as well put us in a zoo where it's safe to pet us, watch us mate, or eat each other. Look around, Sam, and what do you see? Any nice two and three flats? Any black faces behind the counters in the stores around here? Hell no."

Foster stopped. The room filled with the silent echo of his anger. Sam sat quietly, less stunned than surprised. He knew that he had been granted a gift. Foster's confidence came to him unasked, and Sam understood that the trust that lay behind Rube's words could last a lifetime. He felt foolish, too. He didn't want to compete for misery, as a Jew, with Foster. But he had wanted to establish common ground. It had never occurred to him that it might be built on talk.

Sam stood. Offering his hand, he spoke, "Thanks, Rube. Thanks for the instruction. I was wondering. You got a game this afternoon, you know, the American Giants. Mind if I grab a seat?"

"Shit, darlin'. I thought you'd never ask. Tell you what. You just show up at the gate at four 'clock. You won't be the only white man in the park, so I'll tell 'em to look out for a nice Jewish fella. You'll have the best seat in the house. How about that?"

"I can't wait. I've never been to a colored game before. But I guess you know that."

Sam turned and walked out the door of Foster's office. Then he spun around, and, grinning, asked, "How they gonna know I'm the Jewish fella?"

"I was gonna describe the schmatte you got on. That incredible jacket you got there, you know, the thing with all the wrinkles and the short arms and the tight ass!"

At 3:30 that afternoon Sam Weiss, his suit coat now draped over his arm in self-conscious indifference, nodded and smiled at the ancient

ticket-taker who waved him through the turnstile. Despite what Rube had told him, Sam sure felt like the only white fellow in the crowd spilling into the stands. He walked slowly up one of the access ramps, feeling the cool spring air mingle with the smells of popcorn and beer. Men, mostly, accompanied by a few boys and even fewer young women, pressed on either side of him as he flowed up toward the landing behind the curve of the structural skeleton that supported the grandstand. They seemed to come, Sam thought, from all walks of life, working men on their way home from the mills and independent packers, haulers and lifters, in denim and scruffy newsboy hats from the docks walking shoulder to shoulder with shoe salesmen and clerks, plumbers and carpenters. Occasionally Sam thought he saw a few men with an almost aristocratic bearing, tall and slender, their bodies in a posture that spoke politeness, even refinement. And then he noticed that almost all of these men wore the blue caps, the ones with even darker, shiny black bills of the Pullman porter. Some of the men marched together in groups of twos and threes, rolled up newspapers in their hands, gesturing and talking loudly about the day's pitching match-ups, or arguing over the inning when their number, that is the number they had picked, of runs would score. Others, usually those with women on their arms, strolled more leisurely, patting the hands that cupped their fingers around their biceps, as if to protect them from the essential maleness of their surroundings.

There were, Sam realized, no reserved seats at the ball park. First come, first served. And as he made his way down to field level, searching the grey-green benches to the home plate side of the American Giants' dugout for an empty seat, he suddenly heard his name. "Hey, Semmy!" Foster had turned his attention from the field and put his left hand over his eyes, just under the bill of his soft white ball cap, and waved wildly, "Here's a seat. Right here. Where I can keep an eye on you." Whatever unselfconsciousness Sam possessed vanished as the crowd turned as one, their eyes following Foster's voice up the concrete steps. Sam waved, feigning indifference, rejecting the impulse to bellow "Howya doin' Rube," and instead slid past a half-dozen Negro men who shifted their feet as he teetered toward the seat that Foster had designated. Foster winked and before resuming his place on the bench said, "I told you they'd know who you were."

Sam glanced around him, taking in the crowd, the park, and the two teams as if he were inhaling the entire scene at once. Like Comiskey Park with its combination of boisterous kids, straw-hatted gamblers, and ham-fisted working men, the black folk at South Side Park seemed equally varied — representatives of the entire community come to cheer for the neighborhood team. A handful of white patrons scattered through the stands seemed at home, as if they had been coming to American Giants games for years. The Negroes, Sam thought, displayed a remarkable combination of baseball knowledge and easy banter with each other and with the players warming up on the fields. There was none of that belligerence borne of distance that characterized white baseball, he realized. The Chicago American Giants clearly were part of Bronzeville, and the folks at the ball park knew and accepted them as people first, then as players.

"Hey, Pete," the young black man next to Sam yelled at Bruce Peteway, "surprised you can stand today after what we did last night."

Peteway, glove dangling off his right hand as he kneeled, one knee on the ground the other supporting his left elbow, looked up and grimaced. Then he smiled, ear to ear, and yelled back, "Wonder that you can even remember what we did last night. You was so skunked you never even saw your mama come in the joint." With that he willed his body to stand and jogged off to the outfield to shag some flies.

"I bet he don't get a single hit today. Not after the night he just put in," said Sam's neighbor to no one in particular.

An older man, just to Sam's right and two rows in front, turned, and looking back over his left shoulder, added with apparent wisdom, "Brother, you sure right about that boy. He can't hit hung over. Never could. Never will. Some can, but not that boy, no sir!" As he turned his attention back to the field, the man dressed in the blue uniform of a Pullman porter shook his head a few times, straightened his back, and opened his copy of the *Defender*, examining, Sam realized, the box scores of last week's games.

Bruce Peteway jogged slowly into the outfield. He held out his gloved right hand, snagged a ball tossed by one of his teammates, and gently looped the ball behind his back. Peteway kept on running, but Sam followed the ball he had tossed only to realize that Peteway had only gone through the motions. There was no ball. Yet the group of five players standing in a small circle in foul territory between third and home followed its imaginary flight into their midst. One of them retrieved it and in a single motion pounded it into the well in his glove and stood silently, just for an instant, with his gloved left hand extending slightly from his body at waist level as he bent his arm to place his right hand on his hip. The others stood quietly, their circle stilled.

Each of these five wore a home uniform: white flannel, loose and baggy in the arms and legs, the shirts buttoned up the front to a collarless band. Their sleeves extended down to their forearms before giving way to a grey undershirt that reached to the wrist. The red block letters AMERICAN GIANTS spread across their chests and matched the two bands that circled the long stockings they tucked into their pants' legs just below the knees. The only individual item that varied from man to man were the shoes, which each player had to provide for himself. They were all low cut, soft black leather, but each had his own preference and tolerance. Some could nurse a single pair through the entire season, mending and binding torn seams with adhesive tape which itself blackened within two innings. Others, the same players who also insisted in keeping their old gloves in use for as long as possible, found a way to stretch their pay to allow them at least one new pair of shoes each month. These men, seasoned veterans, knew that, in either case, shoes that ran quick as silver and gloves that stayed soft and supple as the inside of their lovers' thighs were precious.

They stood in a circle, perhaps eight feet in circumference, and, hands held belt high, they began throwing the invisible ball. First simply to each other, clockwise, then counter-clockwise. Gentle tosses, underhand, from one to the next, which they caught barehanded, softly lobbing the ball from one hand to the other, from catching to throwing, as they sent it 'round and 'round their circle. Then they began to alter the routine, changing the direction of their throws. The five men were now less a circle than the points of a star, and the flight of the ball was a crisscrossing of vectors that connected them to one to another. As they picked up speed the players began to vary both the direction of their throws and the style of their delivery. Behind the back, under one leg, catching and throwing just off-balance enough to hitch the rhythm of their motion, the five men meshed as one, each trying to catch the others off guard with a motion none had yet quite seen before.

They whizzed the ball, arms whipping through the afternoon air, their arc creating a dozen staccato images, as they simultaneously strove to remain in synch with each other. Their bodies danced, arms and legs in pirouette, heads turned in profile against the thrust of their bodies, as they worked the ball faster and faster.

Sam had never witnessed their warm up routine before, and he found himself transfixed by the grace and inventiveness of the images that flickered before his eyes. He tapped his feet beneath him, crunching on the discarded peanut shells and popcorn kernels, in time with the patterns of the players' pantomime. And then he felt the rhythms of audience keeping up with the beat of the quintet on the field. The fans around Sam stamped their feet, some even clapped their hands as the invisible ball moved in and out, back and forth between the five black men dressed in red and white that afternoon. Then, almost suddenly, they stopped and brought their hands down to their sides. They stood motionless, frozen for an instant, as if gathering their composure, before allowing their bodies to relax. Then, chatting softly with each other the five men sauntered to their bench.

"Nice work with the shadow ball," clapped Foster as they reached the dugout, and he patted each on the shoulder before turning to catch Sam's eye with a wink.

Foster gathered his team around him, almost like a prayer meeting, and said something softly to them, lowering his voice just out of the crowd's earshot. "We're the best fucking team in Negro ball," he hissed, "and I aim to keep it that way. Play to win." With that the team broke for the field, and the five players who had warmed up together several minutes earlier now fanned out, Sam realized, to the five infield positions taking, like the points on a star, their places with a graceful symmetry. Now, as they went through their warm up routine, fielding thrown ground balls from Leroy Grant at first base, who sported a toothpick jutting out the right side of his mouth, they displayed the same acrobatic elegance, each man moving toward the ball, instinctively guiding its path and calculating its hop, into their gloves. Each knew to keep their bodies low, bending at the knees, asses as close to the ground as possible, and in a single fluid motion they could all, from third, short, or second, field and throw the ball in an effortless but perfect strike to Grant's outstretched mitt.

The Chicago American Giants, Rube Foster, manager, played their interstate rivals, the Indianapolis ABCs, that afternoon. And while Sam would not realize it, even for several years in fact, the game was over in the first inning. But what a remarkable inning it was.

Rube had laughingly told Sam all about the ABCs, managed and owned by their own picturesque manager, C.I. Taylor, a grizzled and wizened veteran of more than thirty years of Negro baseball. He had achieved legendary status not only for his astuteness but for "turning 'possum," a ruse whose sleepy disguise he put to good use on a regular basis. Sloe-eyed and wise-mouthed, Taylor could talk his way around most anything and anybody. Story had it that he had even convinced some less-than-wily umpire one stormy day in Abilene or some such place to suspend a game, on account of bad weather, after six innings and his team losing by six runs. Approaching the umpire, old (he was old even when he was young) C.I. pointed to the sky. "That there is some funnel cloud, yes sir, sure it is. Reminds me of one I saw when I was a young 'un. Back home in St. Louee. You know, well, it musta been just after the Fair there, 'cause I can still remember them singing that song. That one that goes, 'Take me to St. Louee, Lewee,' it's on all them player pianos. Still 'til this day. Just last week, it's a fact, I was having my after-the-game pick me up back home in Indianapolis, that's where I live now, understand, and this fella walks in the joint, and he tells me about this tornado he just saw, and that got me thinking..." When the ump said, "Game called," there wasn't a cloud in the high blue Kansas sky.

C.I. had, during the war years, rounded up many of the best Negro players of his day, and the ABCs always gave the American Giants a good run for their money. And in this case there was plenty of money flowing around the stands, wagers of any kind on any circumstance—"betcha they don't score no runs in the even numbered innings. I'll give you five to three on it"—rippled their way up the rows of benches from the field level seats to the very last row where the professional and not so professional bookies sat, pencils pop-popping away on the newsprint pads they always kept tucked into their hat bands. Some in Chicago thought C.I. stood for the Illinois Central, the I. C., "Only, he's going out of town, the other way, if you know what I mean." His real name was Charles, but no one ever called him that. "Lemme see," he would drawl slowly, "C.I. That stands for where I was born. Sorta nowhere, between Coffeyville and Independence. North of Kansas City, so they coulda named me K.C., but that just didn't sound right. 'Course there was another kid from round there, white boy they called Casey, he playin' for the New York Giants. Not a bad little center fielder, for a scrawny guy. Remind me of myself at that age. 'Course you know why all the Negro teams call themselves the Giants, don't you? Now you do! That's why we are the ABCs. Basic, ain't it." And as he talked, or as the newspaper boys called it, as he blew smoke, he was always thinking, always figuring. In fact, and Rube Foster knew it as well as just about anyone, the more C.I. talked the more crafty he was contriving to be.

Even Sam could tell that Indianapolis featured a remarkable collection of ball players in 1916. Oscar Charleston, whom Foster acknowledged as the greatest center fielder of his time, anchored a lineup that also included the lightning quick Bingo DeMoss, Jim Jeffries, one of the few fighters to give Jack Johnston a run for his money in left, and the incomparable Gentleman Dave Malarcher at short. The most remarkable thing about the game, however, turned out to be not the ABCs' great stars, but the decision that Foster made to start himself in what became the last appearance of his remarkable career as a pitcher.

At thirty-eight Foster had lost about a foot on his fastball, had trouble making his curve break over the outside corner against left-handed hitters—and could no longer back right-handers off the plate by throwing high and tight. But, as everyone well understood, he still knew a thing or two about pitching.

Working with his back to the batters, that is by shifting his outfielders sometimes on every pitch, Andrew Rube Foster kept the normally steady ABCs off balance. He never threw the same pitch twice, never threw at the same speed, and absolutely never to the same place. Foster had already told his catcher, a squat and reliable performer named Red Tomey (and his teammates couldn't resist calling him Red Belly), that he had about six fastballs in him that day, and even before the first ABC hitter scraped his spikes into the batter's box, Foster, keeping half an eye on old C.I. pretending to sleep in the visitors' dugout, busted one over the outside corner, at Belly's mitt, sitting right up, just below the catcher's right shoulder. The whack of the ball, a sound amplified by Belly's own manipulations, made the pitch sound night-train-to-Memphis fast. C.I. squinted his eyes open and said, "Well, that means the old devil's got five more good ones left today," and went back to his feigned nap. But the first batter couldn't be as sure, and the doubt that Foster had injected worked its inexorable way from the batter's brain to his hands, and as if to complete the circuit, back again. It took Foster four pitches, two strikes on curves, the first high and inside, the second low, aimed right at the knee cap, a changeup just off the plate, and then one of the five remaining fastballs, whacked under the batter's frozen fists, to send him cursing back to the dugout.

Bingo DeMoss, slim and wiry and fast as a whippet, took his place in the batter's box and leaned in, extending his left elbow over the inside corner of the plate — daring Rube to come inside. C.I., picking his nose and staring at his feet, signaled for a bunt and DeMoss pushed the second pitch, an off-speed shine ball that Foster had perversely spun low and outside, down the first base line. Peteway charged, bearing down on the ball. DeMoss seemed to be running up the line at virtually the same speed and trajectory, while Foster, whose follow through had taken him to the first base side of the mound, launched himself toward the very spot where the ball, the runner, and the first baseman were sure to collide. "Out the way DeMo, you dumb motherfucker," Foster muttered as he scooped at the ball with his bare hand and in the same motion threw it toward first. As he intended, the ball slammed into DeMoss' back and the runner stumbled, overrunning the base. Foster retrieved the ball, tossed it slowly and sweetly to the second baseman who had finally arrived to cover the bag, and stood, hands on hips as the umpire, now halfway between the mound and first, raised his right fist in the air and said, "DeMoss, you dumb shit, you out."

No matter that C.I. and Bingo screamed bloody murder, gestured repeatedly at Foster, jabbed their forefingers in his direction for emphasis, and threatened to take the team off the field. The umpire, Amos Staley, an elderly gent in Foster's employ who swept the stands after the game for a few extra bucks and a quart of beer, was resolute. "He was in the way. That's it. Dumb shit's out. You don't like it. Write a letter to the commissioner." When C.I. allowed that there was no commissioner, that only Foster, who made out the schedule for the Negro teams in the Midwest, had even the slightest bit of authority, the umpire extended his arms into the air, scratched under one armpit, and said simply, "Play ball."

At that Oscar Charleston walked slowly to the plate, swiveled his hips just so slightly, tapped the barrel of the bat on the base in front of him, and stood quietly, bat resting on his right shoulder, and waited patiently at Foster to resume.

A slashing line drive hitter who more than any of his contemporaries reminded fans of none other than Joe Jackson, Oscar Charleston was in every other way the direct opposite of Shoeless Joe. He could hit with whatever bat he chose to lay his hands on, was a voracious reader of almost anything, hated fancy clothes, and loved to gamble. "Bet I can hit the third pitch," he said privately to Red Belly as the catcher squatted down behind him, "over Foster's right ear, into that gap, there, between short and second, and take the extra base when Amos is scratching his nuts."

Foster leaned in toward the plate, not to hear what Charleston was jabbering (he had played with and against the ABCs' center fielder for years, and knew full well that Oscar loved to jaw) but better to gauge the location of his pitch. Rube knew that Charleston loved to hit the first pitch, and that he always set himself for a fastball. "He just dying to smack this baby into left center," Foster thought and almost imperceptibly he flipped the fingers of his glove, which he kept hidden from the batter by concealing his left hand behind his already ample hip. He knew that his shortstop would see the tiny motion and adjust accordingly. Slowly Foster lifted his pitching hand to his chest, cradled the ball in the palm of his mitt momentarily, and instead of the full, windmill windup that he usually deployed, he pivoted his body toward third, kicked his left leg up and then toward the batter, and with full fury whipped his right arm across his body with a motion that read in capital letters, *fast ball.* Charleston timed his swing, and had snapped his bat toward Foster's prominent head, torquing his body ahead of his hands now hip high, when he realized that Foster had floated a cotton ball, fluffy, and oh-so slow, a regular mother fucking changeup right up, letter high, the center of the plate. And Foster smiled to himself. "Got you," he thought he heard himself say as Charleston's body uncoiled. But fooled as he was, the man many thought as great a natural hitter as Shoeless Joe, he somehow had the quickness and agility to break his furious swing and met the ball solidly with the barrel of his bat. Foster snapped his head over his left shoulder in time to see that the shortstop had indeed cheated several steps to his right into the hole.

At the crack of Charleston's bat, John Henry Lloyd took a single step to his right and dove, stretching his body low and parallel to the ground, right hand reaching as he speared the line drive, fully extended, not four inches above the infield dirt. Charleston had not even left the batter's box, and instead reached into his right hip pocket and let a five dollar bill flutter to the ground at Red Belly's feet.

John Henry "Pop" Lloyd jogged slowly back to the Giants' dugout, passed Foster, slapping his manager hard on the ass, and said, "Next time, throw it out of the strike zone."

"I knew you had it all the way," said Foster. But he thought to himself that Lloyd really was the best he had ever seen, bar none. Sam couldn't disagree, and when he thought no one was looking he circled Lloyd's name on the two-cent lineup card that he had purchased just before taking his seat.

The ABCs' hurler, Smokey Jo Williams, his name as much a description of his brooding angry soul as a tribute to his fastball, reminded Foster of himself a dozen years earlier, all speed and power, with little between the ears to guide his strong right arm. First pitch, fat pitch, and the batter lined the ball just over Williams' head. The line drive hummed its way to center field, straight toward Charleston who stood quietly, hands on hips, as the ball cleared second base. Then, the center fielder took two running steps toward the ball. In the blink of an eye Charleston raised his hands over his head, flipped his legs up behind him and spun his body through the air, landing perfectly, feet together, just as the ball arrived in his outstretched glove.

Sam jumped to his feet applauding wildly. He had never seen anything like that. Never. "Did he really do that? A somersault!" he said to the man in the next seat. The fellow, his newspaper folded open to the sports page, yawned. "Yes. Yes he did. Last week. Last year. It's just an out, ain't it."

Foster leaned out of the dugout and waived the on-deck batter back to his side. He knew he had to win the game early, before Williams found his groove. "Bunt, I want all of you to bunt. There, just to the right of the mound where Williams'll have to step all over his feet in order to make a play. On the first pitch, no waitin'. Got it?"

And before anyone in the park had a chance to settle down after Charleston's incredible catch, Williams found himself on the mound surrounded by plenty of company. Everywhere he looked a Giant danced off the bag, arms waving at the pitcher, like a bunch of pinwheels in the eye of a storm. Three pitches, three bunts, bases loaded, and Lloyd at the plate. Even Foster knew there was only one thing left for Williams to do. Throw at Lloyd's chin, up and in, not far enough to make a wild pitch, but far enough to send Lloyd flopping to the ground, backing him off the plate.

Three times Williams aimed where Foster, Lloyd, and almost everyone else in the park expected, and three times Lloyd calmly craned his head back just enough, leaning his bat back over his right shoulder, to avoid the rising ball. Three times the fastball cracked into the catcher's mitt and three times the umpire called, "Ball." Lloyd looked about as intimidated as a cat about to pounce, and as Williams reared back to deliver his next pitch Lloyd raised his right hand and called "Time. Ump. Time."

He stepped out of the box, looked up the line, and his face impassive, he stared at Williams, "Put the ball down the pipe," he said softly, "you son of a bitch. This here's a hitting man's game. I ain't up to take a stroll." Lloyd tapped the barrel of his bat against the plate, and took his stance. "Throw it, man." Williams, to his credit, gave it everything he had, letter high, tight, and just on the inside corner. Lloyd dropped his hands ever so slightly, and kicked his right foot back as he swung, aiming the ball in the instant before he made contact down the right field line. His line drive, low and curving ever so elegantly toward the line, seemed to gain velocity as it cut between the diving first baseman and the bag, hitting the right-field line with a puff of white dust before skipping into the corner in foul territory, just where the whitewashed outfield fence and the rickety wooden benches met. Lloyd, his bat already skimming the ground behind him, knew instantly that he had cleared the bases, and by the time he looked up from his perch at second, the crowd was on its feet stamping. "Pop. Pop. Pop." Sam knew enough about baseball and almost enough about Foster to fathom that the game had been won then and there.

Eight innings later, Rube Foster bent over, letting his glove and ball hands swing slowly between his ankles, pumped his arms over his head and delivered the last pitch of his career. Foster's fastball, wet enough to wash your ass he would say later, snapped at the batter's lower left wrist before tumbling into the catcher's mitt squarely behind the plate. "Yer out. Strike three," grunted the umpire from his position halfway between Foster and second base. "Game over. Giants win."

❧ ❧

Now, three years later, Sam still believed that Lloyd was the only one for the job. The plan really depended on him. The Sox would, he bet, sign Lloyd, weather the storm of protest, tear up the American League, and emerge as World Champs in 1919. Sure as hell. Sure as the loosely wrapped bundles that those Negroes carried with them from Mississippi.

6

CHRISTMAS 1907

From the porch there wasn't a tree in sight. Sometimes Kid stood there and, when it was really quiet, nighttime quiet, she could hear the trains as they passed through town. The December sun set early, even in Mississippi, and as the black winter night settled in, the rhythmic cadence of the night-freight beat its way north. But you had to be still and it couldn't be Saturday night. Walls' several juke and rib joints lit up the winter sky those evenings, sending shafts of flickering lantern light skyward, luminous rills of music floating on their surface.

Kid shivered. The chill wrapped her in a shroud, cutting through the threadbare muslin that her mother had transformed into a grey tent of a dress hanging from her shoulders. Kid wore it every day — Miss Sweet, her second grade teacher, told her that she had to wear a dress or not come to school. Even the large pin that fastened the material together beneath her neck seemed to have trapped the cold and sent it like some furtive electrical current against her skin. It was one of those nights. Her father has taken the mule to Walls to "get some provisions," and her mother and three brothers were already asleep, curled around the open stone fireplace on the rear wall of the house.

Christmas eve in Walls, Mississippi. Kid knew that her parents had moved up to the Delta from Lewsyana just after she had been born. "And it's good thing, too," her mama said, wistfully, "If we'd a stayed down there there's no tellin' what might have befallen us. City's no place for black folks." And so they settled on their "farm," although Kid knew that their seed, the mule that Pops had taken to town, and, of course, the sway-backed house they lived in, that all of their worldly goods belonged, somehow, in one way or another, to someone else — a white man, John Sprout, who lived down in Clarksdale but who showed up quarterly to watch over his "share." And that's when Pops put on a fresh washed pair of overalls, rubbed the tops of his shoes behind the soft nap of his pant legs, and even took off the sweat-stained brown fedora that he wore day and night, in order to greet "Missa Sprouts." Kid vaguely understood that Pops' manners, his self-conscious courtesy, his mispronunciation were all part of the way he dealt with white people — that he couldn't be himself in their presence. Sure, it was how they all lived in the Delta. "Don't do stuff that'll make the white folk take offense," her mother had always told her. "They like for us to show 'em that we know our place. Uh-hum." That last little phrase was a kind of amen that her mother always inserted for emphasis. But putting it on had a way of signifying to all the other members of the family that this group of black people had no intention of letting Missa Sprouts inside their hearts. Bad enough he came to the front door.

Mama stirred inside, must be getting up to feed the fire, Kid thought, but then sagged back down with a kind of sigh that made Kid's stomach flip over. It was getting late, Pops was due home hours ago, and the children, the boys whose hair she had combed clean just hours ago, hadn't had anything to eat all day. Something crackled out in the dark night, but even when she held herself absolutely still and squatted down in order to peer through the frozen air, Kid could see nothing. She remained huddled against the grey clapboards, her arms wrapped around her knees for a while, breathing softly, and waited.

With the sound of a firecracker he landed, boot-heel first, on the porch, sending a jarring shudder through Kid's body. Gotta be daybreak, she thought, or I'm dreamin' he's finally home. She saw Pops, his shape, not his face, visible in the soft glow of the fire inside, toss his gear into the doorway and bellow. "Old Man's home. Rise and Shine." Mama and the kids scrambled to their feet, rubbing sleep from their eyes as Pops swung a bag off his back, over his shoulder, and with his right hand laid it gently on the floor. The large sack lay there, its contents bulging, wide-knuckled fists wrapped in grey. "Don't look yet," Pops commanded, and he vanished out the door, made more noise on the porch and reappeared carrying a scruffy pine wreath laced with a frayed red ribbon whose embossed gold letters read, "Seasons Greetings—Clarksdale Dry Goods." Kid also noted the date—1906. She decided to remain silent. It was 1907, she was seven and this was the first Christmas her family had ever celebrated.

As Mama scurried about the room, its bare wood walls covered with an assortment of throw-away calendar and newspaper pages, the children (as Kid thought of them) crouched under the one piece of furniture, a handmade wooden table covered with red and white checked oilcloth, that the family did not use for sleeping. The kerosene lamp that flickered its light was the only possession they didn't use for either eating or sleeping. Kid watched, not quite believing her eyes, as Pops lifted his sack onto the greasy surface of the table. "Now don'tcha go askin' where this all came from. Won't do you no good t'know. I came by it honest. That's all I intend to say 'bout it." By this time the boys had circled the table, their eyes at the very height of Pops' hands as he worked the opening of the bag wider and reached in.

For the boys and Mama he proudly presented a fishing rod, a small cigar box (good t' keep the bait), and a bolt of green and yellow cloth with the label "Sears, Roebuck and Company, Chicago, Illinois," stamped on its cardboard core. Kid watched as her family squealed in delight, their eyes bright, the meager cabin filled with laughter. Mama held the cloth up in front of her and exclaimed, overcome with surprise, "I'll make something for everyone with this. Oh. Its just wonderful." And she knew absolutely not to ask how Pops had come by this bounty.

And then he reached into the sack another time. He held the bag high over his head from the inside, and said, "Now's time for a toast." He paused. "To my daughter born first (and he pronounced it like foist) this here I do hoist / 'taint much to look at, but she sure know where it at / So, I takes off my hat and here's what we gat." And with that Pops pulled his hand out from the bag and beamed as he presented his daughter with the most beautiful thing she had ever seen.

The guitar had scars gouged into its body, and its neck was warped but not too much to play. The five strings wrapped themselves around the tuning pegs in random and frayed patterns, and the wood itself looked encrusted with grime. It was glorious and Kid didn't have the slightest idea how to play it. But she knew that somehow she would learn.

Kid had learned to sing, however. That is, she had some knack for following Pastor Hall in his hymns. She loved the way their church smelled, like pine, standing out in the country. Bethel Baptist, the sign read. They just called it church. Hardly larger than the very house Kid lived in, and not any better painted either. But every Sunday folks came, sometimes to hear Pastor Earl Hall preach and sometimes to bury their kin in the small cemetery that lay alongside the brook just off to the side.

Kid adored the way Pastor Hall sang. He had his way of teaching without ever makin' it seem like school. "Steal Away, steal away home," he floated the words out over the congregation. They could all, some better than others, she thought, send the message back to the pulpit, "Steal Away, steal away home." By the time she had been graced with her Christmas guitar Kid had learned dozens of spirituals, each one from the Pastor's way of lining them out. But "Steal Away" remained her favorite. It reminded her of her grandfather, Lionel, who had been a sugar plantation slave "down home," who told Pops who told her about hearing the hymn and how he'd done "stole away one night to the camp meeting where some preacher on horseback had told them that the time of Jubilee was coming." A week later soldiers in blue arrived and announced that slavery was over.

Kid learned that "Steal Away" meant something very different to her life in the Delta. When the crackers got too mean, or when the food wasn't on the table, or when it got too hot, she always knew how to hide inside herself. The music soothed her, protected her, and sometimes she could find new words, even new notes, to sing herself to peace. She could sit on her porch and not let anything in the world find her real self. Sometimes she sat so still she could hear her own heart beating. Once when her parents were having one of their rough and tumble fights, the kind they had when Pops drank too much and didn't come home for days, she just sat, knees up to her chin, on that porch, and was so still that they never knew she was there. Least not 'til her Mama threw the empty bottle at Pops and it shattered on the wall just above Kid's head, showering her with glass raindrops and sticky home brew. But Kid could always "Steal Away," go inside herself and freeze the world outside her.

Christmas morning. Leaden sky, the winter clouds bearing low and dark over the chopped crust of the Delta. The horizon stretched as far as Kid's eye could see but it yielded neither relief nor bounty. Step away from Walls and all you got is cotton fields and cropper shacks.

Some seemed no more than rough hewed log boxes, the size of a caboose, with one opening in the center of the longer wall to let people and animals in and out, to trap the breeze to fan the fire, or to take a leak when the weather got too cold to walk behind the only tree on the share's three and a half acres. Morganfield's place looked like that and Kid could hardly bear to walk over there when her Mama told her to look after four-year-old McKinley. Course they didn't call him that, just like they didn't call her by her given name. She was Kid and the scruffy child just down the dirt road, another half-mile past Walls, well, they just called him Mud. On account of the way he loved to play outside the house and splatter himself with goop after a good hard rain.

Out beyond the Morganfield shack, way back in the clump of scrub oak that dotted the landscape, another house stood watch over the Delta. No one actually dared approach the place. A deep crick ran next to the road just a few feet in front of the house. The water had cut deep into the soil there and to even get a scoop to drink one had to first kneel and then reach all the way down. The local kids were too scared to do this, within glancing distance of the house that is. But one day when Kid tried, she found a stream of remarkable purity, its water, at the right time of day, as blue as the feathers of a jay.

It was said that the man who lived there, just on the other side, and only a few folks ever 'fessed up to actually seeing him, only came out at night. His place—"You gotta be careful out there, no telling what's goin' on," said Pops—had become almost one with the land. Trees and brush grew in and around the frame of the structure, and in winter, the house took on the aspect of a ruin, leafless twigs and branches all tangled and climbing every which way above the low pitched roof, a thousand tendrils reaching into the black-grey sky.

A week later, the first bone chilling night of the new year, at Odell's, the juke joint in Walls, three men set to talking about that old place. The screen door stood ajar, letting in the winter cold. It didn't really matter, because "Odell's Ribs and Chicken," as the hand painted sign announced in faded blue lettering, was hotter'n hell all year round. The open fireplace at the rear where Odell tended his barbecue saw to that. And after a half-dozen beers, three men, counting Odell, couldn't tell either.

There was only one table toward the side of the room. And but one chair. Usually the men stood around the joint telling stories, downing beer after beer, and staggering home at closing time. But, New Year's Day, that was a different matter. The man seated at the table almost blended into the wall. The grey-brown canvas jacket, which he had hung loosely over the back of the chair, a deep blue shirt buttoned up to his neck, dark hat, and black face in the flickering candlelight of room made him appear invisible. Only the pale blue calico handkerchief around his neck betrayed any sense color. Every now and then the man took a sip of his beer, tilting the bottle toward the ceiling, and then placing it down again, almost gracefully, on exactly the same place on the table. Otherwise he sat, his hands gently folded in front of him, feet softly crossed beneath the table, and listened. There was no tension is his body as his shoulders rose and fell with the slow measure of his breathing.

Odell tended his chicken silently, but the third man was anything but. Name's Elmore, he said. 'Course Odell knew his name, he came in 'bout every night after working down Sprout's place cleaning horse dung. Elmore grinned, showing a gold tooth against the deep black of his open face. He talked a blue streak that night — he looked at Odell but it was clear that he aimed his words, his voice rising and falling with the wind that blew outside, at the figure sitting at the table. And the story he told, well Odell didn't really know if he should believe it.

Seems Elmore had once seen a man, the guy who lived in that house down past Morganfield's, walking along the road one night. Full moon, he remembered, last July, and bright as all get out. Well, the first thing he noticed was that the man stopped in the middle of the road and held his palms up to the sky, like he was talking to it, just bent his elbow and turned his hand up. And then he reached a hand into his back pocket and took out a straw hat. But it was the most unusual straw hat ever seen around Walls. Sticking up from one side, from the brim, a red feather, must have been a chicken feather, but there it seemed to glow, catching the moonlight like a beacon. You almost could see its reflection on the dirt, yes, almost.

Elmore paused. He looked at the other, still sipping his beer, watching. Elmore stopped his story for a minute to see if the other fellow had been listening. It was hard to tell. Almost impossible to read his eyes because he had pulled the brim of his hat down over his head as if he wanted to keep the heat of the place as far away from his soul as possible. But Elmore continued. He followed the red feather down the road a bit that night and noticed that the figure stopped every now and then to scratch in the dirt with a stick he carried.

"Must have been some sixteen times because I got so that I even counted 'em. Yes, there he was, walking up and down every side road between here and Morehead, and every time he got to a place where another road crossed the one we was on he stooped down and made his mark. I couldn't tell what in the world he was up to. And then the strangest thing happened.

"It was up by the Southern crossing, down past Percy's place, toward Yazoo, and the fella with the red feather he started walking on the tracks and I followed, not so close's he could see me, but just so I could keep up. To see what was happening. And, I'll be darned, if he didn't go down'n his knees, and turn his hands up to the sky again, like he was giving something way, palms up just like I seen him do earlier.

"Yep. Jus' like that. But this time he started a singing. I couldn't make out the words real clear, but I swear I heard him talking about some dog. Something about crossing the dog. Well, I could hardly believe my eyes, here it was, in the middle of the night, full moon, and a growed man with a red feather in his hat is kneeling by the railroad tracks singing some kinda song about a dog.

"An here's what really got t'me. For just a second I took my handkerchief outa my overhall pocket, see just like this, to wipe my brow, and when I look up next, all I can see is the moon light streaming down the tracks, over my shoulder, and not a soul in sight. No sir, not a single solitary soul."

At that Elmore looked around the joint, just to make sure that the man in the corner and Odell were still listening. Just to catch their eyes. And yes, they both sat just were they had been, the one in the corner sippin' his beer and Odell still turning the chicken, just as slow as slow can be.

It wasn't but a minute that the man at the table looked up and said what a fine story that was, but did they know where to find the fellow with the red feather. Nope. Never saw him since. Guess I'd better be going now he said, maybe I can find him myself. I've been looking for him for a spell. He rose gracefully from the table and unfastened the top button of his shirt. Then he loosened the knot of his handkerchief and, with the thumb and first finger of his right hand, lifted a dark leather pouch from inside his shirt, one tied with a lace which he undid. As he reached in with the same two fingers the contents of the pouch chimed, like shells moving in the tide, and he handed the silver dollar gracefully over to Odell, touching the owner's shiny palm with the tips of his fingers. Gotta be moving on, he said. Thanks for the beer.

"Wait," Elmore said, "what did you say your name was?" "Didn't," he said, "but its Esau. Glad to make your acquaintance, maybe I'll be back someday." Odell glanced up at the dark figure, who shrugged his shoulders as he hefted his jacket up around his neck, and wished him a good journey. Esau nodded and left. The screen door snapped back loudly as he pulled his hat down even more firmly over his face, tightened his handkerchief around his neck, and started walking.

After a few minutes, by the time he had passed Morganfield's cabin and headed down the dirt road south toward home, Esau stopped for a moment and, as if to take the pulse of the night, he held his hands out, palms up to the sky, and lifted his head. And then he sang. The song was a simple one, one that he had just made up out of thin air.

It didn't have but three lines, and like the songs that people in the Delta had been singing for a time, and they sang about almost anything — women, steamboats, stubborn mules, sledgehammers — almost anything. Well, he just rolled his eyes and sang.

"Going where the Southern Cross the Dog," yes, "Going where the Southern Cross the Dog," hummm, "Going where the Southern Cross the Dog."

Had anyone bothered to ask where he came from Esau would have said, "Morehead, that's where the Southern Railroad crosses the Yazoo line, you know the Yellow Dog, but down here we just call it the dog." But they didn't and by the time he got to the creek in front of his house he could see the first streaks of dawn, about the color of the feather on his hat, opening up the indigo sky.

Wasn't long after, maybe the second week or so of January that Kid, her face drawn to the sun, whose warmth that day surprised just about everyone, grabbed Mud by the hand and said, "Come on. We gonna take a walk this day. See what's going on by that house, you know, down past yours a bit." The boy shrank back, even he had heard some story or another about the strange house beyond the creek, and he tugged her hand back toward his place. "Stop that, just you stop that," she ordered, "we going and that's that."

Mud in tow, Kid marched down the dirt road, swinging her free arm, imagining that she could sing whereas in fact the only music in her head was the whistle of the 9 o'clock freight for Memphis. They rounded a bend and came to the creek that cut a narrow winding path between the road and Esau's house. Unable and certainly unwilling to resist the charm of flowing water, Mud pulled Kid's hand and in the same motion bent down, his hand already in a scoop.

"Don'tcha drink that," she ordered, knowing that the creek that spilled eventually into the Mississippi was surely brackish, especially in winter. She pulled the little boy up by his arm and caught a glimpse of the water out of the corner of her eye. Then she bent down and cupped her hand. The cold water sat pale blue against the pink of her palm, clear as day, crisp too. Kid slipped her legs under her and looked deep into the bed. The water there too ran clear, it must have caught the light of the winter sky. And it was the same blue, like that faded shirt Pops wore every summer, sleeves rolled up around his strong arms.

The man standing beside her reached down and touched her shoulder, "Don't mean to 'larm you. You'n the boy want to come in and have some breakfast? It's early but I could fix you some grits and bacon right quick." He wore the hat with the red feather over the canvas coat and the dark denim pants that he had on the week before.

The daylight revealed an open face, shiny black, its lines running in all directions, crisscrossing at the bridge of his nose and radiating out over his forehead. But his eyes were fresh and they looked kind. "Don't be scared. I won't harm you. See, here's my word," he said softly and pulled the leather pouch out from under his shirt.

The small shells, mottled white and brown, no larger than the last joint of Kid's pinky, clicked together, their shiny patina smoothed by years of wear. Esau held them gently in the palm of his hand, "My mojo," he said, "you hold it. If you gets fearful just rattle 'em together. They'll do their job."

With that he extended his hand like a cavalier, and helped Kid and Mud step-skip over the creek. Kid held the shells in her other hand knowing somehow that this gentle man presented not a lick of danger.

"Name's Esau." He glanced over his shoulder. "Seen you come past from time to time and wondered when you'd get curious to come in. Just knew you'd be the one. Just knew."

They pushed through the bare branches that grew everywhere around the house and Esau, now standing on the porch, reached to lift the children up. Kid's eyes opened wide. She couldn't believe what she saw. Standing in the corner, leaning against the wall of the house—a guitar as bright and clean as hers was nasty. "Oh, that is beautiful. Can you play it? Could you show me? Oh." She beamed and looked down at Mud, who had already taken a seat at the edge of the porch where he dangled his legs, kicking them gently, rhythmically.

Esau schooled Kid starting that day. She thought he had more music in his head than ever existed in the world. Not only that, he could make it up on the spot. Like that Yellow Dog song, a blues he called it, that he loved to sing when he thought no one was listening. Soon Kid learned that what was important about singing was singing. Esau sang about anything, being places, losing things, wanting folks, working, worrying, wishing, there wasn't nothing he didn't sing about.

And at first it always sounded the same even if the words were different. He'd just pick that guitar out of the corner sit down next to Mud, who just couldn't take his eyes off him, and begin to play, his feet tapping against the few boards that still clung to the side of the porch.

Soon Kid learned that what made his music different was the feeling that he gave to it. Esau seemed to grow when he played. Walking along side her, he seemed maybe a head taller, but when he sat down to play and cradled the guitar like a baby, his hands soft around its body and neck, he towered over her. And when he began moving his hands, well, she was sure it was magic. This slight and gentle man who never took off that hat of his, the one with the red feather, just played.

"This here's what I do," he almost whispered, "to make it sound like it gonna go and grab you in the insides." And he reached in his overall pocket, the one over his chest, and pulled out the neck of an amber bottle. He slipped it over the ring finger of his left hand and began to slide it up and down as he beat the strings, in a series of alternating rhythms, moving the bottle neck to his left, away from him, two strikes at a time, and then back to the middle of the guitar neck where he started a series of strokes that made the instrument wail as if it had a voice of its own.

> Down on the hard road
> the moon was shinin' bright
> Down on the hard road
> the moon was shinin' bright
> Prayed to heaven up above
> "Lord, take me home tonight."

He looked up at the winter sky, shook his head at Kid as if to say you follow me, don'tcha, and played some more.

This time his eyes were closed and the steel strings of his guitar vibrated under his glass finger with the hard harsh sound of jagged metal. Esau finished, put his guitar on the ground, the neck leaning back up against the porch where the three of them sat, legs hanging over the side, looking out at the rising sun. It was almost as if you could hear, in the pulse of his right hand, Kid thought, the cadence of the night train as it passed through town.

Kid drank from Esau's hand and from his heart. Some nights they spent looking up at the black winter sky, facing north, just under the Big Dipper, the night ablaze in white light, and sang. Others, in the summer with the sun's rays suspended on the horizon 'til almost midnight, they played their guitars back and forth to each other, Esau saying, "Here do it like this," and dancing his long slender fingers along the neck of the guitar so quick Kid thought it sounded like someone else was playing at the same time. This was how he taught her, evening by evening, song by song, lick by lick.

And then one day, it must have been two years after Kid had first come to visit, in the winter of 1909, the little man vanished. Just plain vanished. Kid appeared at the creek and the house ahead felt still, its crown of brambles and twigs a hundred darts pointing upward. The cabin was clean empty, and as Kid walked away she understood. Esau had upped and moved on.

Now it was up to her to follow her music wherever it took her. Of course, that meant telling her mom and Pops about what she had learned. And she wasn't sure she could do that. Not yet. Pops had been let go, again, by the Turpentine factory at Stovall's and mother barely had enough money to stretch to the next season. The boys were still children, still too young to really help out. It was, she knew, up to her. Reason she got away in the first place, to be schooled by Esau, was that the rest had been too busy to really notice. They hardly had time to notice if she went to school.

Miss Sweet presided over the fourth grade in the local school, just a one-room shack where Kid always sat quietly, watching and listening. A little old lady who said she was from Memphis, Miss Sweet, as everyone knew, came from Helena, Arkansas, but was too ashamed to admit it. How she got that name Kid never understood, because she was the most sour person Kid had ever ever met. "Didn't I tell you," she said slow and mean, "that you here to learn your letters and stay quiet. Nothing else. So just stop your…"

Most days Kid spent looking out the window, waiting for the train whistle, the high hoooooot that told her school was over. Even before its vibration had left the room, the schoolchildren, all forty of them, scraped their shoes under the long benches where they had waited hands-clasped and asked, "Miss. May we be going home now." And Miss Sweet, as she always did, looked down at them over her steel-rimmed glasses and said, "Now yo'all go right home. No dilly-dallying down at Shine's." They all knew what she meant — even if they didn't all obey — that Shine, the geezer in Walls who sold a bit of every-thing, was a mean and hateful man.

Too small it was, Walls, to have even a Negro part of town. The townsfolk had accommodated what the politicians in Jackson and Memphis called Jim Crow by letting colored folks use the stores, and there weren't but two of 'em anyway, Shine's and the Chop-Suey restau-rant and laundry, for an hour in the early morning and then again in the late afternoon. All the fourth graders loved to congregate in Shine's, and even if they didn't have a cent they hung around waiting, for some-thing, anything, before scuffling home for the afternoon chores. As always Shine, and that's what everyone, white and black, called him, stood at the entrance of his store, hair slicked back over his large head and a white apron around his ample waist. "Don't you go touching nothing you can't buy," he grumbled, as he did every day, and he reached out a long paw to swat away what he was sure was the furtive reach of a sloe-eyed boy of twelve who kept on moving through the maze of oak barrels and glass-covered bins.

"Yessssir," the boy replied, his gaze firmly on the floor, "Yesssssir, I didn't mean nothing by it." Satisfied, Shine grunted, placed his fists at his waist, elbows out, and turned his attention to three more kids who clambered up the steps to his store.

Kid, penniless, watched as the boy, Richard, still in the back, slipped a brown cylinder into his pocket and without expression saun-tered past Shine and slipped the candied root beer barrel into the pocket of his younger sister, who entered the store ducking her head ever so slightly past Shine's left elbow. "Don't you be coming in here again without no money, you hear," Shine followed the boy with his eyes down the steps. "Yesssssir. Yesssssir," the boy responded, the back of his head bobbing up and down, rolling his eyes to the heavens.

Richard lived only 'bout a mile past her place and as Kid walked home later that afternoon, the sun a red-orange ball falling over her right shoulder into a deep indigo sky, she smiled. She'd known Richard all her life but never caught his eye. And now she knew a secret about him. Until that day he seemed just another boy who drifted around Walls, going to school when it pleased him, boosting candy from Shine's when he felt like it. But that root beer barrel in his sister's pocket, that gesture, fleeting and sweet, moved her. She hummed as she walked, thinking of Esau, of the music inside her head, of the road between her and Richard, of how the porch on her house felt every time she set foot home.

The boy's figure, his shoulders swaying left and right as he walked, became smaller, a cutout against the late winter sky, grown suddenly grey and sullen. Kid lingered, her mind wrapped inside her imagination. She walked without seeing along the dirt road as if in a dream. Day turned to night, the light of evening translucent and crinkly, the road's dark shadows a thousand fingers spread across the dust. Pulling her coat closer, Kid hunched forward. Up ahead she saw the lamp flickering through the kitchen window, the one under the porch roof where her mother liked to stand waiting.

With a movement that surprised her because it seemed silent, like someone sneaking up behind, the storm overtook Kid and sent the road boiling with bubbles of sand and water. The cold rain fell, a wavy curtain before her, breaking what little was left of the evening sky into random spirals and flashes of light.

"Come in the kitchen, girl," she heard her mother say as she jumped onto the porch, "You'd better come on in my kitchen baby, its goin' to be rainin' outdoors." Kid could feel the song in her head even as she heard the winter rain pounding down.

> Winter wind's a-blowin'
> Gonna get cold tonight.
> Winter wind's a-blowin'
> Gonna get cold tonight.
> You could be sittin' pretty here
> And feelin' pretty tight.

Lizzie Douglas had only heard of Memphis once or twice and only then as a mysterious place one went to or left. So it sat in her imagination on the porch in Walls, hazy and dream-like, until one day when Richard came sauntering up the road, sashaying like he always did, carrying a newspaper under his arm. He looked a head taller than he had that day seven years earlier when Kid watched him lift the candy from Shine's, and he no longer wore the short pants of a country boy. Kid patted the grey floor boards but Richard stood over her, gazing, admiring the way she sat there, legs crossed under her skirt, eyes broad and inviting. "See here," he said and he tossed the *Defender* down next to her. "I told you that we'd find a way to get outta here. Paper say that the President gonna send soldiers to the war, to help."

Kid looked up at Richard's overalls, imagined for a moment that she could see her father just like he looked before he took off that night, and scowled. "What you talking about. They don't want no colored soldiers in that army. They'd as soon shoot you as pay you." She held his eyes in hers. Thought of the way he liked to stand close to her and press his body into her, how it made her lean her head back so she could see the sky as he held her. "Not the army," he said. "Up there. You know, Memphis, St. Louis, Chicago. Up North. To work. Someone'll have to work. There's gonna be jobs up North. No more working for Shine and smiling, no more cotton choppin' for a nickel an hour. Real jobs it says here. Two bucks a day, even a place to live."

They looked into each other. He's leavin', she thought, and he don't know how to say so. "You got enough money? I hear that it's dear up North, that everything costs. I got some money saved you can have if you need." Richard shifted, moving from foot to foot like he did when he was uncomfortable, as if some bug'd got into the heel of his shoe. His eyelashes looked so fine, curving, thin, black, clear against the white of his eye. She reached her hand to the place between his legs and pressed her palm against him. "Baby, I want you to come with me. I don' want to go by myself," she heard him say as he swayed above her. "I can't even think about going without you."

She knew that he meant it. And she also knew that he'd break her heart. "Soon's I tell Mama," she heard herself say, "soon's I tell Mama. Then we can go north."

Richard covered her hand with his and closed his eyes. "You bring your guitar, okay. Then when we need some money you can sing. That way we won't be so needful of white folks when times get hard."

Kid took her hand away. "Where's that paper say t'go?"

Richard sat down, slapped his left knee with the still folded *Defender*, and said, "Memphis. Then Chicago. But first Memphis."

They sat for the next hour, the silence falling around them, and Kid felt the bleached boards of the porch grow cool with evening. In her mind she reached for her guitar, but her hands remained enfolded with Richard's. The future seemed to stretch out before them, blending with the night. "You better come on in the kitchen," she said softly, and guided him into the house.

She left Mama a note, "I'll write to you when we find a place to stay. Tell the boys I love them." She signed it Lizzie. She couldn't bear to tell her, like she knew she should, face to face, couldn't bear to see her mama cry. And as she sat on the only colored car on the Chicksaw freight that took them from Walls to Memphis, she didn't know if she'd ever come home to Mississippi again.

∾ ∾

The rooming house where they found a small bed to sleep during the day — "You shares it with the others, them who works at Schwab's Dry Goods, so you be out by 6 P.M. sharp" — was around the corner from the barbecue joint where Richard found a job, on the very first day in the city, working from 8 P.M. to sunup. "What'm I supposed to do while you working and they in the room," she asked. Richard, whose eyes grew hard, answered, "That up to you, babe. That up to you."

Memphis in the late summer of 1916 lay as open as a city could lie — "She just spread her legs at night and never close 'em up during the day," explained Little Kokomo later to Kid. "No city like this one. Well, 'cepting maybe Kansas City and New Orleans. You ever been there, honey?" It was about three in the morning — a Monday morning, but the crowds seemed thick as molasses that night on Beale Street.

It hadn't taken long for Kid to realize that Beale, which was about the only part of Memphis she could live and walk in without being hounded, was all con. "It means, you knows, trickery, like the opposite of what it sounds like, confidence. They tries to con you into believin' this and that, but it ain't so. It's the opposite," Richard had said, his voice rising high just like Miss Sweet explaining how to figure out the times tables. "Just the opposite."

Richard poured buckets of beer, a red kerchief tied around his hair, six hours a day. "What you wearing that thing on your head for," Kid said the first night, only their third day in Memphis. Richard looked down at his boots, grimaced, and said, "I ain't got enough money to get it conked. So the manager, Tiny, he told me to put this here rag on." While he poured Kid wandered up and down Beale. She felt too dizzy to play yet, and didn't have any idea that a bunch of strangers would want to hear the music in her head anyhow.

The bars that lined Beale between Hernando and Fourth where Kid shuffled along opened out onto the street. In each doorway a man in dark pants and light shirt with sleeves ballooned by garters tickled the crowds, inviting, cajoling, daring them to enter. She soon realized that each establishment had its own customers. Swell folks, dressed to the nines, ran in and out of palaces with names like The Monarch and the Panama. Others, working men and women who could easily drink in one evening the buck they had made during the day, walked jauntily through the swinging doors of the Hole in the Wall, put their nickels on the bar, and occasionally tossed a bit to the bucket boy. "Hey country," they called out to Richard, "get yo ass moving. Time's a wastin'. Move it."

Kid spent that first week in Memphis watching — watching the fancy men in their jaunty bowlers leaning into women in dime store satin, watching clusters of card and dice players conspiring on dimly lit street corners, watching kids, not much younger than she, darting in and out of alleys that led down muddy, fetid paths to the outhouses and swamps that bathed Beale with a brew of foul odors that defied description. It dizzied her senses, and made her numb. She watched too as Richard came out each dawn, his face exhausted, his breath a river of stale beer and cigarettes, only to hang on her shoulders and say, "Baby, take me home."

And so she did. Taking his shoes off, rubbing his shoulders 'til she felt him sag into a dreamless sleep, then staring up at the dingy ceiling 'til she too drifted away. Their rest lasted only as long as the whores upstairs allowed. Usually by 11 o'clock they woke to bottles breaking, screaming, and occasional sounds of "Oh, Honey. Do it to me. Jus' like that." Kid and Richard would hold each other, nose to nose, feeling their toes touch, for an hour 'til one of them said, "Well, might as well go see if we can't find a little something to eat. Gotta greet the day."

One early afternoon a month after their arrival in Memphis, they awoke and stumbled down the street exhausted, bone tired, until they came to Pee Wee's Saloon, about a block from the Hole in the Wall where Richard continued to work. The dimes and quarters that Richard made each night barely got them through the day, barely paid for their miserable little room, barely sufficed to buy a pickled pig's foot for breakfast. Kid knew that sooner or later she'd have to start pulling her share of the load, and she began taking her guitar with her when they walked around Beale in the afternoons.

Richard, his hair shiny and smoothed out, and Kid, denim overalls hanging from her body, still looked like country. And Kid knew it. "Look, would ya look at that fella." And she pointed to one of Beale's most notorious characters, Mac Harris, standing just in front of Pee Wee's, leaning against the building, one leg bent into a V, the sole of his boot pressing into the brick wall. Harris snorted in disapproval when he saw Kid and Richard, took a chew off the end of his cigar and spat. "Go on home to the Delta, its past your bedtime," he said out of the side of his mouth, and looked up at the sky. To do this, Kid noticed, he had to tilt his Homberg, his black Homberg, and squint, a motion that caused just a slight wrinkle in his impeccably tailored Chesterfield coat between his lapel and sleeve. He smoothed it out and took another draw on his cigar, sliding just enough to his left to allow Kid and Richard to pass through the doors of the saloon.

Here's the place, Kid thought, as she led Richard inside. I just know it's where I was meant to play. The idea remained mute, she knew that it would be a huge step. But for the last two weeks she had taken her guitar out on the street, down at the corner of Fourth, and played her songs. People stopped and listened and most of them, she was amazed to find, tossed a nickel or a dime into the open cigar box that she placed at her feet. One night she counted more than twenty dollars in change. More than Richard made in a week, more money than she had ever in her life seen at one time. "Come on baby," she said earlier that morning. "I got something to show you," and she grabbed his hand and led him down to Pee Wee's.

"Gonna be amateur night at Pee Wee's next Tuesday," the short man told her the night she raked in all the silver. "You ought to show up and strut your stuff." He was a tiny black man, dressed in a checked jacket, leather pants, and a cap the deepest blue that she had ever seen in her life. His eyes twinkled and as he doffed his hat he clicked his heels silently and waited. "I heard you play all night. I know you good. Why not show all the swells."

Kid looked inside herself. The music felt like she needed to sing it. So she glanced back at the little man, caught his eye, and said, "What time?"

"They audition at 2 P.M. sharp. Then the ones they choose come back that evening at 11. Tell Vigello that I told you to come."

"Who in the world is Vigello?"

"You'll see. Yes, sir. You'll see."

"Wait. Who are you?"

"W.C. Yep. Just W.C. They'll know me at Pee Wee's. You'll see. I live just down there," and he tilted his head toward the river, "on Jeanette, over in Greasy Plank. See you Tuesday night."

The audition had gone smoothly. A group of white men, more than Kid had ever seen together in one place, sat in wooden chairs in the fully lit room and asked her to play and sing. After one chorus of "Yellow Dog," one of them, she couldn't tell exactly who, said, "Okay. That's enough. Come back tonight around eleven and play two numbers. Make sure you get ridda them rags. Wear something that'll show your boobs."

Kid held her hand over her eyes to look more clearly at the voice below. "I ain't got no clothes like that."

"No matter. Here's a fin. Go up to Schwab's. Tell that Hebe to fix you up. Tell him Vigello wants it ready for tonight."

As Kid moved off the stage the man turned to his right and reached out for the telephone that sat on the small round table next to him. Kid had never seen one before. He spoke firmly. "Watcha mean you can't pay the Vig. You think I'm some easy touch? Listen, you dumb fuck. You bring the bag today, and I mean today. Got it?

"Imagine, this asshole, just because I send him some business from time to time, he thinks he got something special going with me. Fuck him."

Then he turned to Kid. "Whatcha waiting for? Ain't ya never seen the inside of a club? Hey, hey, see this girl from the farm, first time here. Waddaya think," he said to no one in particular, or to everyone. Kid couldn't exactly tell. "Okay. Okay. Call up Skinny the shiv and tell him there's a stiff to take up to the Parlor. And tell him to hustle his wop ass.

"See, honey. We got lots a stuff to do here. Ya know. So, get moving. Tonight. Don't be late."

Vigello Maffei looked around his joint. He smiled at the class. All the action and it looked good too. He rubbed his hands together, took a sip of espresso from the tiny porcelain cup next to the phone, and straightened the knot of his tie against the wing collar of his starched white shirt. As Kid and Richard walked out the door into the mid-afternoon sunlight, they couldn't help but notice that Vigello's pearl grey suit exactly matched his spats and shoes. "Oueee," Kid said softly to Richard. "What kind a man is that?"

❧   ❧

Kid couldn't believe how quick the woman's hands were either. One minute she had some shiny green material draped over Kid's shoulders and in the next she had pinned a dozen seams and darts, which she had taken from an invisible spot just over her own left shoulder, into the shape of a dress.

"Lower. Pull the schmatte lower, Hannah. You know he likes them to be falling almost out. There. Just a bissel." The voice came from the small grey haired man standing just off to the side, a faded yellow tape measure shawled his neck, a piece of white peeking out between the thumb and first finger of his delicate right hand. "You know, Hannah. Lower."

"Ve're almost done," the woman said, her 'v's and w's sliding in and out of each other. "Just a moment more, right Simon."

The older man glanced up at the clock. The one on the wall between the signs that read "Colored" and "White" that led back to the divided commercial floor of the store. "Yep. Ve're almost there. What time you going on young lady? What time did Pee Vee tell you to come back?"

"Pee Wee?" asked Kid, squirming to find a place to stand comfortably without letting the top of her almost dress fall. "Who is Pee Wee?"

Simon and Hannah Schwab both laughed. Poor child, they each thought. She hasn't any idea of what she's getting into. Or with whom. No matter. Mr. Maffei always paid his bills, always sent girls to get their dresses from Schwab's, and always offered them good protection to boot. No one on Beale did much of anything without Vigello Maffei, without Pee Wee's help. Not Nine Tongue, the craps shooter, not Mac Harris, not Guido Antonio the undertaker. Pee Wee had them all.

"He told me to come around 11. And he said to wear my dress like you made it."

"Don't worry, sweetie. He says that to all the girls. You ain't the first birdie he set his eye on, you know."

Beale Street's ensemble of bars, saloons, barbecue and chicken joints, gambling parlors and whorehouses, though it was often difficult to tell which was which, brought the street alive every night. Between midnight and early morning their lamps and banners, ticklers and shills attracted all seekers of pleasure, so long as they were black. But it was music that made Beale Street jump. Rumor had it that Pee Wee started his tradition of tryouts a few years earlier, just on the eve of the Great War in Europe, to try to bring a new clientele into his club.

He had arrived in Memphis at the turn of the century from Baltimore where his parents, Carmine and Rosa Maffei, had come from Sicily a dozen years earlier. Connections with some policy bankers and other assorted gamblers on the East Coast had given him the cash and reputation to establish himself in Memphis, in the heart of its black quarter, just as the city began absorbing the waves of black farmers who left rural Mississippi in search of opportunity. Whatever it was that they were looking for Vigello made sure they got it.

By the time Kid and Richard returned to his club they had been fighting with each other for most of the evening. The pint in Richard's pocket had only taken the edge off his anger.

"Why you got to go dressed like that, anyway. You just look like some black man's whore," he said over and over.

"Hush. It ain't nothing," Kid heard herself say. But she knew, and she was afraid that Richard knew too, that it wasn't nothing. It was something. She knew that she felt both scared ("Oh my, what would Mama say if she saw me") and powerful ("Is this what the men always is looking for? Is this what they really care about?") but for some reason that she couldn't understand she didn't feel the slightest bit nervous about playing.

It was as if Esau had touched her spirit. From within the body that poked its way out of that too tight green satin dress she could feel his presence, calming and as blue as the water that flowed in front of his house. It gave her an inner radiance that found its way in the flash of her eyes.

"What you looking that way for," Richard almost barked as they eased their way into the door of the club. He seemed angry, resentful, stirred up, his face a mask of leaded eyes and a frozen smile. It was not a question, she knew, only an accusation.

"Mama Mia, wouldya take a look at that," Pee Wee clapped his paw on Richard's shoulder but couldn't take his eyes off Kid's breasts. "Them Schwabs, they outdid themselves. Waddaya say, huh?" he asked, as she realized he always did, to the room. "Waddaya say?"

Kid felt her mouth open. But she found no words. She felt herself moved firmly to a place behind the small stage that covered the club's floor in the back, just off the door to the kitchen. Richard, his face frozen in a frown, disappeared into the crowd that had already gathered, standing on the wood boards that seemed to flex with their weight. Dozens of black men and a handful of women surrounded the stage, dressed to the nines. Kid wondered how many of the women had been to Schwab's, and she squirmed against the too tight fit of her bodice.

She quickly realized that she was hardly alone there behind the stage, but had become part of a long line of uncomfortable looking black folks, mostly her age she reckoned, who stood shifting their weight from foot to foot, primping their shiny hair, pulling in their waists, pressing their chests out.

Suddenly the room went dark. All she could see was the single light that blazed from the ceiling, its white circle shimmering against the darkly painted floor. A man appeared, the little guy she had met earlier on the street, the one who called himself W.C., still wearing his peacock blue hat, leather pants and checked jacket. Kid hadn't realized how small he actually was, only now, seeing him just a few feet before her, he came up no higher than her chin. But he spoke with a wonderful ease, warming the audience up for "What you-all done come here to see, the best local talent that Pee Wee's can provide. Yes, sir, ladies and gents, Pee

Wee's presents for your amazement and amusement, the Best of Beale." And with that the audience hooted, whistled, and howled.

"Hey, W.C., which one you think it'll be?"

"Bring 'em on W.C., bring 'em on. Show us your best stuff." "Oh, my, W.C., lookit the wings on that dove. You know, the one in the green. She sho look fine."

W.C. held up his hands. "Okay, Brothers and Sisters. You said enough. Time for the show. You have plenty o' time to vote for the one you like best."

"Only election we ever get to vote in."

"You can say that again, brother."

"Amen to that my man, amen to that."

About thirty-five seconds into the first number, a kind of shuffle-shout by a boy in his teens whose voice hadn't quite finished changing, the crowd got restless. "Hey, send him home to his Mama," someone shouted. "Which one," came the answer. "What would you know 'bout Mamas, you 'bout the ugliest thing here tonight."

The boy danced faster, his legs kicking higher and higher, frantically trying to salvage his performance. The crowd picked up his panic, and began clapping over his rhythm, taunting him to catch their beat. The harder he tried the faster and more ragged they clapped. Harder and faster, each bar further and further off his cadence.

Kid heard W.C.'s stage whisper. "Get out there young'un." He put his hand on the small of the back of the girl standing next to Kid and shoved her out onto the stage, so that she less landed than flapped, arms and elbows akimo, up next to the dancing boy. Hair in pigtails, which she had fixed in bright red ribbons that jumped, Kid thought, like fishing bobbers, the new girl lifted her skirt in both hands and began stomping her feet alongside the boy, who seemed relieved to have the crowd's attention focused somewhere, anywhere, else. The two of them, now, danced side by side, kicking left and then right, arms, bent at the elbows, pumping up and down in unison.

"They ain't nothing but two farm kids going to milk the mules."

"What you talking 'bout. You ain't never seen no mule milked. All you ever seen's his ass."

"Hey, W.C. This the best you can find fo' us, tonight. We's done paid our two bits to see a couple kids imitating some crackers."

Kid held her breath. There was only one other person, the boy to her left, waiting to go on. She felt a butterfly flutter its wings against the inside of her belly. This wasn't what she thought it was going to be like.

The boy was tall and thin as a string bean. Wore a rough blue wool suit, buttoned high up his chest, the newest fashion Kid wondered, and flashed white cuffs through the sleeves of his coat. He stood next to Kid now, his hands clasped behind his back, his eyes staring straight ahead, following the two dancers who by this time had the presence of mind to link arms and step in sequence. The crowd stilled for a moment, sensing that the two performers might have saved each other. But that confidence lasted only long enough to allow the boy to start stepping higher and higher, kicking his brown boots awkwardly out toward the pressing audience. Then, thought Kid, his fatal mistake. He began to sing. But instead of a song there emerged from his mouth, open wide enough for the night train to St. Louis, a squeaking-croaking kind of a sound, somewhere between a child's cry and a sheep's bleat, that sat there in Pee Wee's, heavy as the night, before it crashed down upon them.

"Get this outta here. Before my ears pop."

"Hey, W.C. Whatcha trying to do, make us leave the joint?"

"Give 'em the hook. The hook."

At that the crowd began to hoot and then boo. First in random patterns, an eruption here or there, and then together, until they drowned out the poor fellow, whose head gradually fell to his chest as his feet stopped. Still holding the hand of the pigtailed girl next to him, the boy began to cry. He broke from her grasp and ran off the stage, through the audience, and right out the front door.

The bobbing girl just froze in fear. She stared out, blankly, looking at the door, hands extended in front of her, as if to pull back a lost lover, her chest heaving in exertion. Stringbean appeared next to her, the sting of W.C.'s hand still on his left buttock, and he began to sing. The crowd stilled. They seemed ready to give the boy a chance. His voice, sweet and high, had the lilt of something familiar. And so too did the words. "Life is like a mountain railway," he sang, and as he did the audience flickered to life. A church hymn on Tuesday night. It seemed blasphemous. "With an engineer that's proud." They were shocked. What's this angelic pole of a choir boy doing in a joint like Pee Wee's anyway? What's wrong with his people, they'd allow him to do such a thing. Don't he know what this place is for?

They were silent. The boy's spiritual ricocheted off the walls and onto their now deaf ears. Saturday night's for hell raising, Sunday for sermonizing. And Tuesdays, they's for trying out for Saturday! Hush, let the poor boy sing, he don't know no better. Well, he sure ought to. Damn fool.

The boy sang his heart out. Kid knew every word. He looked up at the saloon's tin ceiling, knit his hands with great piety, and let the music flow from his soul. But good as Kid thought he was, he simply could not win over the audience, who, having had their sport, were in no mood for serious religion. Certainly not at Pee Wee's, and certainly not Pee Wee himself.

The owner, who rarely strayed far from his bar which lined the front half of the place and which served as the repository for one of the only two telephones on Beale Street, moved forward, insinuating himself into the audience. Pee Wee raised himself up to the top of his feet, which with the lifts that Simon constructed, made him almost five feet tall, and tried to catch W.C.'s eye. When he finally did he made a gesture so faint and so unmistakably familiar that only W.C. caught the trace of Vigello's pointer as it touched his Adam's apple.

W.C. jumped out quick as a flash. "Well, isn't this just amazing friends, just a wonderful example of local down-home talent. Pee Wee's always brings you the best of what's good, and what's new. Speaking of what's new, here's our last entrant. I know you'll just love what she can do for you." And, grabbing the skinny singer by the crook of his arm, W.C. marched him off stage as fast as his short legs could carry him. As he disappeared into the darkness he tipped his hat at Kid and gave her the thumbs-up sign.

Kid bent down, holding her neckline tight with one hand, and reached for her guitar with the other. It was the same instrument that Pops had given to her ten years ago, still scarred and battered, but now she knew its heft and feel as if it were an extension of her fingers and her heart. She lifted it to her chest, ducking under the ribbon that still read "Clarksdale Dry Goods" and riffed her way up the neck, taking the measure of the audience which she knew still thirsted for the kill.

"Good evening everyone, my name's," and she paused, vamping an A chord, the pinky of her left hand rising and falling with her breath, "my name's Minnie." It just came to her, the name, out of the blue, something she heard once and stuck in the recess of her memory.

"Yeah, Minnie," someone called out. "Sing it girl."

She rode the neck again, starting the song where she knew it would end, picking the run faster now, letting her fingers tell the strings how to sing along with her. Kid could feel the crowd still, oblivious to her green satin dress, listening to their music. She could see W.C. out of the corner of her eye just off to the side of the stage, hands clasped in front of him just below his chin, his blue cap slightly a-kilter.

> Oh, the blues got me thinkin'
>   just like a woman now.
> Oh, the blues got me thinkin'
>   just like a woman now.

But she didn't just sing the blues, not this night. She sang 'em from her gut, letting her voice fall and then rise, from deep in her throat, then from the back of her head and down again.

> Don't matter where you be, chile
>   Don't matter anyhow.

Then she turned the song around, brought it back to the beginning, working the steps back to A, filling in sequences of three notes as she climbed back to where she had begun. But this time she took the simple form of the song, its three chords and its rhythmic drive, and added the tricks that Esau taught her. Riding the bass strings, she used the fingers in her right hand to pick new notes right over the chords. It made her think of the kind of intricate lace — its patterns delicate and lovely — that her grandmother had passed on to her mother so long ago.

> Come on in, baby
>   where you been so long.
> Come on in, baby
>   Where you been so long.
> I'm waitin' in my kitchen
>   Time you came back home.

She stopped for a moment, suspended, and looked at the audience. They stood rapt. Quiet. Listening.

"This here is called "Moaning the Blues." It makes me think of home. I'm from Walls, you know, Walls, Mississippi. Anyone else out there from the Delta?" Like a store full of clocks they began to chime. Not all at once, but here and then there. "Yes, we from Greenville," and "My kin's in Clarksdale," or "Cleveland," and then even one who said, "Tupelo." Someone else said "Tupelo ain't the Delta," and then another voice answered, "Don't matter. You just keep singing, Minnie. You in Memphis now. Why don't you call youself Memphis Minnie."

> Hello blues, hello blues
> How are you today
> Hello blues, hello blues
> How are you today
> You got me on my knees
> And now I'm gonna pray.

She didn't have the burnished bottle neck that Esau once used, so she slid her left hand all the way down the neck of the guitar, ran her index finger across the strings, and chopped her way back up the fretboard, rasping the nails on her right hand harder and harder as she frailed. This time, when she found her place back at A she struck a final note and just let it glide out over the audience, hovering above them, snapping the high E string in exclamation and celebration.

Kid found herself transported by the moment, found the woman within her, discovered the feelings and desire within her own body, in the curls and dips that her satin dress unveiled. She sang as a woman, her hands and voice, one.

> Oh the blues got me thinkin'
> just like a woman now.
> Oh the blues got me thinkin'

And here, instead of completing the lyric she just allowed her guitar to sing, to play the notes of the song into the minds of the audience, let them sing it inside their heads, let them hear her two voices, to allow the guitar to speak the words to them. She closed her own eyes now, looking inside herself, and found the place of feeling and emotion to attach to the last line of the song.

> Don't matter where you be, chile
> Don't matter anyhow.

Opening her eyes, Kid Douglas, born Lizzie, became Memphis Minnie. As she finished the blues, as she picked her right hand through the song's ending riffs, she thought she had discovered a new life.

❧ ❧

When she got back to the rooming house just as the sun had begun its rise — they had asked her to keep playing and even Pee Wee hung around 'til closing — Richard was gone. His suitcase no longer sat next to the cardboard dresser under the window, and his bone-handled knife, his only prized possession, was not there on the sill, where he put it, she thought, every morning just before goin' to bed. As she fell back on the bed she remembered how he looked and felt on Mama's porch. And then she slept.

Sunday morning in Memphis. The city's south side, the rail depot, the loading docks down at the levee, the Pullman Boarding House, Beale Street, even Lorraine's Clean Rooms over on Second, had finally closed up. Kid's green satin dress sat in the corner of her room, accordioned down into itself, catching the light on the ridges of its folds, watching. Only footfalls of the dozen waiters and busboys who had to scurry to work the early shift at the Peabody Hotel disturbed the silence. Asleep and hung over the city rested, its black folk grateful for the respite.

At 11 when Kid awoke (it was her Sunday for the room, she recalled thankfully) she began to cry. The last verse of the song she had played echoed in her head, and there was nothing she could do to get it out.

> Got up in the mornin'
> Had that feelin' in my head
> They tole me that you gone, chile
> Maybe gone and dead

She rocked her head in her hands sitting there alone. "Oh, Richard," she moaned, "what must I do."

The idea of praying didn't sit well with her. Somewhere, sometime, she knew she'd have to go to church and make her peace. But not now, not in this city. Looking out the window, down on Beale, Kid could see the first churchgoers, dressed like it was Saturday night, she thought, as they strolled past the rows of saloons and dance halls. "Not for me," she said out loud. "Not for me." Still, something within her pushed her out the door into the bright sunlight of midday. And without thinking Kid merged slowly into the stream of tall, elegant men and women who had walked from their flats down by the river to follow Beale toward the three churches that stood guard over the neighborhood, their towers already casting a shadow across the open space of Church's Park, two blocks to the east.

So stately and silently did they walk that Kid wondered if she had become part of a funeral procession — these were no ordinary going-to-church folk. The men wore dark suits and the women white linen dresses with collars and sleeves decorated in delicate filigree. The patterns on their parasols matched the cutouts on their dresses, and they strolled with such ease and grace that Kid imagined she might be inhabiting a dream. 'Round Church's square they walked, the women holding lace handkerchiefs to protect their gloves from the handles of the parasols, the men gleaming in pearl-gray. And, then as the clock struck noon they turned sharply down Wellington Street and disappeared into the city.

The square stood empty save for the few souls who lay sleeping under the clump of trees in the center. Kid held herself silently for a moment, taking the measure of the park, mapping it in her mind, gauging the pitch of the sidewalk that bordered it. She felt the breeze touch her arms and she folded them across her body and said, "Richard."

"He ain't comin' back, you know. So, don't waste your eyes a cryin'. That's just the way it is."

The man just held her. Not moving. She could feel the tip of her head against his nose, and the warmth of his hands on her back. No, it didn't feel like Richard at all, more like someone whom she could trust. And she looked up at a giant of a man, dressed in dark pants and a deep blue shirt, whose black Stetson folded down just a mite before it tipped back up in front. Kid took a step back and said, "Who might you be, Mister? I never seen you before."

"They call me Little Kokomo. On account of where I'm from and what I like." And with that, eyes twinkling, he bowed from his waist and said, "At your service." As he did so he reached for his hat and without moving his eyes he lifted it forward and tilted his head just slightly to the right. "And who might you be, young lady? And what you doing out here by yourself anyway." Kid told her story and the man listened carefully. How would she know, she realized later, that he had heard it a hundred times before.

Sunday noon on Beale was the saddest time of the day. She was just beginning to understand that between going to church and playing the blues in the juke joints and saloons there was another world of loneliness. They sat together on one of the park's benches. Didn't even have to say "Colored only." Not in Church's Park. Only black folk went there anyway. Not even the sailors on leave from their station up the Mississippi came to the park. They were welcomed to Beale on Saturday night, but none ever showed their faces on Sunday. Or at least that's what Little Kokomo told her.

By the time she looked up Kid realized that the sun had crept lower in the sky, hanging over the place she knew the river lay, down behind the bluffs and gullies, its rays streaking the sky eastward toward the dark. Little Kokomo had twice offered some "vittles" and Kid had politely declined. But now she realized how hungry she had become. "Come on over to Pee Wee's," he said softly. "I want to talk with the boss about something. We'll fix you up with some good Eye-talian food."

Like the other places on Beale, Pee Wee's opened late on Sunday nights. Didn't want to offend the churchgoing folks, explained Little Kokomo as they walked back up the street. But the side door cracked open easily and they walked into the dark space filled with the aromas of tomato sauce, cigar smoke, and cologne. Hard to tell which was which. The tables and chairs were still stacked one atop the other all over the stage where Kid had performed just the night before. Only a solitary round table and three chairs sat under a single light, just to the left of the long polished bar. The phone was still and Vigello Maffei sat sipping from a tiny cup.

"Ah. Mr. Arnold and the little lady in the green dress. Watcha doin' out this way? Hey, sidown. Pull up a chair. Yeah. Over here. Coffee? Over there. At the bar, you know. Help ya self. I been thinking 'bout you all night. You sure had 'em eatin' out of your hand last night, y'know. Them Schwabs did't hurt you neither. So, I said to my pal Mr. Arnold here, I said, hey, go find that girl and offer her a contract. No. I said, go find that girl and bring her back here. I want to offer her a contract."

Kid glanced at Little Kokomo, who nodded at her and then at Pee Wee, who grinned.

"Sure, kid. What's that name they gave you last night? Memphis Minnie. I sure like that. Sure. This here is the place where all the colored singers, from here to Biloxi, sign up. We're your agents. We get you the places to sing and when you sign up with us, we take care of everything. Everything."

While Vigello rambled, his eyes darting from her face to Little Kokomo who had slipped behind the bar, Kid sat transfixed. She couldn't quite fathom what was happening to her, only that some white man who couldn't take his eyes off her chest for very long was offering to let her sing for money and in places all over the South. She'd even be able to send money home to Mama and the boys. She looked down at the plate of steaming spaghetti doused with a thick red sauce flecked with cheese and realized how hungry she was.

"Sign this here. Right here," Pee Wee was saying as he pushed a contract across the table. "Just has the usual stuff. You know, how much you make, and other jazz that the lawyers make me put in." He seemed proud of his use of the word, jazz, that had just begun to make the rounds of Beale. It had a nice zing to it. His hand, resting on the bottom of the single page, obscured the title under his name. Kid would wonder later, but not for too long, what exactly this Theater Owners Booking Agency (TOBA) was really all about.

"Tough on Black Asses, baby. Tough on Black Asses." Kid sat, feet dangling, on the platform, just up from the brick station house as the man standing next to her spat a wad of tobacco juice onto the tracks. "You got to be tough in this business," he said speaking down to her. "Ain't no one gonna take care of you. No one but you."

"But I ain't even got enough money to get home," Kid said. And my Mama lives two stops up the line, in Walls." She gestured across the levee with her eyes. It was too high to actually see the Mississippi from the station, but everyone in Helena could hear it and smell it. It controlled the rhythm and the reason of the town's life. "Helena, Arkansas. What kinda place is this anyway," Kid whispered. "It's the saddest town I did ever see."

The train station formed a tee at the end of Helena's main street which ran north hard against the levee. It also marked the boundary between the white and colored parts of town, anchoring the meager storefront barbershops, rooming houses, pool halls, and juke joints that lay in a strip bleeding west. At the end the lurid blue stucco of Joe's Tamale Shop gave way to random unpainted wood frame houses surrounded by vacant lots, unfettered pigs and sheep, and a kind of greyness that seemed to hover over the town.

Even the white part of town, Kid noticed, the two blocks that packed general stores and the King Biscuit Flour warehouse next to the Regal (colored only in the balcony and only on Saturdays and Sundays at midnight) theater, was grim. Standing in front of the theater earlier that morning, she could see back down past the station where the Helena Silage Company and Gin watched over the entire town, black and white, its four stories towering even above the levee as its long tin arms delivered corn and cotton to the barges moored in the river. Caught between Memphis and Natchez, the town of Helena never really had a chance.

Kid had been on the road for TOBA for only two weeks, but she knew that this was not the life she had bargained for. "They said they'd pay me when we got done here last night," she sniffled as the man next to her continued to spit into the tracks. Her cardboard suitcase and guitar lay on the platform to her left, their shadows already like tombstones as the summer sun broiled against her forehead. She and the others, two dancers, a small troupe of jugglers, and a man who called himself The Professor, actually a teenaged boy who wore a pickaninny wig and a red, white, and blue Uncle Sam costume and sold magic cures in small brown bottles containing molasses and crushed beetles, had arrived on Friday, done three shows each on Saturday and Sunday, the last ending at 4 A.M. When they had gone to the box office to collect their wages the lady with the fat hanging down between her eyes said, "We ain't got no money. That's for your TOBA man. He'll be here in the morning. He said to wait."

Even Mrs. Witlow's Boarding House, one of the two for Negroes just up the street from the station, refused credit and Kid found herself sitting by the station waitin' first for the morning sun and now for the TOBA man.

Oh, he'd appear all right, he always did, sooner or later, either drunk or hung over, and with some story to tell. Quit? He'd pull a piece of paper out of his pocket and pretend to read, "This here says, that so and so (that's you, honey, that's you) being of temperate comportment, contracts with the Theater Owners Booking Association (that's us, honey, that's us) to perform exclusively at our venues (that mean our theaters and nowhere else) for the next year. And see, down at the bottom, next to Mr. Maffei's name, right there, is you. Kid Douglas, you signed, as Memphis Minnie. Now, here's what we promised you. Get yo ass on the next train and be in Batesville by tomorrow."

He'd hand her a little envelope with a ticket and a few dollars for the next week's room and board, and head down the street to the nearest saloon where he'd shoot pool, drink a half-dozen bottles of beer, and get the last train to Memphis.

Kid walked slowly into the red brick station and nodded at the ticket taker, who gestured to her from behind the "Colored" sign over the window. "Got something for you," the man said and he slipped a soiled envelope under the brass frame that separated them. "Here."

"Be in Jackson tonight. Two shows tomorrow. Pay your own way. Here's the fare and an extra two bits for some food." Vigello Maffei had signed the note.

Kid counted the money, walked out onto the platform, picked up her burlap King Biscuit sack and guitar case, hitched her cotton dress up on her shoulders, and looked north, up the tracks. She thought for another moment, turned on her heels, and struggled with her burden back into the station. "Is this enough," she asked the agent inside, "to buy me a ticket to Chicago? It's all the money I got."

Two hours later Kid Douglas boarded the train for Chicago—for the Promised Land. "Free," the word snagged in her mind. She thought of Richard, and sang quietly to herself.

Ride on, baby, ride that freedom train
Ride on, baby, ride that freedom train
One day you'll want your woman
But she won't be home again.

Then she slept.

7

JULY 1919

"One thing I ain't about to let happen," Comiskey said in his best tough-guy voice, "is let that Irish fucker McGraw beat me to the punch. You think I didn't know it when he asked Foster to teach Mathewson how to throw a shine ball?" And then he looked right down his nose, over his reading glasses, and belched. "Or that he still figures to make a pile of dough playing dark teams on his days off? You think I'm stupid?"

The men sitting in leather chairs, cigar smoke curling from their nostrils in blue tendrils, all grunted in assent. "But, Charlie, you gotta take care. Bring in one of 'em, pay 'em a few bucks less, sure. But, watch out. It could backfire."

Comiskey thought for a moment. "It'd better not backfire. If it works, we win the pennant, and make a bundle, and if it don't, well…"

Old W.F. Swift took a swig of his brandy, set the glass down on the tray that the maid held for him just at elbow height, and snorted. "Don't be such a wet rag, Henry," he said, elevating his nose in Armour's direction. "It's not as if he's actually a strike-breaker. Just the possibility of a Negro ball player on Charlie's old time plantation. Right, Charlie?"

Comiskey tightened his legs, as if he needed to pee but didn't know how to stop the flow of the conversation. And besides with that Negro girl, the one who had been sent by Mrs. Binga, all wide-eyed and expressionless, hovering over them, he could hardly stand up and say, "Fellas. Gotta go take a leak."

"Well gentleman," he said softly, "I'll be back in a minute. Hey, uh (and now he stumbled trying to remember Kid's name) kid, how about another round for the gentleman before I return."

Kid busied herself with proffering ample portions of amber drink into the cut-glass stemware that Comiskey kept for special occasions. The half-dozen well draped men, each casually regal in their black evening clothes, collars open in studied relaxation, settled back into their leather chairs, puffed their cigars, and silently toasted their good fortune.

Their talk, once Comiskey returned to his inner sanctum, revolved around the same subjects it always revolved around — politics and money. And for the magnates assembled in Comiskey's Near South Side mansion it was difficult to say which begat which. It was abundantly clear to all of them, however, the packers and the bankers, the merchant princes and the team owners, that the war had changed everything. "You really can smell it," one of them said. "You can smell the money in the air, ripe as a spring lilac, ready to pick."

"Sure. If we can count on the Mayor," another replied. And the Irish and Polacks who we need to vote for him, he thought silently.

At that moment Sam, holding the front door open for a man in a dark hat, his collar pulled up to his ears, gave a soft whistle. "Pssst, Mr. Comiskey, they're here." As the two newcomers entered Sam could feel the room's emotional posture change. He glided off to the side, near where the Negro girl, Comiskey's new maid he guessed, stood. Same one who he had seen playing that night, he remembered suddenly. Sam felt himself blush and then he thought of Miss Ruth. Kid remained passive, her tray in hand, her white apron still crisp against the stiff black fabric of her uniform.

With uncharacteristic formality Comiskey stood, extended his hand and said, "'Evening Mr. Mayor. Pleased you could grace us with your presence, busy as you are and hot as it is this summer."

"Cut the crap, Charlie. We both know the score. Right fellas?"

The assembled notables winced inwardly; they failed to appreciate the presumption of camaraderie, the assumption of equality, in the Mayor's tone. Outwardly, however, they smiled, nodded, and stood up gingerly to return his greeting. A couple, Swift and Armour, furtively glanced around to see if anyone else had accompanied the Mayor that evening. Probably scared shitless that he might have brought along that Oscar DePriest. Bad enough that the Mayor openly conspired with the city's first Negro alderman, but he also seemed to actually enjoy his company.

But the Mayor, William Henry Thompson, known to all as "Big Bill," was up for reelection in the fall. And as much as the new patricians of Chicago needed his anti-union republicanism to feed their coffers of privilege, they also knew that Thompson depended on the expanding Negro vote as a hedge against the Democrats. As long as their Irish, Polish, and Lithuanian workers insisted on their unions (Lord, don't they even remember those anarchists dangling from the gallows?) the magnates and the Mayor both needed the new Negro immigrants more than the poor devils could ever realize. Sam suddenly thought, "Hell, Comiskey and Thompson, they're both in the same boat. Without Negro votes and Negro players they're cooked." And that, of course, was the unannounced and never to be expressed reason for Big Bill's visit that last evening in July 1919.

But partnerships of convenience and devilry are never simple contracts. They require — no, demand — a celebratory ritual to cement the alliance by elevating it beyond the plane of self-interest that, of course, both parties know but never acknowledge to be operative.

Sam remained in the shadows of Comiskey's salon. For an instant the room grew silent and he could almost hear Kid's breath come to a halt. "Sit down, fellas," Big Bill commanded in that too friendly voice of his, "don't have to stand on ceremony with me."

The men settled back into their leather seats, crossed their legs, picked up their glasses and tried to look relaxed. But Thompson's entry had clearly altered the proceedings and Sam listened attentively.

After about a half-hour of chatter about the Sox, the extraordinary pitching of Eddie Cicotte and the thunderous bat of Joe Jackson, Thompson turned to Comiskey and smilingly asked, "What say we go try out this new joint some of my South Side pals told me about it. What say? Your treat, of course, Charlie!"

Comiskey thought, "Up-yours pal," and instead replied, "Great idea. It'd be my pleasure, gentlemen, for you to be my guests at an evening spot of the Mayor's choice."

A tall white-haired gent cleared his voice. Sam recognized him as Henry Dalton, the Hyde Park realtor and local stalwart of the Republican machine, who had been buying up block after block of South Side apartment buildings. "I'll have my chauffeur bring the car around. You'll be my guests tonight."

Sam caught Comiskey's eye and with a slight nod the old Roman signaled him to come along. The heavy night air, wet with mid-summer humidity, greeted the group as they descended the serpentine walk from Comiskey's private side entrance out to the street. There a large dark car, a Packard, waited, its double rear doors held open by a Negro chauffeur whose equally dark uniform was set off only by the strip of brass just above the brim of his visored cap. "Evening Mr. Dalton, sir," the man said with a diffidence flavored by just the slightest hint of irony — like a scent barely perceived and never identified. "Yes, good evening, Bigger." Dalton spoke with a kind of gentle softness that seemed equally evanescent. Sam took the front seat, next to the driver, and rode in silence as they sped their way east to the just completed drive along the lake shore and headed north toward downtown.

The lights of Navy Pier, its Ferris wheel a blur of yellows and oranges, swirled in the distance as Dalton's car made its way through the newly executed park that connected the city with its shoreline along lake Michigan. It looked, thought Sam, incredibly gay and cheerful, a city ablaze in revelry, in celebration of its own prosperity and pleasure. The virtually deserted parkway, an avenue of curves that terminated at the Loop, made their voyage — Sam increasingly had the sense, perhaps from their proximity to the lake — seem as if they were on a boat sailing the nighttime waters toward some mysterious and exotic destination.

Quickly the driver guided the car off the drive and began to turn first west and then back south, up State Street, past the Armour Institute, toward 35th Street. The night sky gave off an incandescent glow, a red and indigo mixture of color and smoke that cast the street, its buildings, and its inhabitants in its hue. Sitting in front enabled Sam to take in the scene, which for all his experience on the South Side he had never before encountered.

Nightfall transformed the intersection of 35th and State into a fantastic cityscape whose bustle and energy came alive. Newly installed neon lights, silently dark during the day, announced the neighborhood's pleasures. Blinking, glowing, and sputtering in a kaleidoscope of garish yellow, red, and blue the signs beckoned, invited, and seduced. *Eat* *at Sam's, Drink Blatz, Club Bronzeville, Liquor Sold Here, Save your Soul, Bar-B-Que, ComeOnInn, Hair Do — Anytime, and Ten Cent Billiards* flickered and sang their siren songs to the throngs strolling up and down the ever-crowded intersection.

Look up and you find a whole other world, of women standing in windows, their frayed red negligees transparent and shiny; of holy-rollers, eyes and hands raised toward the gods who seemed just beyond the cracked plaster ceilings of their tenements; of Irina's Seances where folks lined up two deep to speak with the dearly departed, those who had recently and not so recently passed; of families selling glasses of whiskey and joints of fried chicken to their neighbors to help them pay off the long overdue rent; of men and women in naked, sweaty, passionate embrace, the lights reflecting off their skin; and even of old folks, their time past, now confined to a single room, the world spread out below them, with little to do but watch.

And below, on the street, along State and around to 35th, just short walk west to Comiskey's park, and just a bit longer east to the residential center of the Black Belt, strolled these new migrants to Chicago, the Negroes from Mississippi, from the Delta, who now made the city their home.

They promenaded, walked, even strutted singly and in pairs — women in satin gowns tight across their rumps and breasts, arms linked in the yellow suit jackets of men who cut the guts out of the hogs six days a week and lived for Saturday night. In doorways and just around corners that gave way to alleys they might embrace, saying, "Oh, baby, that feels so good." Side pockets bulging with pints, the men stopped to speak with others whose rough clothes bespoke their recent arrival. "Say, brother. You sure need to find you some new threads. Whatsa matta, your mama can't sew no more?" Or, tipping their new black bowlers, ones they wore jauntily on the backs of their heads, they might stop and laugh. Bright-eyed and full of life, they marched along State Street that Saturday night. Closer to the storefronts, away from the curb, another breed of men, in tightly fitting pants and checked shirts, some sporting puffy newsboys' caps, stopped to banter with shop girls, young women in cotton dresses hanging loosely from their angular frames, their hair short, their jewelry bright. Their hues, these teeming women and men from the South Side, were as varied as their imagination. Ebony black, yellow, tan and brown, chocolate and almost albino cast the spectrum of "the race." But the South Side that night, Bronzeville on Saturday, welcomed all comers. It seemed only to say, come on, have a good time, spend your money, and leave in peace. White men and women, usually in the company of Negroes, found themselves out for the evening, their faces flushed with pleasure, their bellies filled with food and drink.

"We call it the stroll," announced the chauffeur, "but it's not quite where you folk is going," and with that he put the car into gear and moved out from the curb only to slam on the brakes, lurching all the swells in the back seats forward, then snapping them back. He cursed quietly under his breath, "Fucker." An open car breezed by, just missing Comiskey's, and Sam had only a moment to glimpse the driver and his companion, her green scarf trailing in the wind as the car sped down State Street, south, into the Belt.

Bigger shouted, "Hold on," and turned his own car in a tight spiral U and spun the wheels on State toward the Loop. Immediately, however, they turned right, toward the lake and eased into a narrow alley, between 34th and 33rd. The car crept down the cobblestone street, lights off, blending into the night. The occupants in the rear fell into silence and for the first time seemed to be aware of their surroundings. The sputter of the dozen cylinders had become the only noise to interrupt the night. And then, suddenly, lights blazed before them.

Just off the alley, tucked into what might have looked like a small park carved out within a large city block, emerged a long and low building, its circumference marked by a necklace of oil lamps attached to its lattice foundation. The wide steps up to the entry porch were lined with elegantly potted palms, and Bigger darted quickly from his raised driver's seat and circled around to the other side of the car. He opened the double doors and announced, "Watch your step gentlemen," as he held out his hand while Comiskey's party emptied out of the car.

Sam trailed discreetly behind the flock of black-coated magnates as they strode up the stairs, past the liveried Negro doormen, their gold epaulettes swinging with the motion of their salutes, into the open ball-room of the Panama Cafe. "Good evening, sir, good to see you again," announced the maitre d', his top hat and bowtie contrasting with the brilliant white of his shirt. Comiskey had already begun to slip his hand out of his pocket, but Big Bill interrupted. "Thanks Roberto, its always a pleasure. Tell Tony that we're here at my usual table," and with that he palmed a fifty dollar bill into the glove of Tony Overton's right hand man and partner.

Roberto nodded quickly to a young woman who, clutching a dozen menus to the front of her silver gown, shimmied forward and said, "Follow me boys." They did, their gaze measuring her hips as she made her way to a table in the middle of the room. Her long, wavy hair, set off by rhinestone combs, and her light brown arms, a dozen bracelets jangling from wrist to elbow, gave her just the touch of tawdry elegance the club's owners desired.

She seated the Mayor last, patting him on the shoulder gently, then trailing the tips of her fingernails across the nape of his neck. "Have a wonderful evening, Bill. You know where to find me," she said as she pivoted around, the silver sequins tinkling delicately in her wake. Sam slid his chair between Comiskey and Dalton and looked around. He had heard of the Panama, knew that it had been closed a dozen times by the vice squad before Big Bill had become mayor but had, since 1915, remained in continuous operation. But he had never before been invited to share its pleasures.

The Thompson party was seated at a large, in fact the largest, round table front and center, with an unobstructed view of the slightly raised bandstand which dominated the room. Between the table and the stage a wood dance floor marked a neutral zone where couples might find each other without approbation. Chandeliers hung by the dozen and their reflection flickered against the black cast-iron ceiling like a thousand stars in the night.

The two dozen white covered tables, elegantly appointed with crystal and gold-edged china and crisp linen, were all filled by the time Comiskey's party filed in. For the most part well-to-do men and a scattering of beautifully turned out women sat in relaxed splendor, dining on opulently prepared pheasant or lobster, quaffing flutes of champagne, their lavish appetites matched by the number of digits that would appear, later, discreetly, on the bill, or as the management called it, The Facteur.

This last indulgence brought howls of quiet laughter to the lips of the Negro waiters, all men, who had themselves recently arrived in Chicago, some but a few weeks or months removed from life and work chopping cotton. Back home the idea of a factor, the usually sleazy and always greedy agent who weighed and appraised their crops before assigning value to their share, had an entirely different connotation.

The white clientele at the Panama Cafe seemed at ease with the club's unspoken racial policy. Less so the club's Negro waiters, not only recently arrived from the South but whose skins were "so black they looked blue," according to Armour, who seemed to be the first person in his group to take any real notice of his surroundings.

Trays held high above their shoulders, this chorus of waiters circled the room with remarkable silence, emerging from the quiet of their attentiveness at the whim of a patron's summons. But these men only served and never spoke.

The young woman in the silver sequins reappeared behind Sam's left ear and said silkily, "Gentleman, this is Myla, she'll be glad to take your orders and see to your every need." And as the men at Sam's table ordered their luxuries Sam could see, now, that each table at the Panama was attended by a virtual duplicate of Myla, young, café au lait, slender women, hardly more than girls, dressed simply in gold, their hair piled atop their heads.

"Ladies and gentleman," announced a smooth voice projected from within a stubby, black megaphone, "ladies and gentlemen, Cafe Panama has spared no expense to bring you tonight's entertainment. Turn your attention to the stage and feast your eyes and ears as we present The King and his Court in their exclusive Chicago appearance."

At that moment the waiters converged on the tables, cleared the empty dishes and simultaneously extinguished the tallows that illuminated the chandeliers. They then retreated to the periphery of the room, where they stood, mute, arms crossed, and watched with expressionless eyes. Only the light over the stage remained, its incandescence bathing the small combo, a group of five black men who began to play. As their syncopated music, its beat sustained by a tuba, its melody by a cornet, energized the room, the lights dimmed and then enlarged their focus to reveal a line of young women who paraded across the stage. Kicking their legs high, they stood in front of the band and faced the patrons. A dozen light brown young women, in fact the same girls who had earlier taken patrons' orders, moved from left to right, linked arms, and danced in unison. It was, as almost everyone in the club knew the latest dance rage, the Black Bottom, and the girls obliged the now entranced male patrons by turning their backs to the audience, and bending over. With their hands on their knees, they tossed their rear ends and their thigh-high flounced beige skirts skyward. As the crowd applauded the girls turned around and bowed just enough to let their breasts hang out from their scooped lace necklines. Then, quickly they raised their heads, smiled, kissed the air, and ran off stage.

Within moments, though hardly had the lusty applause ceased, they reappeared. The drummer lay down a steady beat accented by the bass drum as the young women circled across the stage, arm to shoulder, this time clad in jungle costumes, feathers and bones adorning their wrists and ankles. The band wailed as the beat changed into a steady drone, thumping the room with its vibration. As the rhythm picked up so too did the motion of the young women, their feet bare, their eyes closed in apparent ecstacy. They led the audience into the bosom of their ritual, whirling and then finally collapsing to the floor in spent conclusion.

Then almost demurely the troupe picked itself up, stood in a single line, held hands, smiled pleasantly and bowed. The music shifted to the piano, the lights came back on, and the audience applauded.

Sam couldn't help but think of the girl at Comiskey's house. The one in the apron, quietly serving drinks, her dark skin and serious eyes. The applause around him startled him back to the moment and he heard the megaphone say, "And now, the best jazz this side of New Orleans." The band resumed playing and Sam fixed his attention on the young man with the shining silver cornet. His round face and even rounder cheeks, puffed with the exertion of his music, gave way to large expressive eyes, which even at the age of nineteen revealed their watery, almost glassy gaze.

His playing, Sam realized, was that of a virtuoso. The few jazz bands Sam had heard since the end of the war a year earlier had played a music that bounced, but did so in a kind of patterned unison, each musician finding his individual place in the whole. But this cornet player made his own music. He seemed to string notes together with a furious, yet steady beat, transforming the ensemble into a band that backed the heat of his own expression. Every now and then he would lower his instrument, and using his left hand, wipe his forehead with the large white handkerchief that he held in his palm.

After a few minutes many of the men in the audience abandoned their tables and searched the sides of the stage where they found, first with their eyes and then with their hands, the young women who had danced so fetchingly earlier. The couples walked to the dance floor, white men in black evening dress, their arms around younger light-skinned Negro women, and held each other. The waiters remained, arms folded, on the edge of the room, and watched.

Comiskey's party, however, lingered in their seats—with the exception of the Mayor, who found one of the waitress-dancers. She called him softly, "Wild Bill," and giggled as he led her onto the dance floor. But twenty minutes later he returned, hitching his pants, patting a few shoulders, and resumed his place at the table.

"Gentlemen, another round of drinks is in order," Comiskey announced with self-importance which he decided to lace with generosity. Comiskey straightened his back, squirmed his rear end into the seat of his chair, folded his hands in front of him and said, "I've made the decision that I had introduced you to earlier. Now, I want to hear your opinions, and then gain your support."

He fell silent for a moment and let his eyes move around the table and stopped briefly to catch Mayor Thompson's return look of cynical curiosity. "Thanks to Sam here," and he gestured to his right where Sam sat as unobtrusively as possible, "I've begun negotiations with my old friend Andrew Foster to obtain the services of his extraordinary shortstop, John Henry Lloyd, for the White Sox. As I'm sure you all know," he added, knowing full well that they did not know, "Lloyd played for the Negro team here, the American Giants. And now I want to sign him for the White Sox."

Comiskey's announcement left the table silent. Chicago's millionaires didn't know what to say first. Each of them knew exactly what Comiskey meant, understood firsthand the value of bringing Negroes to the workplace, and the relationship between costs and benefits that might accrue from such a decision.

They had, after all, to a man used colored workers from the South to fill the positions vacated when their immigrants had gone first to war and then, when they returned, to the unions. Colored workers were cheaper, less trouble, and easier to manipulate.

But they argued with Comiskey that evening. Baseball wasn't the same as meat packing, they said. Sure, all the owners cooperated, as was normal and proper, to set standards of wages and prices, and sure the workers needed their benevolent protection. But, come on Charlie, a guy living in Joliet or Brooklyn, what did he know or care about the color of the man who had stuffed the sausage. And, believe-you-me, the kind that come to the ball park, well, they don't want to watch 'em play, no less sit with 'em. Jeeze, Charlie, you got enough to win the pennant anyway without changing everything. And, you know I really have nothing against Negroes, why I let my children be brought up by them, but besides, they aren't up to scratch. Sure, Charlie, they can run and hit, but when the pressure is on, they fold. And with that Montgomery Ward unhitched his diamond cufflink, rolled up the sleeve of his silk shirt, and grabbed himself by the throat.

"Lemme ask you something. You guys all got money, power, prestige. You got a place in this world," and Comiskey paused in part to get hold of himself before he allowed his resentment to get the better of him, "so why do you employ Negroes and at the same time tell me that I'm the revolutionary for wanting to sign just one? I'm not talking about a whole team. Just this one player. If I don't do it someone else will, just mark my words."

Big Bill Thompson had, until this moment, remained silent, content to let the money boys do the talking. But now it was time to turn the tide. He moved his chair back, spread his legs, and propped his elbows on the table and ordered, "Honey, a bottle of champagne for the table. No, make it two. And put it on my tab." And as the hostess wiggled off, Mayor William Thompson addressed his congregation.

"Boys," he said letting the false equality settle under their skins, "boys. Let's get down to business. We need these new Negroes. We need their money, their work, their rent, and we need their votes. And if we don't get it someone else will. It's as simple as that. I wouldn't be mayor today without 'em and I sure as hell won't win this fall without 'em either. The Democrats may sound like they love Wilson and all that segregation crap, but he's a vegetable now, and the days of kissing Southern ass are long gone. So, I say, let Charlie show us the new way, because if we don't the alternatives are a lot worse. And besides if it fails it's only one colored ball player, and Charlie still has the best team in the business."

The others at the table began nodding their assent. Not that they wanted to acknowledge Big Bill's importance, for they still controlled the purse that allowed him to be mayor. But to a man they clearly understood the gist of his words. If the correct interests of Chicago could not succeed in keeping the Negroes on their side, then the colored would have only to look toward the Democrats, the unions, and the white workers for allies. And that, even Dalton had to confess, that would be a disaster.

The only thing left to do, said Comiskey softly as he left the club a half-hour later with Sam at his side, is tell the team, and he knew just how he would do that. Yes he did. "What about Foster, Mr. Comiskey?" Sam asked as they walked toward the car idling at the curb.

"Waddabout him?"

"Well, I just thought, you know, it's Foster's contract. Don't you need to buy it?

"Hell no, Sammy. Hell no. Dontcha know. These Negro teams have no reserve clause. Lloyd's free to sign with me whenever we give the word. That's what makes us different from them. Foster can't keep the same team together for two months, they're always revolving. Come on, dontcha know nuttin?" And Comiskey smiled ear to ear, tossed his tux over his shoulder and jumped into the back seat of Dalton's idling car. "Home, boy."

The next morning was an off day for the Sox. Kid Gleason decided to call the boys in for a workout. They had played well, he thought, in St. Louis but the dog days of August were upon them and the Red Sox were coming to town the next day for a four game series. That fucking Ruth was not only scheduled to pitch the third game, but they had him playing right field most other days and he was hitting the hell out of the ball.

Gleason looked at the diamond. The ground crew had cut the grass short, banking the soft brown dirt from home to first and third just ever so slightly to keep cutters down the line fair. Not that his team bunted a lot, but he wanted Weaver and Gandil to make as many chances as possible. He reminded himself to tell Lefty Williams and Cicotte to pitch Ruth on the fists, that way, he reasoned, the new slugger would over-stride, and pull an inside pitch foul or skim it toward the forewarned Gandil.

The team had assembled an hour earlier and already had taken the field in their home uniforms. Comiskey had told him that to save money the Sox would have only one home uniform and the players could tend to the laundering themselves. And now, in mid-summer, their home whites had, all except the one Collins sported, turned a dull and mottled light grey, dirt and sweat congealing in all the usual places, in some cases all but obscuring the black stripes that otherwise distinguished them. But, thought Gleason, still they looked grand. He loved the way SOX appeared on their chests, a large S inscribing the smaller o and x in its upper and lower curves. It seemed to be an emblem of their prowess, an insignia repeated above the short bills of their caps, which they wore back on their heads as they worked on the field.

In foul territory, in front of the dugouts, the players had arranged themselves, as he had required, in pairs. And, in unison, also as he had prescribed, they tossed a dozen balls back and forth, oblivious to the warming summer sun. Gleason always worried that Comiskey would look down from his office and see the fellows goofing off and so he told them time and time again that baseball was a business, an important business which they'd sure as hell better take seriously.

Exactly five minutes later he put his fingers to his lips and produced a piercing whistle. The players responded and as if choreographed; half of them dropped their gloves, disappeared into the dugout, and returned with bats. The two lines then proceeded to play pepper, tossing the ball underhand and by half-swinging tapping it back. Good for the reflexes. And for discipline.

Another whistle and this time Gleason motioned the players on the first base side to move into the outfield while those off behind third base now assumed their infield positions, Gandil at first, Collins at second, Risberg at short, and Weaver at third. They pawed the ground in front of them with their spikes, spat, except for Collins, tobacco juice into their gloves, and waited.

Gleason sauntered over to the on-deck circle to the first base side of home, picked up a fungo bat and began banging out ground ball after ground ball to each of the infielders. The smack of the bat sounded as regular as a riveting gun as he sprayed the ball from first to third and then back again, pushing his fielders to their right and then to their left. Twenty minutes later, his players drenched in sweat, uniforms ripe and heavy with their perspiration, Gleason called out, "Get two." The drill continued. Gleason said nothing, working his infield until he felt they had the kind of precision of what he and Comiskey called a "well oiled machine." He always told them that if they did it right in practice, and did it the same way time after time, then they would do it right in a game. Leave nothing to chance, he liked to say, but that was before Hal Chase had his head handed to him for betting.

The hair on the back of Gleason's neck stood up even before he realized that Comiskey had walked up behind him. "Good practice, Kid," he muttered. "Risberg and Collins look good on the double play," he allowed, "most of the time." Gleason grimaced imperceptibly and nodded, spitting tobacco juice at his feet as he replied, "Yea. Thems not so bad." He and Comiskey both knew that their two middle infielders never spoke with one another, only occasionally grunted when the other made an especially good play.

Their mutual resentment, of Collins the politely educated college man and of Risberg, who worked in the paper mills during the off season, was legendary. At least Risberg threw Collins the ball correctly during practice and in ball games. Not like Gandil, who took some secret pleasure in leading Collins into sliding runners when forced to throw to him at second. Still, Gleason knew he had a winner, a damn good team despite all the personal bitterness and the intervention of the Old Man.

"Tell 'em I want to see them in my office after practice. First Collins then Swede."

❦ ❧

Swede Risberg saw Collins leave out of the corner of his eye and wondered what was up. First Comiskey comes down to practice and then Collins goes upstairs. Risberg sat in the dugout, tossed his glove onto the apron of the field, and closed his eyes. It was only his third year on the team and for the first time he was playing more at short than at the other infield positions.

Gleason liked to move him around, playing third sometimes to give Weaver a rest and even at first when Gandil looked as hung over as he actually was. Not bad for a kid whose parents spoke no English, and who had been content to work for a living ever since he had turned fourteen. He also knew that his value to the team depended on his willingness to play well anywhere in the in field. Compared with Jackson and Collins or even Weaver his .258 career average didn't mean shit. That Collins, what a stuck-up pain in the ass, always acting like he's better than everyone else. It really made Swede angry that Collins not only made twice as much as he did but even more than Jackson.

And he couldn't keep his face out of other people's business. On the train the other day, coming back from St. Louis, in the lounge car where Collins never went anyway, we were just sitting around chewin' the fat. A couple of pitchers, the regular guys, Cicotte and Lefty Williams and I was just listening, you know, lettin' 'em bend my ear. They were showing each other stuff they do to the ball, how they shined it to make it swerve, or how they wished they had a catcher who'd scuff it against their spikes to rough it up. And Williams, he had a ball in his hand and was letting Cicotte show him how to do this stuff and along comes Collins and the son-of-a-bitch looks down on us and says, "Hey, fellas, don't you know that doctoring the ball is against the rules?" Against the fucking rules.

"You know Eddie," Comiskey said in his office just moments after his prized second baseman had knocked on the door, "I think that the deal I made with Connie for you was the best move I have ever made in my long association with this great game of ours. In fact, just today I was saying that you are the White Sox version of Christy himself."

Collins didn't know if he was being conned or flattered. Both he decided, and kept his reply to a polite, "Thanks Mr. Comiskey, it sure is good to hear it from the boss." Collins wasn't above the same game.

"I've been thinking, Eddie. How are things going between you and Swede? I mean everyone knows that you don't get along off the field. Tell me," he leaned forward across the desk, jutting his face closer to the still standing Collins, sweat pouring off his forehead, his hat dangling from his right hand at his side, "is the kid up to scratch? Can he pull his weight? I want to win the pennant again and I need the best players I can get."

"Well, Mr. Comiskey. You know I've always been on the up and up with you. And to tell you the truth Swede's a good ball player, in the field that is. He can go 'bout anywhere and reach almost anything that's hit between me and Buck."

"Come on, Eddie. I can see that with my own eyes. He's a good fielder. No doubt about that. I want to know what you think about him. Let's just say you were the manager, what would you say?"

Collins wondered what was up. "He's a good ball player, don't get me wrong. But it's his attitude that gets to me. He's always ready to go with his fists, he's always looking for an angle, and, well, maybe because he's from the sticks, you know that mill town in California, he's looking to make a buck on the side."

"I know just what you mean, Eddie. Just what you mean." Comiskey paused. "That's why I asked you to come up here. I have an idea for our club, but it won't work Eddie, unless you and some of the other fellows on the team go along with it."

"Okay, Mr. Comiskey. Shoot."

"Here it is, Eddie. I want to sign John Henry Lloyd, the shortstop on Foster's team, to play for us for the rest of the season. I think he'll be good for the team, guarantee us the pennant, bring us lots of new customers, and give us another bat for those days when Swede is on the schneid. Which I notice he is often. What do you think, Eddie? You went to college with Negroes. I figured you'd be just the guy to help me with the rest of the team."

"Well, Mr. Comiskey, I don't know. Sure, I got no problem with Lloyd. I hear he's the greatest ball player on the Americans. And I don't think he'll be any problem. But, the fellas on the team, well that's another story. Lots of 'em don't like me. What will they do with a Negro?"

Comiskey dropped his voice in a whisper. "Listen, Eddie. This is a job for you. You are one of the leaders on this team, and I need you to make it good with your friends. You know, soften the blow. I want Lloyd to take Risberg's place but we can't risk the rest of 'em getting pissed off. I need your help. Can I count on you?"

"I'll do my best, I'll work with the fellas who talk to me. But I can't promise about Gandil and some of the rest of 'em."

"That's okay. Eddie. I have some ideas about that. Just do what you can."

"I sure will, Mr. Comiskey. I'll do my best, honest I will."

"Thanks, Eddie. I won't forget it…. Oh. Tell Gleason I want to see Risberg too."

An hour later Swede closed the door to Comiskey's office behind him. He had never been summoned to the owner's office before, and Comiskey's last words still rang in his ears. "Thanks Swede. I won't forget it."

Swede hoped and assumed that Comiskey meant more money. He sure could use it and so could his friends. Even Joe Jackson, well, with the taste he had for looking swell, he was always out of money. Of course, all of them knew that Collins had the highest salary on the team, and Risberg felt that somehow Comiskey was playing them all for fools. He even considered talking to some of his old union friends from home, from the paper mills in Red Bluff, but he knew Comiskey would show him to the door the minute word got out that he even thought about ball players organizing.

And he had no idea if Comiskey was giving him a load of bull about the Negro player, that Lloyd, from the American Giants. Said he wanted to sign him to take some of the pressure off Collins, that Lloyd would bring new fans to the ball park, and that he needed Swede to make it smooth with the other guys on the team. Comiskey said, and Swede remembered it exactly, "I'll really be in your debt if you could find a way to help me out in this. I'm not sure Collins would understand it this way, but I know, Swede, that I can count on you."

He "Yessed Mister Comiskey" and "Yes-sirred Mister Comiskey" all the way out the door of the swank office. Always bullshit a bullshitter, his pal Gandil told him when he first joined the team several years earlier. But, playing with a Negro. He really needed to think about that one. Oh, he could do it all right, but what about the guys on the team from the South, like Joe Jackson? What in the world was he going to say to him? "Like I said, Swede, I am sure counting on you for this one." At that Swede closed the door to the Old Roman's office, and shaking his head began to worry about how and what to say to Jackson, Weaver, and Gandil. As he walked down the corridor back to the clubhouse he couldn't help but notice the scent of perfume that seemed to linger in the hall outside Comiskey's office. Swede wondered, and then turned his attention back to Lloyd. Anything to make that stuck-up sap Collins feel the heat. Anything.

Swede usually didn't frequent the Palmer House. But he decided to talk with Jackson on his own grounds. It was a long walk from the boarding house that he lived in on the West Side, but the early evening brought a welcome cool breeze in from the lake as Swede made his way through the Loop. The rush-hour crowd had begun to thin and even the streets offered some breathing room from the congested tangles of street cars, hacks, and horse-drawn wagons that daily plied their wares downtown. Shop girls hurried to waiting suburban trains, and men in bowlers and starched collars seemed less to stride than to stagger home.

The elegance of the Palmer House, all polished brass and mahogany, its deeply dark tables separated by frosted glass etched with scenes of historic Chicago, made Swede hunch up his shoulders in anticipation. This joint was just too grand, he thought, wishing he had been strong enough to suggest the neighborhood taverns where all the barkeeps knew his name and kept a tab.

Over in the corner of the cavernous room, attended by a half-dozen beefy waiters sporting handlebar mustaches and white aprons, Swede caught a glimpse of several heads peeking up from behind one of the partitions. The two men were already engaged in secretive conversation and they each spoke in hushed tones, spinning the amber bottles of beer between their palms as they conversed.

Swede slid in next to Gandil and across from Jackson. He knew that they were the key to Comiskey's plan and that they would jump at the chance to show Collins up. "Whadda ya say, boys," he announced jovially, as he signaled one of the waiters to bring him a bottle of beer. "Two bits," the waiter grunted, his hand attentively at his side. "Jeeze. Costs a nickel over by Bughouse Square," Swede said under his breath.

"Okay Risberg," barked Gandil, "waddid you bring us to this joint for anyway. Two beers and I'm already halfway through my meal money. That cheap son-of-a-bitch Comiskey. Always shavin' me."

"I'm all ears," Jackson pronounced and he loosened his tie and stared right through Swede.

"Fellas. No beating around the bush. The old man called me in today and told me he's gonna sign a nigger to play for us. Wants that old guy Lloyd, you know, the shortstop for the American Giants down on Wentworth. Says Lloyd will be good for the team and that he'll play some for Collins."

"Shit," was all Gandil allowed.

"Nigger ball player, I'll be damned," said Jackson.

It took Risberg an hour to talk his teammates through their objections. Why should they go out of their way to help Comiskey get even richer anyway? Why should they let the niggers back on the field? Who was this guy Lloyd anyway? "I tell you. I done thought about this all day," said Risberg. "We go along with Comiskey on this one and Collins looks like a jerk because sure as shit he's gonna squawk when he learns that Lloyd'll play some for him, maybe even for Weaver too."

What Risberg didn't tell them was how the news of Lloyd's signing made him all tight in the gut. How he imagined that Comiskey was gonna use him at short anyway and that the stuff about Collins was all bull. But, he said to himself, what if it wasn't. Well, he could be sitting pretty, and if that were the case it didn't much matter what the color or the skill of the guy playing next to him was as long as it wasn't Collins. He knew Gandil would agree with him a hundred percent. But he was worried about Jackson.

"Hey Swede. Ever play with a colored ball player?"

"Hell no, Joe. What do you think?"

"Well I have. Dozens of times. Down home."

"So?"

"So. If you don't mind they smell different and don't mind they don't talk to you after the game, tell you what. Some of 'em, and I heard lots about Lloyd, they can play the hell out of the game." And then he spoke with a kind of seriousness that surprised Risberg and Gandil. "But if we allow 'em to play with us. I don't mean just Lloyd, mind you. But a bunch of 'em. There go our jobs."

Swede found himself stunned that Jackson would admit to some, no any, kind of talk that wasn't bitterly anti–Negro. He expected Jackson to be some kind of plantation Southerner, though he knew in fact that the two of them actually came from the same side of the tracks—the textile mills of South Carolina and the paper mills of Northern California. Add that to Gandil's talking about how he was a roustabout, prize fighter, and boiler maker from Minnesota who had learned to play ball in the outlaw leagues of Mexico and Canada, and the White Sox had a nucleus of players who hated Comiskey for his money and Collins for his acumen — for they all knew Collins made almost double their salaries.

"Here's what I say," Gandil stroked the neck of his beer bottle with the thumb of his left hand. "Here's what I say. Let's give Lloyd a chance. He's just another working stiff like us. And, if we don't like how its going, well…"

"Its not like he's gonna live with us. He won't even be able to eat with us in some joints. And Comiskey'll probably make him sleep in some boarding house in every dark-town between St. Louis and Washington." Swede looked at Jackson. "You in?"

Shoeless Joe Jackson, from Brandon Mill, South Carolina, "just up the road from Greenville" where he learned to play ball for the company team, and the greatest natural hitter in the history of baseball, nodded his assent. "Pop Lloyd. Well, I'll be damned."

John Henry Lloyd shifted from one foot to the next. He didn't like this kind of waiting. Made him feel really uncomfortable. Hat in his hand, too. What the fuck are the two of 'em possibly talking about, he wondered as he looked at the gold etched letters on the door: "Chicago White Sox Baseball Club. Charles Comiskey, Owner."

The wavy glass made it impossible to see in, but he could hear the voices, less arguing than discussing something clearly important, in hushed tones, and for a long time. Too long. Too damn long.

Comiskey sat stoically at his desk and listened to Foster.

"I tell you. This isn't gonna work, darlin'. Your players will think it's a Trojan horse."

"Listen Mr. Smart-Ass, what the hell is a Trojan other than a rubber?"

"Mr. Comiskey. Begging your pardon. Unless you find a way first of all to pay me for Lloyd's contract — you see here, he has signed his name to this piece of paper promising his services to me and the Chicago American Giants for 1919 at two hundred dollars a month…"

"Foster, you are not as smart as you think. I can pay him ten times that."

"Sure, but you won't. Don't have to be Solomon to know that. And, that's not what I'm talking about anyway. I mean that if you take a colored ball player from a colored team in a colored neighborhood you sure as shooting" (and here Foster opened his jacket for emphasis) "better make sure you pay the freight."

"Let's say I do. What about this Trojan stuff?"

"You take Lloyd and folks'll think he's the first of an invasion. That you plan to turn the White Sox into the Black Sox."

"But you know, damn it *you* know, that's not what I want."

And Foster jumped, sensing that he finally could close the trap. "That's why you, Charles Comiskey, the owner of the Sox, must purchase the contract of John Henry Lloyd from Andrew Foster, owner of the Chicago American Giants. It's clean, it's legal, and no one's gonna sing about taking what isn't yours. See?"

"What are you trying to sell me, mister?" Comiskey seemed to bristle with the force of Foster's argument.

"You know as well as me. We may be partners but it's gotta go both ways. I get my cut or you don't get Lloyd."

The two men looked hard at each other. Perhaps, thought Sam, who sat quietly off to the side listening to the two men duke it out, perhaps there really is a chance for Foster to live up to his dreams. But Sam kept his peace.

"Besides," injected Foster, "I'm taking a chance here. You think you'll get the credit for being some kind of Lincoln to baseball. But if it don't work, I'm the one gonna pay for leading my player into your hell." And that is already telling him more that I ever wanted, he thought. This mother, he really has the chance to change things and he doesn't even know it. It's a real gamble and if we lose the whole race loses.

Foster felt the pain in the back of his head reach its fingers around to his eyes and press even harder. For a moment he shook his head as if to clear its intensity. Then he fixed his gaze on Comiskey. "Come on, you old goat. Look at all the shekels you paid for Jackson and Collins. I ain't asking for even a quarter of that. But, we're both in business here, and if you sign Lloyd outright it's just like stealing. There's gonna be hell to pay with the sportswriters anyway. Why make it harder on yourself?"

Comiskey sat quietly for a moment, a rare occasion for him. God-damn Foster was right. Why the fuck was he going to do this anyway? He must be out of his mind to even consider signing Lloyd.

But he knew full well why. If he didn't then McGraw would be the first, sure as shit. And, as his conversations with Collins and that dope Risberg showed him, Lloyd could be just what he needed to really control the team. Power and money. So, what else was new.

Comiskey took a breath. "Sam, get a contract ready that will authorize the purchase of John Henry Lloyd from the Chicago American Giants for two thousand dollars. Rube, I assume you will be taking your usual," he said, his smile a combination of grin and leer. "Oh, and Sam. Ask my Lloyd to come in now please, will you."

John Henry Lloyd, suit jacket buttoned too high, shoes too tight, hat in hand, entered the room as Sam closed the door gently behind him. The bright August sun shone through the window behind Comiskey, filling the room with white light and casting the shadow of Comiskey's head across the top of the desk that separated the two men. "Come in, come in," said Comiskey with a joviality whose insincerity Sam hoped Lloyd would not notice. "I'm very glad to see you. Rube, here, tells me that you are quite a ball player." Lloyd almost grinned.

Foster interjected, sensing Lloyd's discomfort, "He's a Chicago kind of player. He's a real country hitter and fields like Hermes — quick, you know," and he dropped his eyes and added, "Mr. Comiskey."

Comiskey nodded and looked at Lloyd, allowing his eyes to follow the contours of the black man's body from head to toe. Lloyd shifted uncomfortably under the owner's gaze, and nervously jingled the change in his pocket.

"Have a seat, please, Mr. Lloyd. Please. Do you have a good guess as to why I asked you here today? Well, I'm gonna tell you. Foster here says you are the best and I want the White Sox to be the best. So here's what I'm going to do, John. I hope you don't mind my calling you John?"

You can call me whatever you want, Lloyd thought. Just get on with it.

"We want you to play for the White Sox for the rest of the season. I'll pay you double your salary with the American Giants and if we go to the series I can assure you at least a half share. Rube here has agreed to sell your contract to the White Sox. What do you think of that, John?"

Lloyd kept his thoughts to himself. He'd only sign, he told Sam earlier, if Rube got his cut. He hadn't expected that. Now he smiled inwardly and pursed his lips. Before Lloyd had a chance to speak, Comiskey broke the silence. "Of course this is going to be hard. Not everyone is going to approve of a colored man playing in the major leagues, and even some of your teammates are going to be difficult. But I want you to promise one thing. Simply this. That you'll be a good Christian, turn the other cheek, and let your playing do the talking. Can you promise me that, John?"

Lloyd, who made more money than Comiskey had offered by working overtime for the Quartermaster, laughed inside. Sure, he'd promise anything. He just wanted to get on that field and show them what a real ball player could do. Fuck all that other stuff. "Why sure, Mr. Comiskey, anything you say is all right with me. I sure 'preciate the opportunity to play for the White Sox and especially the generosity of what you be offering to me."

That ought to satisfy the old goat, Lloyd thought to himself before adding, "Yes sir, sure is an honor."

8

FIVE DAYS: AUGUST 1919

Kid shuddered. She could feel him even before she could see him, peering into her room. His eyes, small and squinty, seemed to bend their way 'round the slight opening in her door and settle on her hands. She stopped playing. It wasn't music meant for him. One thing to work for the old buzzard, another thing to let him look her over like a piece of meat. She'd already heard enough stories about Mr. Comiskey, or as the other black folks in the house called him, T.A., old Tight-Ass Charlie, to know that he presented a danger and a challenge.

By the time she looked up he had gone. But she could smell the cigar aroma he had left in the hall as it trailed his footsteps out past the kitchen and up into the house. But, my, what a house, she thought. It seemed to go on forever, bigger than anything she'd ever seen. Bigger'n all of Walls, even bigger than Pee Wee's. Hard to believe that she'd been in this huge house, this enormous city, for a week.

The woman at the Urban League had taken her hand, patted it and said, "Honey. I got just the job for you. A dollar a day, a room of your own, and as much as you need to eat." Just like that. But she also told her the rules.

Kid had never met anyone like that woman, Mrs. Binga she called herself. She had imagined someone like her, but white, not Negro. Just the way she held her head, tilted slightly up, her sharp nose almost pinched together at the nostrils, and looked at Kid through those spectacles of hers, made Kid feel small and out of place. Every finger of her right hand sported a different ring, and she wore a silver brooch, looked like a sunburst Kid thought, a garland across her white blouse which closed tight around her neck. Black skirt, loose to the ankles, just touching black shoes completed her appearance. But most startling of all — her eyes. Green. Shining translucent green eyes that pierced Kid to the core. "You must remember young lady that you are now a member of the race," she said. "No more Mississippi nonsense now for you. Be polite and respectful, get rid of your head rags, don't make noise on the trolley, and put your money in the bank."

"Yes'm."

"Young lady. That's exactly what I meant. Get rid of those Southern ways. I'm not, never was, never will be, your white mistress. I said be polite, nothing more. You're a member of the race now. Do you understand?"

"Yes, Mrs. Binga, I do."

"That's better."

Mrs. Binga fixed Kid with her eyes and then reached out to touch her, extending her hands to Kid's shoulders. Her eyes smiled and her face softened, and Kid could feel the smooth café au lait skin that brushed against her arms.

Mrs. Binga told Kid about the job at Comiskey's, gave her the carfare to get there, and said when Kid began to walk up Michigan Avenue to the next trolley stop, "Now don't you forget to put your money in someplace safe." Kid nodded, placed her burlap and guitar case down, and waved. "Soon's I get some." Later, as she sat in the streetcar, its open sides filling her with the smells of the city, seeing more people walking along the street than she had ever before seen in one place, she glanced at Michigan Avenue just as they crossed 22nd Street. The sign that stretched across the double-wide grey stone building its brass banisters glinting in the sun proclaimed BINGA NATIONAL BANK. "Oh, my," Kid thought. "My, oh, my."

What amazed her even more when she had time to think about it that morning, the hazy Sunday that marked her first week in the city and her first day off from Comiskey's, what amazed her the most was the lake. They called it a lake, Lake Michigan, but it was like no lake she had ever seen before, the endless stretch of blue-green that merged with the horizon, its surface filled with every boat imaginable — large rusting freighters bound for the iron cities of the north, gleaming mahogany yachts with their pennants snapping in the breeze, alongside every size and shape of sailboat, tracing its way over the surface, a thousand slashes, white against the water. Running alongside the lake, a white-brown band of sand extended south as far as she could see. Dotted with bathers and picnickers, ball players and exercisers, the beach along the lake seemed a wonderful extension of the city itself, yet at the same time a step removed from the town's whirl and racket. It surprised Kid to see men hurrying along the street, oblivious to the sights and smells of the water so nearby. That one, she suddenly remembered, picking out an angular white man with a straw hat tilted forward as if to guide his purpose, walked with such a peculiar gait. He's the one from the station. Or from Mr. Comiskey's. Feels just like the day I met Esau, she thought to herself. Then she shivered.

The man's hips and legs seeming to inscribe shadowy circles on the noontime pavement as he forged ahead. She could see the sweat circling out from under his arms and his suit jacket flapped against the back of his white shirt from the hinge of his finger where he held it just behind his ear.

Mid-summer in Mississippi, she thought, no one ever hurried, not at midday at least. But this Sunday, this was a time to slow down. Today, she thought, she would have her first day off and she determined to spend it by herself. Kid had tossed her traveling dress over her shoulders, shimmied and then pressed it down her legs, glanced at the black maid's outfit with its short white apron sitting neat in the small closet in the corner of her room and said aloud, "So long. I'm good and gone." She tapped her guitar with her hand and walked out into the sunlight. Her first real day in Chicago.

"Just remember where the lake is," Mrs. Binga had told her, "and you'll never get lost." It only took her a few minutes to walk east on 22nd Street before she saw the tracks that separated the city grid from the lake shore beach that she knew was her destination. "And don't forget, you go to our beach and not theirs." The rickety wood overpass reached its praying mantis arms across the IC railroad tracks and Kid could see its walkway filled with people — all of whom where white. She knew that it was all right for her to take the streetcar, to sit anywhere, but also that it wasn't all right to walk and swim anywhere on this stretch of the beach. Wasn't too hard to figure out, she realized, not when she stopped to read the sign tacked on the street lamp that stood watch next to the first steps of the overpass: "NIGGERS STAY OFF," and in small letters, "Chicago Property Owner Protective Assoc."

A few blocks south, just beyond 26th Street, Kid could see the crowds of black folks making their way across the wooden trestle overpass. The sun had reached its midday place in the hazy sky, and she could see the south shore of Chicago as it spread out into the lake, the black hulks of the steelworks barely visible in the distance. Caught up in the throng as it moved toward the beach, the sand itself hidden from street level by massive boulders, their green-grey surface specked with silver, Kid felt completely among friends — though she did not know a soul. Families, children holding onto long hands extended down, plied the narrow bridge and their pace quickened as they saw and then smelled the water. Even the bathhouse, freshly whitewashed thanks to the "Prodigious Efforts of Alderman DePriest," seemed welcoming. Picnic baskets swinging gaily between them, the revelers lifted their heads to the sky and seemed to breathe more deeply. The men had already rolled up the sleeves of the white shirts, loosened their ties, and some even carried their shoes. Kid could only imagine how they embraced the respite from their labor at the packing houses and steel mills, or how the women, no less tired than she from shifts bent over laundry tubs and slop buckets, looked forward to a day off. Chicago's bounty, its fresh air and sand and water, seemed a fair trade now from the city's hardships. No lazy water hole alongside the bend of the river, still the lake offered repose and wonder.

Now atop the wooden bridge Kid could see the city at her feet. She stopped for a moment, hands on the railing, its black-grey splintered surface edging into her palms, and looked north, back toward the Loop. The heat shimmered off the sand below, and her gaze followed the tracks downtown all they way to the Central Station's imposing clock tower, which, as if on signal, chimed its first midday toll.

She marveled at the journey. How far she had traveled since that day, marooned in Helena, taking her heart in her hand, now in the promised land. The breeze caught her dress, pushing it against her legs as the sun warmed her back and neck.

It seemed like the first moment of solitude, even in the midst of the crowd swirling around her, that she had experienced since her arrival at the station off in the distance. Kid closed her eyes for a moment as she steadied herself against the railing. Around her the laughter of a hundred black folk, inside only her voice.

> Train's at the station, you can hear it blow
> Train's at the station, you can hear it blow
> I'll be on that train, baby
> 'Fore you even know.

The three young black boys ran past Kid with a speed and fury that pushed her flat against the rail. Like a locomotive, she thought without thinking. Turning, she could see them, barefoot, disappearing down the stairway, away from her, back toward the city, their arms braced against the wooden banisters, torsos tilted, clambering, running, two steps at a time. Like a storm's sudden spiral they twisted past her and then were gone.

A dozen indistinguishable voices followed howling in their path, a rush of angry sounds containing the meaning but not yet the words of human speech, filling the void where she had been dwelling so peacefully. Finally something emerged from the sudden chaos. A single person bellowed, "There they are. Over there. On the other side," followed by a new storm, this time of angry white faces, red, florid, appearing all at once at the top of the overpass, from the lakeside stairway, gathering force as they rushed and squeezed their way onto the bridge in twos and threes, pushing their way, shoulder to shoulder, onto the walkway.

Kid could see them now at the top of the stairs, to her left, too many at once to squeeze onto the trestle where she stood completely still. Then with a burst of energy the human mass popped through the stairway opening and flooded onto the bridge. Arms raised, fists shaking, sleeves rolled, the men in grey and brown caps roared down the walkway. "Get the goddam Niggers. Get 'em before they get away."

Kid flattened herself against the rail as the mob pushed past her, a blur of emotion and color and excitement. And then, as fast as they appeared, they were gone. Down the other side of the overpass, running, tripping, stumbling over each other as they negotiated the stairway and then the street below. Felt like a swarm of locusts. Something told her that even in their midst she was safe. The clock pealed louder as it reached noon.

Spinning, she followed in their wake and found herself on the other, the city side, of the overpass, looking down and Westward along 26th Street. From her vantage point she could see the three boys, shirtless, the sweat glistening off their chests, arms pumping as they ran toward Michigan Avenue. One of them, he couldn't be more than twelve she thought, stumbled, his bare feet spreading instinctively for balance, and then fell. The others in front slowed as they turned around at the boy's scream. Blood poured out of his right foot. He had run over a broken beer bottle, slicing his instep which now left prints of mottled red where his hobbled foot landed on the pavement.

The two boys in front spun around and caught their friend by his shoulders, ducked their necks under his arms, and tried to run, the injured boy swinging madly on one foot between them, as the blood continued to flow from his heel to his toe with each step. Frightened, the three Negro boys looked behind them, each wide-eyed in frenzy to escape. A block away and perched still on the overpass Kid could hear the men crying in pursuit.

"Get 'em. There. Little fuckers. That'll teach 'em. And so'll this."

"Hey, Ritchie ... you get the one who's bleedin'.

"'Kay."

"We'll take the others."

The white men, only now Kid could see that they too were boys, hardly older than the three black boys whose fear, fatigue, and burden had slowed them, drew ever closer. Their ranks thinned as the fastest of them overtook their quarry, leaving a remnant of running and panting boys to dot the street all the way back to the overpass. Those closest in pursuit sensed their prey's last gasps and even slowed in their stride to gain a better angle from which to attack. "Hey, its okay, fellas. We just want to talk wid ya. Yeah. Sweet like, to esplain the rules. Yuz just didn't know where t' go, did yuz."

And with their taunts rising over the three Negro boys now stopped in their tracks, each one wild with fear, chests heaving, the white gang set about to beat them, it seemed to Kid, as close to death as possible. Within thirty seconds the first rank of whites had been joined by the rest of the pursuers, about twenty-five in all, who took turns pummeling the three Negroes, now a tangle of arms and legs twisted in blood and mucus, with fists and sticks. "Fuckin' niggers. This'll show 'em."

One of the white boys, a young man dressed in knickers and white shirt, his long socks pulled up to his knees, drew back from the knot. The front of his shirt had come out from the waist of his pants, and his hat twisted so that the tiny brim half-covered his right eye. Holding his hands to his sides, elbows out, he began to bend over, falling, as he stagger to the curb, where he suddenly kneeled and vomited.

Somehow others in the gang noticed their comrade and began to separate themselves from the melee, half ashamed, half exhausted. One by one they walked away, back down the street toward the lake, some shaking, others joking with their neighbors as they came closer to the overpass where Kid remained, transfixed.

They passed on both sides of her, a river's swelled current, brushing the sides and dress of this Negro girl, without even seeing her. Some muttered, "That'll show 'em where they can go. Fucking right, they'll swim in their beach next time." But others looked hollow and stared empty-eyed ahead toward the water, whose blue-green surface no longer seemed to beckon.

Down the street where the three black boys lay collapsed in each other's arms, their torsos smeared with blood, their sobs audible even on the bridge, Kid could see the blue clad figure of a policeman, sweat pouring down his brow under the wool uniform braced in yellow and silver. A large man, he had been standing in the shadows of the tenements that lined the street, tumble-down brown-grey boxes, waiting for the crowd to finish its business.

The cop waved. His back toward Kid, he seemed to be looking up the street, back toward the city, and as the square black wagon approached he gestured even more acutely, his arms windmilling, the whistle in his mouth suddenly piercing the summer air with its shrill call. "Take 'em up the street to Mercy," he said to the white-coated attendants who jumped from the ambulance. The two white orderlies looked queerly at the cop.

"You know they don't take niggers there."

"Just take 'em outa here. I don't care where. Just get 'em outa the street. It's a Sunday."

Sam had decided to walk over to the beach for an hour of sun before catching the Giants' late afternoon tilt against the ABCs. He was as astonished as Kid to see the Chicago police officer, face florid, slightly bent at the waist, pointing toward the South Side as the two ambulance orderlies stood palms up, shrugging their shoulders. It took Sam a bit longer to see the three tangled bodies of the boys lying at the feet of the arguing men. Sam had been amazed too at the way the girl on the trolley had looked at him not a half-hour earlier as he strolled along, coat tossed over his shoulder, on his way to the white beach. He had wondered who she was, couldn't quite place her. Then he saw the keen sparkle in her eye, and had taken a short breath.

"Look Callahan, the hospital won't take these kids."

"I don't give a good god-damn, just get 'em the hell out of here," the cop replied, lowering his voice as a small cluster of Negro onlookers, Sam oddly in their midst, moved in.

"Did you hear. Beat near to death. Three boys, over there, out on 29th, just off the hot and cold. White guys did it."

"These boys need our help. Fucking cop. Didn't do nothing. Just stood there. Lookit 'im now."

"Hey Paddy. Take your Irish ass home. We'll take care the boy."

With that the twenty or so young black men surrounding the ambulance, the orderlies, and Callahan began rocking the wagon. In a moment they had it overturned, on its side, beached. Someone produced a club and smacked the exposed undercarriage and the street filled with the unmistakable odor of gasoline. Another tossed his cigarette into the clear liquid and the wagon blazed into fury. The crowd retreated, the heat growing in intensity. Sam could feel their anger, palpable and hard.

"You white guys. Y'all get outta here. We'll take our boys. Just get out before it's too late."

Callahan began blowing his whistle, louder and faster, waving his arms again, gesturing the crowd to move back. But they were too many. They circled the burning ambulance, the fire reflecting in their eyes, the sweat of the midday heat flowing down their foreheads, darkening the fronts of their shirts from neck to waist.

His wits about him, and surprised at his own fearlessness, Sam screamed, "I know a place. Let's just get these boys out of here before more police come."

He was thinking of Provident, the all-black hospital that his old teacher Miss Norman had helped found down by Washington Park more than twenty years ago. But the crowd would have none of it.

"What you talking 'bout white boy. This ain't your problem."

"Don't trust no fucking hospital, they just as soon let us die."

"If we don't do something soon," Sam said holding his ground, "they're going to die sure as I'm standing here. Come on, pick them up, and follow me. It's the only way to help. We gotta do it now!"

A couple of the men nodded in agreement and urged the others to take Sam's lead. "Come on, its our only chance. We got to do something."

Two others dashed across the street and grabbed the bridle of a dark brown horse whose flatbed wagon bore the sign, *Holly Springs Provisions — Best on the South Side* along the side. Quickly they picked up the three boys, who moaned silently, loaded them onto the wagon, and told the driver, a large gangly black man in a straw hat and overalls, "Let's go. We gotta take these kids for some help." Sam hopped up on the front of the wagon and said, "I'll show you the best way," as the driver picked up the reins with a snap and guided the horse out into the street, away from the beach, away from the lake, away from the wood overpass where Kid stood, mesmerized.

The wagon moved westward into the city, on its bed the three boys, their broken bodies in a heap surrounded by half a dozen men, feet dangling off the side. As they drove away the driver cocked an ear toward Sam sitting alongside him. The ambulance, now a smoldering skeleton, lay on its side in the street, while the two orderlies sat on the curb, heads in their hands, uncomprehending. The cop had disappeared, and the street, bathed in heat, lay quiet, its silence interrupted only by the crackle of the embers settling into the paving stones, red rivers of coal glowing and then dying.

As Kid made her way home that afternoon, she passed, as if in a waking dream, marauding bands of young men, no less angry than those she had observed earlier, prowling along the almost empty streets. When she spied, or as was more often the case, heard them ahead, she quickly darted into the shadowy frame of a doorway, twice dropping down to the safety of the cellar entry, beneath the steps of the grey stone houses that lined the way back to Comiskey's house. In groups of tens and twelves the young men, chanting slogans in unison, marched through the neighborhoods just off the South Side offering protection and revenge. "We're the Colts / and don't you mess / We'll get the Niggers / We're the best."

It took Kid three hours to walk the dozen blocks. By the time she arrived back at Comiskey's the old goat had pulled into the driveway and was stepping out of his car speaking to his chauffeur, who stood at attention. "Only a couple of 'em killed. Nuttin' to worry about, it'll be over by night. Go get Sam first thing in the morning and bring him to me at my office. I want him there soon's I arrive."

"Yessss Sir, Mr. Comiskey, Yessss Sir," the Negro driver said, lips quivering.

Hot before it even got light. So fucking hot might's well be in the South. Face them crackers. Damn. What a way to meet the day. Well, darlin', might as well see how it plays.

Rube Foster had waited for a dozen years for this day. And now he wasn't sure. Connie Mack and John McGraw had as much as promised in 1903 that soon, "Soon, son, one of you'll be in the bigs. Just a matter of time" before Negro ball players would make it. Foster had planned a long time for this. Making peace with Comiskey, that god-dammed gonoff, he thought, and then chuckled at the idea of replacing the intertwined CC that the old Roman had sewn onto his custom-made shirts with the initials GG. He'd have to tell Sam about that, the young lawyer'd get a kick out of it. Question was, where'n hell was Lloyd. He had to find him, and find him this day so they'd be able to ink him to the contract Comiskey had promised.

Loved Mondays, Rube did. Cubs and White Sox rarely played on Monday. Travel day. Coming or going. To New York, or St. Louis, Philadelphia, Washington. But not playing on the first day of the week. That meant, he had learned long ago, that the Giants would have the city to themselves. And that's why he always scheduled Monday games for 6:30, just after the shift changes at the packing houses. Men didn't even have to go home, just change back into their street clothes and walk to the ball park. Easy as pie.

Rube Foster had lived on 55th, now Garfield, for the past ten years. Figured it was not his lot to live with the people who went to his games—not that he didn't appreciate their business, but Foster was hardly some Johnny-come-lately-pickaninny, and didn't want anyone thinking he was either. Even the Bingas had finally invited him over to their joint on the lake, and that was the way he liked it. Swell spread. Candles, even a couple of servants wearing white gloves, plenty of booze. Made Comiskey look like the piker he was.

The heat of the late mid-summer afternoon took his breath away. He suddenly wished that he had not chosen to walk down Wentworth toward the Giants' park. He stuffed his cap into the pocket of his brown jacket, unhitched the knot of his tie and crossed the Boulevard to stroll down the shady side of the street. "Just like Ulysses," he mused, "staying cool 'til it was time to move on." And he chuckled thinking about how good it felt.

It never failed to satisfy. The late-afternoon walk to the ball park. The feeling of anticipation that filled the air as he merged with the streams of black folks who flowed, boisterous and celebratory, through the city streets. Often they carried their black lunch pails in one hand, swinging, sometimes stopping at a local tavern for a quick one, just to wet the whistle, before the game began.

Black revelers, he thought. Come from the South to the Promised

Land. Hardly. Not when they had to move quickly and quietly through Bridgeport. "Can't get their Irish up," some said. But as soon as they had cleared the IC overpass at Federal they knew they could relax again. At least they had the American Giants to look forward to, and Foster was proud of that. And proud that soon, even this week, he could do something more. Damn. Where in hell was Sam when he needed him.

Foster looked up, his reverie interrupted by shouts. Ahead a group of Negro workers had begun to run down the street. Behind them an even larger number of white men, clubs and fists raised, gave chase. Like two swarms the men moved eastward, the distance between the two constant. Screams and then shots, unmistakable, rang out. Foster could see, less than two blocks away, the puffs of grey-black smoke, the spit of red, and then, to his right, a Negro man falling, his body collapsing in the street as the group of whites, guns still drawn, grew bigger, closer.

Foster's first instinct, to reach for the pearl handled revolver in his waist band, gave way to caution. Police whistles and bells reverberated along Federal Street and Foster felt, suddenly, at the center of chaos. The white and black knots of men had merged into each other when a wedge of blue uniforms, billy clubs raised, went about the business of prying them apart. The black batons found their mark. The Negro men in the melee, some falling to their knees, others clasping their hands to their heads, struggled to flee. Down the street they ran, toward the other side of Federal, toward safety. Whites stood, hands on hips, chests heaving, yelling, their faces twisted in anger, following the string of Negro men down the street with their eyes. And, as fast as they had come, Foster suddenly realized, the cops disappeared, melted into the late afternoon furnace of the South Side.

But there he was. Alone on the street, just half a block in front of a mob of a dozen angry, exhausted, and frustrated white men. One of them, unshaved, wearing a soldier's khaki shirt, its AA arm patch worn and frayed, stood out above the others. A young man, Foster noticed, hardly more than twenty he guessed, the man's bright blue eyes looked alert, somehow alive inside that hard shell of a body.

Foster fixed the man with his eyes. Tried to look into his very soul. Like my old man, he remembered. Stand tall. The other man struggled inwardly, never taking his eyes off Foster, but something about the way he held his upper body, as if the anger had fled, let Foster know the danger had passed. "Let him pass. He's okay. I know him." And the white men, in virtual unison, began to move away from each other, disclosing a path between them through which Foster began to walk.

"See you at the game tonight, Rube," the blue-eyed veteran shouted. "See you at the game."

Andrew Rube Foster had less than ten seconds to enjoy his free passage. The whine and smack of a gunshot twisted Foster's head around, torquing his body back toward the white men. They all looked, fingers pointing upward, across Federal, toward the lake, craning their necks, gesturing and shouting all at once. At their feet lay the blue-eyed man, the back of his head no longer there, his hands crossed over his chest.

"Up there," one of the men shouted, pointing to the roof-tops, "I seen him. Nigger with a gun. He's the one who shot Carney."

And then one of the men turned and faced Foster.

"Well there's one of them right here. And he ain't got no gun."

Andrew Rube Foster, the greatest Negro ballplayer of his day, the best pitcher in Chicago, hated to run. But he did this time. Pearl handles or not. There were twenty or more angry and frightened white men who'd just as well shoot him as look at him, and the only thing left to do was git — deep into the South Side, east, as fast as he could.

It didn't take long for Foster to lose the men in the tenement alleys that twisted behind the wood houses that lay scattered across the South Side between Indiana, Prairie, and Calumet. On the avenues hollow-eyed three-story grey and brown stone buildings, already carved into kitchenettes, conveyed a ghostly prosperity to the neighborhood. But along the side streets and alleys sat rows of mean and squalid shacks. Unpainted and brooding among the weeds and vines, these city shotgun houses reminded Foster of nothing less than home.

Ducking into the alley with sweat pouring down his neck, Foster finally stopped to catch his breath. He could feel the gun press into his side, the shirt wet to his back and chest. The rows of houses, their unshuttered windows quartered and dark, seemed coated with soot, so dark were the clapboards. From their second stories extended crude wood entries, rickety staircases that angled downward into the grey vegetation, threadbare and limp, that lined the dank alley. Panting, Foster leaned against the rough supports of the rear-entry stairs, finding a moment of shade beneath the landing above. He stood silent and waited.

For a moment he thought they were the same group of men who had been chasing him, and he shrank back deeper into the shadows and pulled his gun, holding it to his chest. A dozen of them now in pursuit of another single Negro man rumbled into the alley, their white shirts ablaze in the angled sunlight. To their rear was a single policeman, pistol drawn. The white men, Foster soon realized, were older than those who had pursued him, wore white straw hats and sported red handkerchiefs sprouting from their back pants pockets.

In his haste to clear the wood fence between two of the back yards the Negro caught his foot and tumbled to the ground. The pack was upon him in no time, and soon their victim simply disappeared before Foster's eyes. Only the fists of the white men, hammering blows upon the now invisible Negro, remained above this artificial horizon, a silhouette of madness accompanied by the sounds of a hundred thuds.

Foster felt his muscles tighten, his lips push back against his teeth in agony. What he was seeing, he thought, was impossible. The world had gone crazy with violent hatred. He felt hunted and the anger welled up inside him until he could no longer contain it. His whole being shook with outrage and he stood.

Two steps out of the shadows he began to scream.

"Well. Looka here. A nigger. Nicely dressed, too, don't you think? Wonder where he came from. Where'd you come from, boy?"

Rube's fury burst. His voice and hand spoke with a startling crack. "Awaaaaaayyyy!!!!" he screamed as he slammed the butt-end of his pearl-handled pistol into the forehead of the largest of the attackers, who crumpled to the ground instantly. "GettttAwaaaaayyyyy. GettttTheFuckAwaaaayyyyyfrom him," he yelled even louder as he bent down to pull the hand of the Negro who lay at his feet, pleading with his eyes to be saved. The white men stood stunned for moment. They had never seen such rage. Foster's wrath came, he understood instantly, from a place he had never been before. His intensity surprised him almost as much as it frightened his antagonists.

Foster lifted himself to the full height of his frame, extended his arms upward to the sky, and bellowed once again. The white men, first startled and now completely surprised, turned as one and fled down the alley. Chest heaving, Foster lowered his arms and bent over the other man who lay crumpled at his feet.

Only then did the two police, their guns drawn, appear.

Remarkably, the poor fellow who had suffered the terrible beating, worst one Rube had ever witnessed, had all his faculties about him and gradually forced himself to stand. Shaking, he began to tell his story. But it was no different, Foster slowly realized, from his own encounter that day. They had both been set upon by a group of angry whites out looking for a solitary Negro to beat. And as the police listened sullenly Foster realized that these incidents had not been isolated. The beatings had, he now understood, been going on all over the South Side.

When the two police offered to escort him home he declined. "Take him," he said pointing to the other fellow, now sufficiently recovered to walk but still shaking in fear, "I can take care of myself. Don't you worry none about me."

He knew too, that the Giants wouldn't be playing that night. That something awful had changed in the city. He just wasn't yet sure what it was or why. Slowly and carefully Foster walked through the heart of the Black Belt, the sun low over his left shoulder, the dark of evening just beginning to show on his right. The streets were empty. But every now and then Foster could see, a half-block up or down from where he was, the remnants of violence — heaps of old furniture smouldering in the street, small clusters of men talking in hushed tones before darkened doorways, and then every so often, the silhouette of a figure in a third story window, looking up and down the street. Perhaps, Foster thought, with a gun drawn.

It made him think of Homer. The night between battles— on the plains of Troy, small groups of men, caught in their own thoughts, the scars of war about them, glory or death in front of them. And then he spoke out loud to himself. To nobody. To everybody. "Oh, Lord. What have we come to. What have we come to."

He sat at home all that night and well into the next dawn. The throbbing in his eyes reached around to the back of his head and made him weep. And that was how Sam found him the next day.

Comiskey's car had picked Sam up and delivered him to the old man's house early. "Drink this," the Old Roman said with an unexpected touch of solicitude, pointing to the glass of red liquid Kid held out on a tray, "and listen up." Comiskey swept his hand imperially across the room. "You know Sam, I got big plans. And this stuff out there, this crap with Negroes going where they ain't supposed to go, without asking us permission, this here's gonna mess it up for everyone."

Comiskey fixed Sam hard with his eyes.

"Yes, sir, Mr. Comiskey. What do you want me to do?"

"Help me get Lloyd under contract now, now before it's too late. That's what I want you to do. Just do your Jew stuff, make it happen and I'll be happy."

From the corner of the large drawing room, the one with all the ugly white statues of women with curtains draped around their waists, Kid watched silently as the two men talked. And when the younger one, the one she had seen before, looked up at her she read the glint of recognition on his face as well.

Sam tried to act as if he had not caught Kid's eye, and looked away, speaking simultaneously to Comiskey, his voice rising as if in secret compensation. "Why don't I go up to Foster's and bring him back here, Mr. Comiskey. Then we can just finalize the deal later." Comiskey adjusted the black velvet belt of his scarlet brocade robe, opened the door and said, "Do it. Take the car and bring him back here in an hour."

He looks like shit, Sam thought as Rube opened the door, his elegant clothing rumpled, his starched shirt collar standing up, bent away from the unbuttoned neck of his stained shirt. "You look like shit," Sam commented.

"Ain't as bad's I feel, not a lick."

Foster's weary and bloodshot eyes stared back at Sam and then closed down.

"I suppose the old man wants to talk about Pop."

"Right."

"I'll get dressed faster'n Mercury, darlin'. Be right with you."

With a tip of his hand Foster disappeared into the back room and emerged five minutes later, fresh, as he would say, "as a daisy in Waco." Sam couldn't quite believe the transformation.

"Step lively, Sammy. Step lively. The man wants to see us. You and me. Jewbaby and Black Ruby. Can't keep him waitin', can we now?"

Foster clapped Sam on the back as if it were a night at the Elks Club, ushered him to the door and followed him down the stairs whistling a tune. Sam recognized "St. Louis Blues," but thought to keep that to himself. As usual Foster really had him baffled.

Kid bent over, her black maid's dress (old man Schwab must have a relative in Chicago, she thought the first time she put it on) pressing out against the white embroidered apron that she wore like a bib. She offered the coffee first to Foster, who barely looked at her, and then to Sam, who couldn't take his eyes off her no matter how nonchalant he tried to appear. They both sat on the green velvet sofa in Comiskey's drawing room and as they balanced their cups delicately on their knees Kid moved quietly off to the side and pretended indifference. Comiskey stirred his own cup noisily, then took a sip, placed the saucer on the mantel, and tightened his scarlet robe tightly around his ever widening girth.

"Rube. What in the world is it with your people. All hell's breaking out in the city. Even the Governor, I just read in the *Tribune*, that weak-kneed son of a bitch, even the Governor is thinking about calling up the Guard. Unbelievable. Just unbelievable. Don't you think, Sam?"

Sam and Rube responded at the same time. But Sam backed off and let Rube finish his sentence. Instead Sam settled back just a bit into the green velvet materials and tried not to sneak a peek at the girl out of the corner of his eye.

"You ever read the *Defender*, C.C.?"

"You mean Abbott's Negro paper? The one that comes out on Sundays."

"Yes, that's the one. Now, Mr. Abbott, he's no hothead like Black

Tony at the *Bee*. He's just a middle class businessman out to make a buck. Well, you read that paper the last few months, and you'll see. Every time a black family tries to move, even a block from where the Neighborhood Protective Associations think they ought to live, someone tosses a bomb. And when they finished tossing their bombs last month, Mr. Abbott said, enough. We black folks have about had enough. We better get together and fight back if we have too. It's all in the *Defender*. Been there for weeks."

Comiskey looked past Foster. "Rube, you know most of us don't read that paper. Sure, we got Negro friends—hell, you're sitting right here in my living room ain't you? But, this stuff about race riots, that's gotta stop, your people they need to know the rules. Without the rules, who knows where its going to end."

Sam cleared his throat. He knew that nothing good could come of this conversation. Nothing except quashing the deal. And he wasn't about to let that happen.

"You know, Rube. It's been crazy. Yesterday, in fact, I took three colored kids over to Provident after the Colts chased them off the 26th Street beach. But when we got to the hospital the docs were just terrific. Six white doctors, could you believe? They hopped-to just like the kids were their own. A real lesson."

And before Foster had a chance to respond, while Comiskey waved Kid back into the kitchen with a silent command to bring fresh coffee, Sam fixed the two men with his eyes and sprang to his feet.

"Don't forget, gentlemen. We have a chance to make history. Let's not let the passions of the moment ruin our opportunity. I think we should go find Lloyd and sign him as soon as possible, make the papers, don't you see, take the heat off all this race-riot talk, show everyone that we can work together."

"You can sure say that again, pal," replied Foster. "If we don't work together we're as cooked as the proverbial goose." And with that he winked at Kid, who already had one foot into the pantry entry. "You can sure say that again, pal." Comiskey smiled at Foster and then looked at Sam. None of them really found each other that steamy summer morning—none of them. Even Kid, who could see as clearly as anyone she had ever met, even Kid couldn't quite grasp what was happening. Comiskey's voice, harsh and guttural, broke into her consciousness. "Sam, let's get

Lloyd. Bring him over to Foster's park this evening and we'll get the contract done. Tell one of your Jew-boy partners to draw up the papers. Its time to get the show on the road. Let's meet at 6 P.M., sharp."

Comiskey looked at Foster and then at Sam. Seeing neither dissent, he wiped the sleeve of his brocade robe under his nose and left the room. Foster smiled ironically at Sam, went to the door, picked up the morning *Tribune* and read aloud, "Quiet returned to the streets of the South Side this morning when Governor Lowdon, at the mayor's behest, ordered three thousand National Guardsmen to their posts."

"See here," he pointed, with his pinky finger, holding the paper for Sam to read, "see here."

Sam read from the back page. "Negro kills unarmed white man on Wentworth. Whites call for protection." He looked at Rube, started to say something, and instead looked down. He closed the door softly behind him.

❧   ❧

It took Sam much longer than usual to walk downtown that morning. Cottage Grove, where it cut over to Indiana, was completely cordoned off by National Guard troops who patrolled the streets in threes and fours. These were, Sam realized, not young men just enlisted for the task. No, they were battle tested veterans, full of alertness and swagger, rifles slung over their shoulders, walking the streets of Chicago. Michigan Avenue, even as he approached the Loop, was no different. There, late morning crowds of office workers streamed out of trams and trolleys, careful to avoid looking each other in the eye, even more careful about making physical contact with each other. Negroes seemed especially wary that morning — walking next to the buildings, even rubbing their shoulders against the stone foundations as they passed by. The city was neither at rest nor at peace.

Turning West on Madison in the heart of the city, Sam let his eye wander up Fifth Avenue. Hundreds of young men and women, especially women, their shirtwaists crisp in the morning light, their black high-button shoes freshly polished, swarmed into the rows of dark red brick houses that lined the street. Many carried burlap sacks bulging in their hands. Sam knew, knew all too well, that these immigrant daughters were on their way to work in the warren of cubbyholes and lofts that lay all along the fringe of the Loop. They sew all day for less than a dollar and take home more piece work in those burlap bags. The men, in black suits and dark round hats, looked swell. But they too mounted endless flights of stairs to sit in darkened offices copying figures into large account books, their white sleeves covered in dark material from wrist to elbow to protect them from the slow drying ink on the ledgers. The humanity and the labor overwhelmed Sam. Not a Negro face in sight — they would never find jobs in Chicago's sweat-shops.

As he crossed the Chicago River, just a few blocks further west, Sam took a quick left and slipped down a concealed iron stairway that led from the ramp of the bridge to the embankment below. To his left the grey ribbon of Montgomery Ward's warehouse empire snaked snug against the bank of the river. Ten stories high and a half-mile long, the hive of commercial retailing serviced fleets of boats and trains disgorging and consuming the nation's commerce at its docks and bays.

But to his right, directly up the river, sat the dark and brooding hulk of the Reaper Works, its twin stacks pouring black smoke out into the sky, the brackish, still water of the South Branch barely catch-ing its reflection. Sam knew that the factory belonged to McCormick, who had in turn merged his company with International Harvester years before, but like everyone else in the city he continued to call it the Reaper Works. And this, he thought, was where he hoped to find Lloyd.

Entering the rear of the factory, the floor already bristling with the activity of two hundred workers in groups of eights and tens assem-bling iron tractors and implements, Sam walked through the building to the riverside loading dock. There he hopped down to the ground, holding one hand on the steel plate that encircled the wood platform, and descended a stone staircase directly underneath the dock.

The early morning coolness of the river and the surface immedi-ately gave way to something heavy and oppressive, and as he walked down the flights of steps he stopped at the succession of corrugated iron landings to shed his coat, then to loosen his tie, and finally to roll his sleeves up past his elbows. Still, each landing brought only more heat and humidity, and soon the sweat poured off his forehead and ran down his neck and back. Finally, facing a roughly seated steel door, with block yellow letters proclaiming, "Chicago Tunnel Company" on top and "Authorized Personnel Only," Sam pushed his way into the world below the city.

The tunnels crackled with electricity. Sparks jumped from the overhead power lines as the small trains, their single flexible antennae sliding above, screeched their way along the tracks embedded in the tunnel floor sending more sparks in every direction. Small bare light bulbs, which marked the cross streets on the surface, barely illuminated the labyrinth, and often only the sound of the four-car wooden trains provided warning of their proximity. From where he stood Sam could only hear the rumble and clack of the approaching freight before he saw the dancing showers of light as the miniature train moved toward him out of the shadowed cavern — like a creature that lived deep in the earth, dark and unseeing.

Someone had chalked "Wells" and "Madison" on the corners of the concrete chamber created by the convergence of two sets of train tracks whose paths mimicked the grid of the city's surface streets above. The crossroads of hell. Sam wiped the sweat from his eyes and peered down both tracks, standing tentatively in the iron bound square where they crossed. He had sent Lloyd a message that he'd meet him at this underground intersection at 9, the time he thought Pop would be leaving his post with the Quartermaster General's depot at the end of the tunnel line.

Impossible to tell where the trains were, he realized. All the tunnels connected with each other, and through a complex system of custom the two-gauge cars ran north-south on the hour and east-west on the half hour. Impossible in theory to have two trains collide, they bragged. It hadn't happened since the Armistice Day, the previous November when several of the tunnel engineers lost their watches and miscalculated, sending a pair of trains running toward each other along the State Street axis. They closed the whole system for the entire two weeks before Thanksgiving in order to clean up the mangled cars filled to overflowing with coal for the Palmer House and Marshall Field's. Both places remained chilled to the core for another week, until their furnaces had been restoked. Sam chuckled; he had met Comiskey one day that month at the Palmer House for lunch. The old chazzer had to keep his fur-collared coat pulled up around him the whole time, barely concealing the shivers that made him quiver as he picked at his cold salmon and capers.

So, here he was—standing at this subterranean crossroads, waiting for a Negro to appear, listening for the sounds of an onrushing train. He could hear the metallic hiss and crackle of the electric lines echoing up and down the tunnels, but he had no idea where they came from on the grid. The noise rushed out of the four tunnel openings into the chamber where he stood silent, still, his back pressed against the sweating concrete walls. Every now and again, if a train passed fairly close, the bare overhead light flickered and then went out, leaving him momentarily cloaked in darkness. When that happened Sam caught his breath and only let it out when the flickering dim light restored his vision.

This time, however, it all happened at once. The unmistakable sound of a train approaching from his left, from the western depot he guessed, louder and louder, wheels scraping, electric antenna sparking, fast and close. Sam pressed more tightly against the wall, bracing himself. Then, as the train seemed about to emerge from the tunnel opening, the light that hung directly over the intersection of the two sets of tracks went dark. The sounds and spray of electric fragments from the tunnel's ceiling and tracks penetrated the cavern where Sam had pressed himself against the wall, blinking. He dimly made out the form of the small freight itself emerging from the eastbound track, just to his right. Sam peered into the darkness just as the train scraped to a halt, its antenna sputtering, sending a sparkling shower, tiny red-yellow dots, into the intersection. A large figure jumped from the first car, an open wooden cart actually, and in a single step, the miner's lamp on his forehead swiveled a shaft of light up and down the sides of the chamber, stopping for a moment on the hand-scrawled street signs and then coming to rest on the iron crossroads where the two sets of track converged.

"This here's the place," Pop Lloyd's voice, unmistakable in its not quite Southern drawl, said, "Mr. Sam. You got to be here somewhere."

Ten minutes later the two men emerged from the door underneath the loading dock at the Reaper Works. Sam's clothes stuck to his body, the perspiration soaking all the way through the starched fabric of his shirt, making him feel as if he had gained another ten pounds in water. Pop, on the other hand, seemed cool as a cucumber, explaining, "You gets used to it. Ain't so hard, especially if you from the South." Sam could only grunt as they made their way up the underground staircase, stopping at each landing for him to catch his breath. Once Pop held his palm out for Sam's elbow when the shorter man tripped on one of the steps. Sam looked down into the darkness of the staircase, saw the flicker in Pop's eyes, and turned his head back toward the top of the stairs. "Thanks," he said gratefully. It was about the first act of kindness he had seen in several days, and it took him aback. "Thanks, Pop. I almost fell that time."

They had to walk through the assembly floor at the Works in order to reach the bridge that Sam had taken earlier that morning. "I'll follow you," said Pop in a soft voice. "Just act like you the one in charge. You'll see."

Taking a step in front, Sam turned his head sideways over his shoulder, speaking out of the corner of his mouth. "Just tell me which way to go."

"Take her easy. Right up there, to the corner where the man — that ugly white one — is standing."

Sam scanned the entire factory floor. To his left Negro workers, in teams of four with white shop stewards supervising, worked as wheelwrights and blacksmiths, bending iron bands about the rims of tractor wheels. Two men held the six-spoked wheel while two others took the band out of the small furnace built into the side of the brick outer wall, and then strained to fit it tightly around the wheel. The four worked simultaneously to turn the wheel, tighten and then hammer the red-hot ends together, completing the seal. The sounds of their iron hammers rang out and then disappeared into the vast opening of the factory floor. The two who pounded the iron ring into submission took turns beating the metal. Like a pair of spike drivers, they lifted then struck the wheel, the rhythm of their work rising like a song in the hot summer air, the intake of their breath timed to accent the blows of the hammers.

Finished, they set down their iron tools, arms falling by their sides, and taking deep breaths they allowed their bodies to sag, relaxed. The white floor boss rubbed the ends of his massive mustache with the ends of his fingers and glared. "What you boys doin' now. I didn't hear nobody call about no break. Get back to work." The four Negro workers looked at each other and then back at the white man. For a moment they locked their shoulders, stiffening their upper arms, but then as one they looked down at the floor, picked up their implements and went back to work.

Several white workers from the other side of the assembly floor sauntered by. One, older, all sinew with the close-cropped grey hair of a long-timer, stopped in front of the team of Negro wheelwrights. "Fuckin' strike breakers. Damn scabs. What they paying you? They tell you how much they needed you, too? Did they also tell you that you were making ten cent an hour less than the rest of us? Did they tell you that?"

With each phrase his voice rose and his face flecked with anger.

"Did they tell you that you'd be taking the place of men who'd been working here before the war? Did they tell you that?"

The Negro workers halted in their rhythm, their hammers no longer keeping their labor's time.

"Well you can go the fuck back where you bunnies came from! We don't want you here. Not a one of us."

The Negroes stopped. Put their hammers down. "We don't want no trouble Mister, just a chance to make some money for our family, just like you."

Sam could see the muscles in John Henry Lloyd's neck, feel the anger in his eyes.

The white workers, each wearing a leather apron over denim overalls, glared back. The one with the short hair stood, hands folded across his chest, and spoke with the unmistakable accent of Bohemia. "We don't want no trouble with you boys. Just pick up your stuff and punch out. Leave. The local met last night," and he flashed a handbill signed by Stephan Halecki, President, Local 73, Chicago Metalworkers, American Federation of Labor. "And we agreed. You leave and we stay on the job. You stay and we walk." The men behind him muttered, squared their shoulders, and as one the group walked away.

The Negro workers sagged in defeat. They knew they couldn't win. "Come on," one of them said, "they looking for hog gutters up at the Yards. I know a guy there'll hire us tomorrow. No use staying with these crackers. They'd as soon as beat us as work with us."

"It's the fucking union," another blurted, "we's doing just fine here 'til they come asked us 'bout the wages."

"Not the union. Don't you see? Old McCormick, he's the one. Pay us less. Set us against the whites. Divide and conquer. How long you think they been doin' that? How long you think they gonna keep doin' it?"

The floor of the tractor factory reeked with the sweat of a hundred men. It crackled with their energy and came to life with the ringing sounds of hammers and bearings. But for Sam it felt like the hellhole of Chicago. As the Negro workers left their stations he could feel the eyes of the factory follow them to the punch out. And then he could feel those same eyes fix on Lloyd. Little matter that he'd soon be the darling of the White Sox, to these skilled workers at the Reaper Works John Henry Lloyd was only another Negro.

"Move it along, Mr. Sam. Move it along. Otherwise they likely to beat us both," Lloyd spoke softly and smiled with his eyes.

"What *you* looking at, boy. I told you to follow me didn't I," Sam shot back, loudly. With that he turned on his heels, gave his head a short jerk in the direction of the factory door, and walked out. Lloyd followed, his head bowed.

A half-hour later they reached Comiskey's. Sam opened the door for Lloyd, ushering him into the marble entry. "The old man said to bring you here right away." Lloyd couldn't quite believe his eyes, but kept his thoughts to himself. Kid took Sam's suit jacket, allowing her hand to brush lightly, unseen, across his wrist as he shucked it off. She smiled at Lloyd, who missed nothing in the exchange. "Mr. Comiskey's waitin' inside. He said for you to come right in." She looked at Lloyd and then cast her eyes down — something about the way he wore the handkerchief around his neck made her think of home.

The men entered the drawing room. Comiskey sat in his tall wing-backed chair fanning himself with a copy of the *Tribune* while Foster stood proudly by the French doors that led to the garden at the rear of the house. "Good to see you again, John Henry, good to see you. Make yourself at home." He nodded to Sam. The four men fell silent as Kid appeared from the kitchen with a silver tray — empty save a white envelope at its center.

Comiskey leaned forward, taking the envelope and holding it up before them, a look of anticipation forming on his face, obscuring, Sam thought, the half-formed fear that he knew the old man felt.

"Here's your contract, John, to play the rest of the season with the Chicago White Sox Baseball Club. I've agreed to pay this thief," and he looked at Foster, "a princely sum for the rights to your services, and I've paid this other hustler," this time he glanced at Sam, "an even more outrageous retainer to make it all clean and legal. What do you say," less a question than a command.

John Henry Lloyd took a silent deep breath. He held his hand out, took the contract, felt the sheen of its paper smooth against the tips of his fingers, looked at the careful script, beautiful in its curls and figures, following the document to the bottom where he read aloud, "One thousand dollars for the remainder of the 1919 baseball season." He closed his eyes, then asked, "This seems a very generous offer, Mr. Comiskey. Very generous," and then paused.

Sam jumped in, "It's a standard major league contract. The clause on the next page commits you to playing for Mr. Comiskey next season."

Foster glared. "It's that reserve clause, baby. The reserve clause. Binds you to him like a Joseph."

"Trouble is I ain't got no colored coat," said Lloyd, enjoying the game. "That's for sure. And I ain't gonna work for no slave wages either."

Comiskey held back his surprise already cloaked in silent anger. What the fuck did this nigger want, what the fuck did he know. And who the hell was Foster to be talking like that. "Its really just the same contract all my ball players get, John Henry. Same's Collins and Jackson."

"I read somewhere that Collins makes sixteen grand a season. Don't sound the same to me."

"Oh, you know, John Henry, you can't always believe what you read in the papers. Can you Sam?"

"That's right, Mr. Comiskey. The players are strictly forbidden to talk about their contracts with the press. It's right here in black and white."

Rube Foster stood, towering over the others who remained seated in the lap of Comiskey's luxury. He pulled back his coat jacket (uh oh, here it comes, thought Sam) and allowed the men to see the pearl handle of his revolver peeking out of his waistband.

"Maybe you forgot, Mr. Comiskey. We had a deal for one thousand dollars a *month*—for the rest of the season—including October for the Series." And then he added, "The Reds, you know, they got quite a powerhouse of a team. You'll need all the help you can get. Swede's your weak link and they know it. By my calculation that makes three thousand dollars, doesn't it?"

Furious, Comiskey replied calmly, "Rube, you always had a good memory. Must have been an oversight. Sam'll correct it in the morning. Right Sam?"

"In that case Pop and I'll be goin'. Think you might ask your driver to give us a lift? Don't look too good for two Negro fellows to be leaving your house middle of the day. Not given what's been transpiring in these parts lately. *Verstehen?*"

Comiskey didn't reply. He only nodded and motioned Sam to the door. Rube and John Henry followed and then walked to the curb where they stepped quietly into the back of Comiskey's Packard. Only the chauffeur, his cap pulled down over his eyes, smiled as he closed the doors behind his two guests.

Sam turned back into the house, wondering if this would actually come to pass. He started to speak but found the room empty. Not a soul in sight. He stopped for a moment, thinking. The house seemed empty and noiseless—deserted, the relic of another time. Only the sunlight coming in from the still open front door, casting a shaft of light on the polished wood floor, hinted at life. Sam thought of the Negro woman in the kitchen and began to shift his weight, then thought again and walked out the front door and closed it softly behind him.

As she watched him go Kid sang quietly to herself. "Oh, the blues got me thinkin' just like a woman now."

9

DOG DAYS

Gleason has good reason to believe that he has the best job in the world. Early August and the team is riding high. Not so high that he wouldn't take just a bit of help … like a bit of a snort, he thinks, but still, the White Sox feel like a shoo-in. Sure, there are grumblings. When aren't there? Some of the fellows think that Collins is a stuck-up snot, but he sure can play. And Jackson, he only seems dumb. Dumb as a fox, Gleason tells himself, dumb as a fox. Best natural hitter he's ever seen. Ever.

So, there the team is, out in front by just enough. Just enough that he might even obey Tight-Ass Comiskey's orders not to let Cicotte (and the owner always pronounces it like it's a dish of them Eye-talian noodles) win thirty games. Hated to part with a buck, that Comiskey. Tightwad. Tight fucking ass. Winning really is everything, Gleason reasons. Why else do it. So, it's August, hot as a blast furnace in Gary — the ball park too far for a breeze from the lake, but everything's going just fine. So, why the hell is the old man doing this?

Gleason practically jumps out of his uniform when this thought finally forms in his mind. Bringing in a Negro ball player at this moment. It's insane.

The clubhouse is empty. Early morning. The players won't be showing up for another two hours but Gleason's almost dressed. He walks around the glistening concrete room, more a dungeon than a chamber, smoking. He hears the rhythmic tapping of his spikes on the floor and scratches under his arms, reaching through the unbuttoned top of his shirt. Only his cap, half a size too large for his head anyway, sits on the desk in his "office," the closet just off to the side of the clubhouse that Comiskey reluctantly presented to him early last season.

"It'll give you some privacy," the owner announced proudly, clapping his manager on the back, "keep you away from the scribes. Right fellas?"

The writers, that day in May, had gathered as they usually did in the clubhouse, squeezing themselves in between the pasty white bodies of the players still slick with sweat. With hats tipped back, the writers scribbled on crinkled pads of paper, scratching their codes of pencil marks, cornering their favorite player, searching for a word that would tell their readers that they possessed the secret reading of the day's game. When Comiskey's voice boomed above the room they looked up, silent. Finally one of them grinned, his laugh bouncing off the mildewed walls, and said, "Sure, Kid. Just whatcha need. Some privacy from all us fellas. Right fellas?"

No echoes this morning. Kid looks around half expecting one of the scribes to appear, ready to pat him on the back. Not that they'll pat him on the back anyway. He could hear the questions already. "Hey, Kid. Be square with us. Howd'ya really feel about playing with one?" "Gleason, we all know Lloyd's a hell of a player. But, this here is baseball, not a revolution." And he realizes, as he listens to the ghostly voices in his imagination, that he doesn't have the slightest answer to any of 'em. Not a friggin' one.

John Henry Lloyd wonders what he'll do when he gets to the ball park. Foster had slapped him on the back just as Comiskey's chauffeur had dropped them off at 37th and Wentworth and said, "No sweat, Pop. You'll either make history or a bundle. But not both." Lloyd looked over his shoulder at Foster, just as the black limousine pulled away from the curb. Foster sat in front, next to the driver, his right arm draped over the door. The faraway look on Rube's face made Lloyd wonder. He had played for and against Foster for almost twenty years, and never quite knew what was going on inside Rube's head.

Inside the old ball park, where the American Giants play, Lloyd makes a beeline for the clubhouse, finds the locker he had used until this season, and begins to dress.

The early afternoon silence fills the room, coats the worn wood benches and the hammered clothes pegs that protrude from the green-grey wall at eye level with a film of regret. Lloyd struggles to keep his balance as he bends over to lace up the scarred black spikes buried beneath the folded uniform on the bench. Sam had put them there, he thinks, at Comiskey's order.

The sweat is already beaded on his forehead by the time he emerges from the players' entrance and steps back into Comiskey's car. The chauffeur motions for Lloyd to sit in front, and flips the door open with his right hand as he leans over the shift arm protruding from the floor between the driver's and passenger's seats. Lloyd glances in the back as he settles into the car, relieved that Foster has allowed him to ride to Comiskey's park on his own. He wants to be early. Better to have the Sox players meet him one by one than to make a grand entrance and endure them staring at him. Funny, Lloyd thinks, he'd seen most of them play at one time or another, even took to buying bleacher seats most of the summer and walking quietly in after work at the depot. He sees them, the players, in his mind's eye, quick and strong and grace-ful, bathed in late afternoon sunlight. Joe Jackson's black bat blurs against the frame of catcher and umpire, Cicotte's smooth delivery, and Collins' magic around second, as deft and soft as a butterfly, all flash before him. But he can't remember their faces. It's as if they have no features as men, only the motions of ballplayers.

Rube Foster has seen them all play. Been watching them for as long as he can remember. One thing he's sure of, among his many strongly held opinions, as sure as the day is long, is that Lloyd's as good a player as any he's ever seen — Negro, white, Indian. Doesn't matter. Lloyd's better, smarter, quicker, stronger.

It doesn't take Foster long to walk from 37th and Wentworth over to State and then down to 35th. The streets are remarkably quiet, the National Guard troops in wool khaki uniforms patrolling in twos and threes, rifles slung across their shoulders, have finally quelled the riots, but Foster pats the pistol in his belt just to reassure himself. The center of Bronzeville, a polite alternative to Black Belt, Foster thinks with a snort, seems safe again. These federal soldiers, unlike the Chicago Police, have no stake in racial divisions, they're only here to keep the peace … he hopes.

Foster looks up, and the sun glints into the corner of his eyes, the rays catching him, like a shot, just behind his forehead. The light sparkles into a thousand pieces and then leaves in its place, as if somehow to compensate, a blinding pain so sharp that it drives Foster to his knees.

And then it disappears. Andrew Rube Foster stands. Looks around to make sure no one has seen him stumble; a reprimand forms in his mind, "Fuckin' city. Can't they keep the sidewalks clean? Way they keep us down." He rights himself quickly, pursing his lips and pushing his hands into his pockets as he makes his way across 35th Street.

Impossible, Sam thinks, to erase her face out of his memory. Or is it how she smells, the way he shudders inside when their hands touch? No matter. She's there, inside his head and he doesn't know what to do about it. Turn on his heels and go back and knock on the door, he asks silently as he continues downtown from Comiskey's. It feels as if they knew each other at some other time, some other place, even though it's impossible. Something, he can't say exactly what, familiar in the way she looked at him back there, he'd seen it, just a tiny glimpse, before.

Kid's image dances inside him. He imagines turning back, retracing his steps. She opens the door, the look of delight merges and quickly overwhelms her shock. She opens her mouth as if to speak, and he sees himself reflected in her eyes, which flicker rapidly from side to side, darting, taking his measure. He thinks he can reach inside and touch her. But suddenly, so quickly that it startles him, he finds his hand on the side of her face, his thumb under her chin, fingers gracing her cheek.

She covers his hand with hers, and begins to speak. But the words come out mute. He realizes with a shock that he has no idea of her name, and asks, "What do they call you?"

"Hey, pal. Just keep movin'." A gruff male voice varnished in phlegm pushes Sam away from the corner of the building, its body bending over, broom scraping pavement, to sweep the sidewalk clean. Sam looks up, "Sorry." And shaking his head as if to clear his vision, he takes a deep breath and returns to the business at hand — making sure that it all works out.

Comiskey told him in no uncertain terms to make sure that Lloyd gets to the park early, to "introduce him to all the fellas," and to be careful that Swede and Collins don't talk to him at the same time. "No point in rubbin' them two sticks together is there," Comiskey smiled. Sam allowed his eyes to play on the Old Roman's face for a moment, trying to measure his gaze. But he saw nothing.

"Yes, Mr. Comiskey. I think that's a good idea. Each of them's likely to find Lloyd's presence a threat, don't you think?"

"Don't worry about the thinking stuff, Sammy. Leave that to the professional. Just do what I tell you," and he waved his hand, dismissing Sam in the same gesture.

Marching orders. But the closer Sam gets to Comiskey Park the harder he finds it to concentrate. The damn girl, just won't leave him alone. His mind wanders, back to the lake, to an evening he imagines, his arm around her waist, the water lapping ashore, her hand on his shoulder. She must get a day off. Of course, Sundays. That's when the rich let their servants off. Of course. He had actually seen her. Not just imagined it. Just yesterday. There along the lake, a beautiful Negro woman riding the trolley. And he trembles. Chicago, 1919. One doesn't just walk up to her door and say, "Bye the bye. I was wondering if you'd like to go for a walk with me down by the lake this evening." Not to a Negro girl. Not in the wake of what has just happened. But he also knows that he has to find a way.

Kid can barely imagine what folks at home might say. "Chile, don't you even think 'bout it. Nothin' can ever come of it. Jus' put him where he belong … out of your mind. And the sooner the better." Oh, sure, she had seen black and white together on Beale, but the women were always hookers, and always black. No. Ain't no good gonna come from it. But he sure seems different, that one. Negro or white, doesn't matter. He's gentle and soft-spoken, his eyes kind. When she grazes his hand it feels like a current passing between them, and she tingles in memory.

The Old Man had already left the house. "Goin' to the ball park," he announced to no one in particular, "I'll be back late. No need for dinner." And then he looked at Kid, a gaze that cut right through her. "May's well take the afternoon off. Go to the ball game," and he tossed a pass on the entry table and slammed the door shut behind him.

She knows not to wear her Memphis Minnie dress. Not today, not to the ball park. Not… And, as she brushes her hand over the two other print dresses that hang limply in her closet, she wonders. Richard. Leaving Walls. His leaving her. Wouldn't it be remarkable to find him up here? Maybe that Mrs. Binga can ask about him at the Urban League office, or at the Y. And maybe someone knows where this man Sam lives. He could just as easily walk right back into Comiskey's house, his long legs take the steps two at a time, and smile, "I just left my umbrella behind the front door." Kid grins into his eyes holding her hands behind her back, clutching the umbrella, aware of her body beneath her black uniform.

"I been wonderin' if you'd show up," she sings. "Its rainin out, ai … isn't it."

Sam nods, and stands just before her. She realizes that he's only a few inches taller, and she smells his summer sweat. So quick that her motion surprises both of them she takes the umbrella out from its hiding place, and laughs.

"Looking for this, Mister?…" But she leaves the question hanging in the air, instead pressing the black iron back one last time against the cotton dress, as if to crush the fabric into compliance with her dreams.

Thirty-fifth Street. The heart of Bronzeville. Negroes and whites eye each other warily as they converge on Comiskey Park. They come from the same direction — the Irish, Polish, and Slovenians from Bridgeport and Back of the Yards, the pads of their fingers still criss-crossed with grime and dried blood, while across the street, their black co-workers from the mills and slaughterhouses have to walk right past Comiskey's park just to get home to the South Side. The riots of the past week have turned each group wary. Even the police and National Guard, young men hunched over as they sit in canvas-covered wagons parked in alleys, others patrolling up and down Indiana, State, and Federal, seem exhausted. They watch through squinty eyes, their fingers hovering above the safety catches of their rifles and pistols.

The city's first public event since the riots, the postponed game against the Red Sox, scheduled for 5 P.M., in the words of *Tribune* writer Hugh Fullerton, "create a stir not seen in these parts since before the Great War." Fullerton had been too young, of course, to see the Haymarket executions, but he had read about them. "Kill that kind of crap," his editor told him earlier that morning. "We got enough trouble with this damn Red Summer stuff without your editorializing."

Sam thinks just the opposite. Nothing he has experienced prepares him for Chicago this summer. Come to think of it, he muses as he pushes his straw boater back on his brow, it seems impossible. He has spent much of his adult life in the city moving between two worlds and made it his business to find common ground. Now, all that seems distant, it belongs to a different time and place.

Someone jostles his elbow, pushing him slightly to his left, into a stream of men waiting in line for tickets just beyond the booths on the corner of 35th and State. "Hey, pal, just wait your turn," one of them says gruffly. Sam smiles, tips his hat, and lets his eyes follow the back of the fellow who rudely rushed by him.

"Fucking rube," is all Swede Risberg can think when Sam, strolling along, hands in his pockets, walks into his path. Angrily pushing Sam aside with his elbow, Swede pumps his arms even faster as he strides to the clubhouse door. His hand reaches for the crumpled note in his pocket but he resists any temptation to read it. He knows what it says. "Get to the park early today. I got stuff to talk to you about. Gleason."

Last time, in fact the only time, that Swede got anything in writing from Gleason, back in his first season it was, the flinty manager had told him that some new kid was coming up from the minors. Comiskey ordered Gleason to play him. "It ain't my idea," Gleason had said then patting Swede on the shoulder, "it's what the boss wants. Don't worry, this busher'll be gone in a couple of days. Then its back to normal." But it didn't feel normal to Swede for quite some time. The other players, his so-called friends on the team, just wouldn't let it go. They ribbed him without mercy while he sat on the bench. "Wassamatter Swede, someone stick a piece of steel up your ass?" Or, as Cicotte delicately put it, "Hey, Swede. You got any relatives in Iowa? The way this kid's playing they be seein' you in no time." Only Eddie Collins kept his yap shut, Swede remembers. Knew that if he didn't there'd be real hell to pay.

Risberg quickens his pace.

By the time he pushes his way into the dressing room Swede's mood is as foul as his mouth. "Where the fuck is everyone?" he announces to no one in particular. The room echoes with his voice. "Where the..." he snarls again.

Gleason emerges from his office, his spikes clickity-clacking against the concrete floor, suspenders hanging loosely from his waist, loops of canvas that reach his knees.

"Nobody here but me, Swede." His voice sounds almost soft.

"Well, Kid, here I am. You told me to get my ass here early. Now what's so important, anyway."

"Now, Swede. No need to get riled up. You remember last week. The boss," and Gleason nods toward the dank concrete ceiling, "was thinking of adding a player, you know, an established veteran, a guy with experience, to help us with the stretch run. Push us over the top, to the pennant. If we win, then we'll all win. You know what I mean, don't you Swede?"

Risberg listens intently. He has automatically begun to shed his street clothes. He stands in front of his locker dressed only in a pair of white undershorts and long black socks pulled almost up to his knees. With one foot on the floor, the other atop the wood bench dividing the room, he fixes Gleason with his gaze.

"Don't bullshit me, Gleason. Comiskey already told me about that.

Said he wanted Lloyd to spell Collins from time to time, ain't that right?

"Sure, Swede. That's part of the plan. Give Collins a day off. This sure is a tough summer. Heat really gets to you. Even seemed to me that you been looking weary the last few weeks. Game or two off for you wouldn't hurt none either. Nope, not a bit." Gleason lets his eyes wander down the walls of the clubhouse, where he stares intently at an extinguished lightbulb. He senses the anger clouding Risberg's face.

"You're bringing that nigger in here to take my job. Ain't that right?"

"Nah, Swede, its not like that at all. You got it all wrong. Lloyd's not after your job. We just want to have him spell you, and Collins, from time to time. Just give you guys a rest to add some extra zip in the lineup."

"I don't believe you one minute, Gleason. Not one fucking minute. You and Comiskey didn't sign that black son of a bitch to have him sit on the bench now, did you? Don't be kidding me. Not me."

Risberg reaches into his locker for his bat, holds it against his shoulder, turns it in his right hand, tight against the handle, as he speaks.

Like to grind it into sawdust, Gleason thinks, trying to mask his smile as the nearly naked shortstop gets redder in the face, shakes that bat, wearing only them shorts and black socks like he's some kind of underwear ad. If he could smack me he would.

And Comiskey told Gleason just the other day, "Don't worry about Swede. He knows where his bread is buttered. Just leave him to me."

"You think I'm gonna let some black bastard come in here and take my job away? You gotta be fucking kidding yourself. Not this short-stop, not after what we just seen in this city."

"Calm down, Swede. Just calm down. No one saying anything about taking your job. Just giving you a rest from time to time. Just a day off, you know, like a paid vacation. Don't do that in the mills, do they." Gleason smiles. He isn't above a bit of that psychology himself, he thinks proudly.

"Sure is dark in here," the voice comes booming in from the hall way. "Can't anyone turn on the lights? Hey, anyone there?"

"Fuck. It's that Collins," Swede whispers loudly.

"It's okay, Eddie. Just me and Swede here talking. Come on and join us, we're over here, by the lockers. Here, just around the alcove," and at that Gleason hitches his suspenders over his shoulders, yanks at the waistband of his pants, and draws himself up as he pulls in his gut.

"Thanks for coming, Eddie. Thanks a whole lot."

"Sure Mr. Gleason. Always glad to oblige."

Swede can't look Collins in the face; instead he takes in the second baseman, who is dressed for an early dinner out in a silk suit and straw hat. "Fucking swell. Who the hell's he think he is anyway," Risberg murmurs to himself.

"I was just tellin' Swede here about the ni ... you know, about Lloyd. I know that the Boss already spoke to you, but Pop's coming to the club today. I'm gonna play him this evening, give you a rest."

Gleason carefully omits either of their names, the "you" hanging ambiguously in the rank air of the locker room. Best way, Gleason thinks, to get through this is to let one of 'em see it my way and step aside. That'll tell me a whole lot.

"Well, Kid. It's okay with me. Whatever the team wants, you know, it's jake."

"Thanks Eddie. I really appreciate that. It's just what I expected from a well-educated fella like yourself. Just what I expected."

Swede stops as he pulls his black socks up to his knees and looks at the two men. "Well it ain't jake with me. No fucking way it is. No black man is gonna take my place. You guys think you're pretty smart, but I see what's on your mind. Wanna shame me into steppin' aside, like hoity-toity Collins here. Well, I got news for you. I ain't no gentleman. Never was. Never will be. So you can take your Pop Lloyd and shove him up your white asses. That's what you can do."

Gleason turns to Collins and says simply, "Thanks Eddie, that won't be necessary. I think I've made up my mind where Lloyd'll play today. I appreciate your offer. Swede, sit by me on the bench this afternoon. I got plenty to teach you about playing ball. Yessir, plenty to teach you."

The three men stand speechless, Gleason at their center, Collins and Swede on either side, as their silence fills the late afternoon. Gleason tugs at his gut, again, pulling his paunch in as he slips his suspenders over his sloping shoulders before snapping the elastic with his thumb. The corner of his mouth twitches slightly, turning lines of black and white stubble into ridges of expression. Swede sights down the length of his uniform socks, black wool from toe to knee, and studies the spread of his feet, measuring their distance, an imagined trajectory. His hands still grip the bat before him, their clenching motion barely visible, his fingers slick with perspiration. And Collins, an expression of blank innocence over his face, stands calmly, waiting. The talc is still dry on his cheeks and Collins slowly raises his right hand and passes it along the side of his head, brushing his dark black hair back, neatly, his fingers skimming the surface between his temple and the back of his neck.

Sam thinks twice about walking in through the players' entrance. Not that he minds buying a ticket. Perhaps he'll get a look at that Boston fellow, Ruth. Rumor has it that the Red Sox plan to convert him full time to the outfield. Rumor also has it that Ruth is ready to hold out for a ton of money. Sam smiles. The Red Sox's owner, Frazee, is about as different from Comiskey as Minsky is from Nijinksy.

Big spender, big tipper, lavish lender, Frazee loves the chorus girls, hates Boston's blue laws, and spends his every idle moment thinking about new ways to indulge his real passion. He loves Broadway shows and vows that he'd do about anything to become a big-time producer. Meantime, Sam reflects, he's still got Ruth, and that's real entertainment.

On the other hand if he sits up in the stands, out in left field, over one of the outfield arches, he'll have a great view of the playing field to follow Lloyd's every move and still feel the mood of the crowd. That's it, Sam decides. I'll go and find Foster and go sit with him. Folks out there won't care, it's where most of the Negroes sit anyway.

Sam cranes his neck and peers out over the crowd marching past him, his lanky body a reed in their current. The colored entrance, by custom the last ticket booth and turnstile closest to the left field bleachers, already has a line before it. Foster, Sam just knows, hates to enter that way, but this week in early August, it sure is the place that even Foster would choose.

Kid walks quickly, as silently as possible, across 35th Street, passing Indiana before catching sight of Comiskey Park. It's about the grandest thing she's ever seen. And the people, so many people, crowding, jostling, walking briskly alongside of her. Like the other day at the lake before all hell broke loose, they flow into a human river that never ends. Then she notices. Unmistakably, a white straw hat up ahead, there, just in front of the gate where all the Negroes line up, clutching their tickets, dressed like it was church, men and women, tapping their feet impatiently as the line moves with deliberate speed toward the turnstile.

Her insides jump. This is exactly what she hoped and dreaded. Sam. Just up ahead. Her fingers tingle, her brain dulls as she moves forward, wondering what direction to take.

"You the young woman who works for Missa Comiskey if I'm not mistaken."

The voice, smooth with a hint of the South, comes from a man who suddenly appears, his large frame towering over her, his hat softly cradled in the fingers of his huge right hand.

"And you, if I'm not mistaken, you are Mr. Foster. How good to see you again. Are you plannin' to go to the game?" she asks in her best been-in-the-North diction, mimicking the vowels that Mrs. Binga had amazed her with only days before. "Can you show me where to go in? I don't even know if it's all right to sit anywhere."

"Just follow me. We can sit quietly, unobtrusively, in the darkie section. Be my pleasure to find your company at this extravaganza." Foster waves his hand, still holding his hat, with a flourish, his wrist spiraling down from his forehead as he points out the way.

"And if it isn't Sammie. *Wie gehts*, Sammie? What brings you to the park this wonderful day."

"Rube," Sam can't hide the hitch in his voice, can't avoid looking at Kid, whose eyes search his face, "Rube, I thought I'd take in the game from the bleachers. See how Pop'll do best that way. Looking right over his shoulder."

"Or, right up his…. Sorry Miss. Sometimes Sam here brings out the worst in me. I almost forgot my manners. Do find it, please, in your heart to forgive me."

"Why what in the world does you mean, Mr. Foster?" Kid answers, her voice rising in the lilt of a Southern lady, at least as far as she can recall.

Foster links her arm and says, "Sammie, have you met this young vision yet? You may have noticed her working at our colleague Mr. Charles Comiskey's house, just the other day."

"Hello, I'm delighted to make your acquaintance." Sam extends his hand. "Is this your first baseball game? I think I heard that you arrived in Chicago not very long ago."

Kid takes his hand gently, coolly, softly.

"Never been to a game. Even the children didn't play this baseball in the Delta. Not when I was coming up, anyways. Maybe you would be patient enough to explain it to me a little bit."

It isn't clear to whom Kid is speaking. But Sam looks down to find that he is still touching her fingers, and allows her hand to drop even as he tries to discover if Foster has noticed. He imagines that the burning in his cheeks has turned his face red and he reaches up to pull his straw hat down over his eyes.

"Sunny day, isn't it, Sammy." Foster's eyes grin as he extracts a pocket watch from his vest. "We best be going in. Game's gonna start pretty soon. This here is history in the making. Let's not be late. After you."

The chauffeur slowly circles the ball park, carefully picking his way through the rills of pedestrians crossing the streets from every angle. Comiskey's words echo in his ears. "Bring him right to my office, Robert. Right to my office. I don't want no scene out there. Not to the player's gate, you hear. Only to my entrance. I'll be waiting. Don't you mess up."

Robert yessed him till he was blue in the face, tipped his cap for good measure, and then guided the Packard out into the city for its mission. Even wore white gloves for the occasion, just in case the newspapers caught wind of the event. Well, not just in case. His older brother, Errol, had been working for the *Defender* for a couple of years. Been begging him for leads. "Leads," Robert said the first time, "what you talkin' leads. I works for Mr. Charlie Tight-Ass Comiskey. He ain't got no news for the black folks in Chicago." Errol had looked at him in that way of older brothers and spoke calmly. "Never know, lil' brother. Never know. Jus' keep you eyes and ears open."

And then only a week ago Robert realized that his brother was right. There was more action in Comiskey's house than fist fights at the Regal. What would Errol say if he knew that Rube Foster and John Henry Lloyd were both at the house. That ought to get him something — a pat on the back and a beer.

"Do tell, you really saw both of them in Comiskey's place? At the same time?"

Robert could only pull the shiny brim of his cap down over his eyes and grin. "Why'd I bullshit you, brother. When'd I ever do that?"

Errol glanced down at his little brother. "When didn't you? No matter. What's happening up there? Just tell me straight."

That's why Errol had gone to the trouble to get his press credentials in order for the ball game. Occasionally, of course, he covered the American Giants, along with the weddings, funerals, and social events that provided the *Defender* with its bread and butter. Even Mr. Abbott knew that a newspaper devoted to the liberation of black folks marched to the tune of Chicago's upper crust Negroes. So, there he sits outside the owner's entrance, waiting for Pop Lloyd to show up and make history.

Little brother doesn't disappoint him either. The Packard eases its way through the crowds and glides slowly up to the curb just in front of the door marked, *Private: No Entrance*. Just where Robert said he'd pull up.

John Henry Lloyd steps down from the passenger seat, nods to the driver, and walks across the sidewalk toward the door. Amazing, Errol thinks, absolutely amazing. From his black stockings to his wool hat with the letters SOX embroidered along the front panel, Pop Lloyd looks like a big league ball player, a member of the Chicago White Sox. But his skin, as black as ebony, his face obscured by the peak of his cap, burns against his uniform. And then as quickly as he appears John

Henry Lloyd vanishes, moves into the stadium, as if he could walk right through the door.

The Red Sox finish batting practice. A few of their players lounge around the periphery of the field, hands resting elegantly on their bats. Warmed by the orange blaze of the late afternoon sunlight, they chat, enjoying the moment of stillness, oblivious to the ministrations of the early crowd and to the nervous energy of the White Sox who saunter over to the cage for batting practice.

A few, including their pitcher, Ruth, stop for a moment as the whip and crack of Joe Jackson's bat, a thin black blur, rifles ball after ball around the outfield, shots that slam and ricochet against the concrete wall. Jackson's swing has its own signature and there isn't a big leaguer who can't tell just by hearing when he is at the plate.

Jackson's teammates trot out onto the field, slapping their fists into worn leather mitts, feeling the summer turf hard beneath their spikes. Some bend down to stretch while others stand in twos and threes, arms folded, chewing tobacco, giving the girls in the stands the eye. With each line drive from Jackson's bat they look up and follow the trajectory of the ball, gauging its speed and distance, and then resume their gossip.

They act, Gleason thought, like it is just another day at the ball park. "I want you to start it off natural, see. Natural," Comiskey instructed him earlier. "I'll take care of Lloyd myself. Bring him in just before the game's gonna start. You talk to Collins and Risberg. Got it?"

Gleason stands, hands stuffed in the pockets of his jacket, just below the steps of the White Sox dugout. Sure, take care of Risberg and Collins. That Risberg sure is steaming mad. A fucking loose cannon, that one. Gleason can only wonder what he might actually do. Sure he's a working stiff, but even so, not the kind of man who'd sit still and see his job taken out from under him. Had too much of the mill in him for that. Comiskey'd never understand that. Still thinks that the guys at the bottom will do whatever he tells 'em. Has too much money for his own good, that Comiskey. Too fucking much.

"Hey, skip, where's the lineup?" Chic Gandil saunters over to

Gleason. The first baseman, one foot resting on the top step, the other, like Kid's, on the concrete floor, crosses his arms. "Ain't on the wall," he nods over to the home plate side.

"Nope. Not yet. Got some things to think about. Go take your hits."

Gandil stares hard at Gleason. Something's up. He just can't tell what. Yet.

Foster settles his bulk between Sam and Kid, making sure they have to talk around him, and points toward the field, "See that fellow, the wiry one with the long black bat. Long enough to beat the sea with. He's the best one the Sox got, call him Shoeless Joe. Can't read, but he sure can count, right bubbeleh?"

"Bubbeleh?" Kid turns her eyes from Jackson's fireworks and leans across Foster to catch Sam's eye.

"Its Yiddish. For pal."

"Yiddish?" she inquires again, this time looking at Foster.

"Why honey. That's the patois of the Jews. Sammy here. He's Jewish. Straight from Maxwell Street. Right, Sammy?"

Sam registers Kid's glance. Better not to try to explain that one. "I'm just an immigrant kid from the West Side, Miss. Only got here a few years before you. My parents are foreigners, migrants, come a long way to the Golden Door. They hardly speak English at home. Rube here, he knows a few words of their lingo, makes him feel very cosmopolitan."

Jackson places his bat carefully against the cage, spits into his hands, and jogs over to Gandil who remains at the edge of the dugout, in front of the stands, between home and first.

"Buck Weaver, now that's my kind of ball player." Foster enjoys his authority. "Watch how he concentrates, puts everything but the pitch out of his mind. He's almost as good a fielder as Pop. Almost."

Sam looks over at Kid. He can't think what to say to her. He's already asked if this is her first game. "No ball in the Delta, then?"

"Not where I come from, anyways. Nosir. No ball games. Just cotton and some singing." Kid can't keep her gaze off the field. Weaver, she thinks, seems to be scowling as he strikes at the ball, like he wants to smash it to pieces. He looks as angry as anyone she has ever seen.

The world, right then, is moving too fast for her. New words, new smells, new rules. She can hardly grasp one thing in her mind before something new pops in out of nowhere. And these two men, the robust Foster and gentle man whose eyes she can't keep from walking inside her head. Too much.

Shifting slightly in her seat Kid determines to hold her balance. Secretly she is grateful to Foster for putting himself between her and Sam. And then again...

Comiskey pats his secretary on her rump. "Get goin'. I got someone comin' in soon. Make yourself scarce, honey." As she disappears through the door between their offices Comiskey pushes the papers they have scattered back into place on the surface of his desk. He shoots a glance at Anson's portrait on the wall, grimaces, stands, and moves to the other door of his office, the one with the frosted glass.

With his hand on the polished brass doorknob Charles Comiskey waits. Behind him, the slatted window that looks down on the field bends the late afternoon sun into hovering bands of light and shadow casting his office in a disquieting glow.

He can see the other man's silhouette ripple across the pane. Before Lloyd has a chance to reach out and knock, Comiskey opens the door.

"Glad you could make it, Pop," he announces to no one in particular, "You look great in the uniform. Just great." And with that the owner reaches up and pats John Henry Lloyd on the shoulder as he ushers him back into the office.

"Come here. Right here. Take a look. There. Waddaya see, Mr. Lloyd. Waddaya really see?" Comiskey stands by the window, pointing down at the field that bears his name. "Yeah. Right down there."

"Lotsa things, Mr. Comiskey. I see lotsa things. But what I see most is ball players like me, most of 'em not as good as me actually, out there on a field where I ain't been allowed to play 'til now." Lloyd pauses, a bit surprised at his own candor. "And I be wondering how they all gonna feel, all them folks out there, about a colored man takin' the field this day. I mean, after this past week. Sure gives me pause."

"Why, Pop. You got nothin' to worry about. My players and my fans, they only want a winning team. Just remember what I told you the other day, willya. Keep your nose clean, don't argue back, and the whole shebang'll be over before you know it. Nothin' to worry about."

Comiskey reaches up to pat Lloyd on the back again, but hesitates, his hand at shoulder level. Pop moves away, just a small shudder that reveals itself only for an instant in the tic of his neck. Side by side the two men gaze out the window, each caught in his own thoughts.

Down below Risberg and Collins stand not four feet apart in the mildewed locker room. Gleason had gone out onto the field minutes earlier. "No crap from you guys. Behave for once, willya. It's the way it's gonna be. That's all there is to it." And now the two players wrap themselves in silence as they strip away their street clothes and methodically don their uniforms.

Collins exudes calm, even detachment. Well, why the fuck not, Risberg broods. He's not the one gonna lose his job to no Negro. And the more Swede mulls it over the more steamed he gets. Makes his blood boil. Somewhere inside Swede knows that Lloyd's color has little to do with it. He knows that he'd feel the same way if they brought in any new guy to take his job. Bastards. But he also knows that Comiskey has fucked with him, probably told Gleason that too. Like a rat in a corner. I'm a fucking rat in a corner with nowhere to go.

The more he broods the angrier he gets, catching Lloyd in the cross-hairs of his emotions. Hadn't felt like this in a long time. Not since that strike a dozen years ago when they brought the scabs into the mills in order to break the union. It had been clearer then, the rights and the wrongs, but this really didn't feel no different. Well, fuck them. Fuck them all. The self-righteous Collins, lookit him, pulling off them garters. Who's he think he his. And Comiskey. Red, pimply assed

Comiskey. He could kiss mine. And Lloyd. Moving in here like that. Risberg has nothing against Negroes. But God help anyone who tries to take his job away from him. Fuck 'em. Fuck 'em all.

Weaver can hit all right. Not like Jackson's firecrackers. Not as sharp and crisp, but his line drives jump, hard and straight, over the infielders' heads. Even from the bleachers Sam can feel Buck working — see the sweat beading on his forehead, staining circles under his arms and darkening the seam between the brim and crown of his cap. A real labor. Gandil follows Weaver and then some of the Sox pitchers, sad-faced Eddie Cicotte, who still dreams of going home to his farm, and Lefty Williams, whose pinpoint control and fade-away make up for his lack of overwhelming speed.

Sam watches at they take their hacks and then disappear one by one into the darkness of the dugout, passing the manager, Kid Gleason, on their way back into the dressing room. Gleason appears stoic, clapping his hands one minute, but then glances up at Comiskey's window, the one overlooking the first base side. Sam wonders.

"When's Pop gonna come out," he says as much to himself as to Rube.

"Oh, you know, Sammy. Only when TA be ready."

"TA?"

Kid felt relieved that Sam asked. It all seems beyond her.

"Tight Ass."

Sam smiles and looks at Kid, finding the light in her eyes.

The crowd fills the stands around them. Mostly black folks, and a smattering of whites—"real" baseball fans Sam appreciates, who want to look in at the plate from behind the pitcher and don't give a damn who's sitting nearby. From time to time a Negro taps Rube on the shoulder with a folded program and says, "Hiya, Rube. Good to see you out at the game. How's your Giants doin' this year?"

Foster tilts his big head back and laughs, pats his acquaintance on the hand and says, "Yesssir. Hadda come see this boy Ruth. They tell me he's the cat's ass. Yes they do. See if he good enough to play with the colored folk."

And then he and the group around him, for Foster always speaks to the crowd, chuckle as one.

"That Foster. Always the life of the party," they say to no one in particular as they work their way back to their own seats. "Gotta get out to see them Giants play soon's they have their next game.... Hey, Rube. Who you playin' next Sunday?"

❧ ❧

Sam closes his eyes. The sun setting behind home angles over his face, dancing light on his eyes, bringing a hint of evening. Sam reaches his arm around Foster's back and as he extends his hand, widening it from thumb to pinky, he barely — and he thinks inadvertently — touches the back of Kid's neck with his fingers. She shivers and leans forward in reflex, raising her arm to point at the crowd of players gathered in front of the White Sox dugout.

❧ ❧

Gleason stands his ground. "I ain't ready yet to put up the lineup. Just hold your water. Game's not gonna start for a few minutes yet. I told ya, the boss asked me to wait."

"Wait for what, he don't know about no lineups."

"Come on, Kid, we got a right to know if we're playin or not, don't we?"

"Just stop your bellyaching."

"You ain't even got who's pitchin' up on the wall."

"Okay. Okay. Williams, get out to the bullpen and warm up."

No one moves from the knot of players gathered around the manager. Gleason barks again, "Williams. I said to get warmed up."

"Must be inside, Mr. Gleason," Eddie Collins speaks from his perch on the bench. "I think a bunch of them went inside a few minutes ago. Risberg came out and they followed him."

❧ ❧

Comiskey wonders how the players will react. It's his team, ain't it. He pays the freight. Who the hell are they to have anything to say about it. And besides, the only one who'd squawk is that weasel Risberg, and he'd taken care of Swede anyway.

The dark corridor that leads from the stairwell to the dugout remains unmarked. Comiskey designed it that way. Didn't want unauthorized characters making their way into the players' inner sanctum. Or to the barely lit stairs that lead to his office.

"Just wait here," he instructs Lloyd, as they stand outside the door. "I want to make sure that the players are on the field. Then we'll walk in and up to the dugout. I'll tip Gleason that we're coming."

The door slams sharply in Lloyd's face. As the echo reverberates through the corridor, Pop peers into the darkness. The light's extinguished, one of those cheap minute lights he guesses. That Comiskey, he's one of a kind, isn't he. Bathed in darkness Pop feels the cool damp air from underground penetrate the soles of his spikes, creep up his arms. He hears voices behind the steel door but hard as he tries he can't make them out.

Pop doesn't have to think very long. He knows the score. Suddenly he speaks out loud. "Why you bein' a fool. A fuckin' fool t'think they want you to play ball with them. Must be that arrogance they speaks of. These white boys no more'n want you playing with them than they do their dicks to shrivel up. No sir, no fuckin' way."

"Must be time for the contest to commence, don't you surmise, Sammie?"

"Well, guess so, Rube. It must be close. I reckon the fellas are just getting some last minute instructions, don't you?"

Foster hunches forward, his back straining the seams of his coat, his hands folding and unfolding, torturing an invisible towel to death.

Kid, finally catching her breath, sits back and questions if these men have any idea what they are talking about. How in the world is this crowd gonna accept a Negro ball player? She doesn't have to know anything about their baseball to know the answer to that one. And, so, oblivious to the crowd's increasing restlessness, she begins to hum, only partially hoping that Sam will hear.

Seven White Sox players gather around Swede Risberg. Their shadows darken the grey floor, their uniforms sag with sweat and dirt, and their hair is wet and matted under their soggy wool caps. Risberg speaks softly. He figures yelling will do no good.

"I tell ya. The Old Man don't treat us no good. Lookit your uniforms—had 'em cleaned lately? Ever been upstairs for the eats he serves his pals … ever get in the door? And what about your contracts. Only one who got a real deal on this team is Collins. You can bet he ain't in here right now. We all know that Eddie here gets a bonus. If he pitches enough. You can bet your sweet ass that's not gonna happen. Even Gleason. You know he's not a bad guy. But he does exactly what Comiskey tells him. Nothing more."

Swede looks up to measure his audience. He's not used to being one of the leaders on the team. But for a moment he knows that he is in his element. These guys, even Joe Jackson standing quietly a few feet away, they know the score. They've all had to shuffle and scrape to make enough dough to get 'em through the month. Swede can tell from how they look at him that they're listening.

"So, I say, when the Old Man comes in here and tells us that we gotta play with a nigger, I say that we tell him that we ain't doing no such thing 'til he makes some changes. Treat us like men, pay what we are worth, and we'll play ball. If not, he can go to hell."

Buck Weaver opens the top button of his shirt and lets out a deep breath. "Oh, Swede. I just dunno. Why don't we just play baseball, and leave all this stuff to the big shots?"

Joe Jackson glances down at his feet and bends over to tie his shoes, which he had secured only two minutes earlier. Eddie Cicotte, however, speaks his mind.

"You guys, you know that we ain't been gettin' our fair share. We got bills to pay, families to feed, and we can't seem to catch a break from Comiskey. This is a perfect time to talk it over with him. Perfect. He wants something and we want something. Maybe he'll even listen."

"And maybe he don't give a shit what you guys think or want. Maybe he's the owner. It's his team. And if you rubes don't like it you'll be on the train to St. Louis or even Iowa before you have time to take a crap."

Charles Comiskey stands before the steel door, its dark frame a perfect outline for his figure. Grey hair and florid cheeks, a suit from the custom shop at Fields, diamond stick pin in his pearl cravat, Comiskey poses himself like a general before his troops. Clenching his fist and then stuffing his hand into his pocket, Comiskey tightens his jaw and glares.

"Any of you guys who don't want to play for me. You can take a hike. I got your releases right here," and he taps the handkerchief bulging slightly inside his left-hand suit pocket. Then, one by one, he fixes each of the players, "with that beady-eyed stare of his," Cicotte remembers later, looking right at each of them until they squirm.

"When you are ready to play ball, I suggest you get your asses back on the field. We got a pennant to win in case you all forgot why you are all here."

"What about..." Lefty Williams begins.

"What about *what*, Claude," Comiskey replies icily, knowing that Williams hates to be called by his real name. "What about *what?*"

Williams, scheduled to start that day, takes a step back.

"What about *what*, Claude? Worried about that Ruth? Maybe you don't wanna pitch today. Maybe that's it."

Williams fumes and says nothing. He looks up, turns to his teammates. "Come on fellas. There's a game to play." Then he reaches in his rear pocket for a chew, stuffs the tobacco into his cheek and walks out to the dugout. One by one the others follow.

"You. Risberg. You wait. Wait right here," Comiskey orders as he reaches for the knob. Lloyd is still waiting behind the door.

From their bleacher perch Foster and Sam watch the Sox take the field for a final warmup, mostly a crisp infield drill and a few lazy fungoes to the outfielders to let them set the ball against the blue-grey summer sky. Gleason has shed his jacket and paces along the steps of the dugout as his coaches begin hitting balls across the infield.

"See, Miss," Foster speaks softly to Kid, still sitting hunched forward at his elbow, "this is when they practice. Catching balls, making sure they loose enough to play when the real game begins."

The infielders whiz the ball back to Ray Schalk, the catcher, who tosses it, gently, underhand to the coach whose long thin bat flutters in the light as he hits two-hop grounders around the horn and back again, his voice commanding, "Get two." Schalk, ribbed chest-protector hanging down between his legs, stands solidly off to the third base side of the plate, his iron mask atop his head, and shouts encouragement. "Way to go Eddie. Way to get to that one," he cries as Collins glides smoothly to his left and filling the hole between first and second, and swoops down on the ball just as it hits the seam between the infield's smooth sandy surface and the burnt outfield grass.

Sam smiles. Something about the game, something about the rhythm of ball, bat, and leather makes him feel that all is well in the world. Comforting, familiar, he knows, but satisfying. For the first time that day he relaxes, enjoying the sounds and images of ball players, of men even older than he, playing a game meant for pleasure, for boyhood, for innocence.

Remarkably, Kid notices first. "Where's the player who stands there," and she points to the vacant space between second and third. "Isn't that a big space for no one to be in?"

"That's where Risberg, the shortstop, the one they call Swede plays," replies Sam, hoping to sound knowledgeable.

"Sammie, my boy. That's where Pop's gonna play. If he ain't there I sure smell trouble. This don't look good to me. Not one bit. Best get your tochus down there an' see what's transpirin'. I'll take care of this little gal while you tending to business."

As Sam pushes his way through the knees and feet of a dozen men and kids seated between him and the nearest aisle, he glances back. Kid is looking down at the field intently, gesturing to Foster. She doesn't see Sam wave as he disappears.

John Henry "Pop" Lloyd, the best shortstop in Chicago in the twentieth century, better than Risberg, stronger, rangier, quicker than Joe Tinker, doesn't wait even a minute for Charles Comiskey. The voices behind the door tell him what he needs to know. Cap Anson's spirit is alive and well in Chicago. No amount of money is gonna help him play on the Sox, not this year, not for any time to come. He works with these guys all day long, in the tunnels. No way they're gonna give their job to him. No way in hell, not after that riot. That prick Comiskey's probably just using him anyway — to bust them. He should have figured that out sooner. But what a dream. To play ball with a white team in Chicago. The first one in almost forty years. That would be some dream come true. But not now. Not in his time on earth.

Lloyd looks down at his legs, black stockings, black shoes, black as his skin. He feels like a fool. Dressed up for some damn parade and no one else there to march. Silently he rips off his shirt, hands tearing at the black "Sox" lettering on his chest, and tosses it in a heap at the door.

That's all Comiskey discovers a few minutes later, a crumpled and torn wool jersey, when he opens the door and announces, "Come on boy. It's time to play ball."

Sam makes his way around the outside of the ball park, quickens his pace, more sure by the minute that something has transpired to throw a wrench into the plan. He reaches his hand into his pocket and twists the ticket stub anxiously as he approaches the outside entry to Comiskey's private office. A Negro man leans against the wall, hat slightly tipped down over his eyes, scribbling on a small note pad. He barely pays notice as Sam pulls open the door and shows his wallet to the guard seated at a desk just inside. "Sure. I seen them go up not too long ago," the guard replies. "Old TA, I mean Mr. Comiskey, and that big Negro ball player, what's his name, from the Giants. I seen 'em both."

Sam stands quite still and listens. He hears the crowd inside the park begin its restless clapping, drowning out, for a moment, the honks and squeals of snarled traffic outside.

"Oh, I also seen when the player fellow he left. Left like he was going home, arms pumpin', didn't even look at me. Had no shirt on either. Just his skivvies on top, you know what I mean. Just happened. Just a minute before you got here."

Comiskey slams the door. No Lloyd. Shoulda known that black bastard'd turn yellow. Fuckin' Foster. Why'd I believe him. Just playing with me. And that Sam. No better than a goddamn nigger. Sneaky Jew. Can't trust any of them.

Flushed, his face red and angry, Comiskey turns on his heels to face Risberg. "What the hell are you looking at? Just get out there and take your position. Tell Gleason you're playing. Move."

"Oh my. My oh my." Foster looks down to inspect his spats. He feels the vise reach around the back of his head again and squeeze. It's all he can do to keep his eyes open and catch his breath.

And then as suddenly as it appeared the pain subsides. Not the first time that day either, he thinks, grasping for breath. They are getting harder and more frequent. Of that he has no doubt.

He turns to Kid, who has moved over next to him. "Did you see what I just saw?" he inquires. "Do you see who just walked out into the field down there? Risberg. The regular shortstop. Something's up. Gives me a bad feeling. I always knew that we shouldn't be trusting these white folk. Always knew it."

By the time Foster finishes speaking Lefty Williams has dispatched the first two Red Sox hitters easily. But now the crowd begins to stir. Ruth, the Red Sox pitcher who bats third, walks to the plate. He's already hit twenty home runs this season, a record that has some observers proclaiming him the new king of baseball. Tall and wiry, Ruth's wide shoulders convey power even as his body reads grace. Two swings in the on deck circle and he bends over home, tapping the dish with the end of his bat as he takes his stance.

Comiskey Park's faithful take him in, appraise him, and begin to cheer. They exhort Williams to give it all he has, to show the bum from Boston how Chicago feels about him, to take the ball and put it in his ear. Ruth taps the plate twice more as Williams moves into his windup. Perhaps it is because they are used to the crack of Jackson's bat, or perhaps they aren't really ready, but no one in the ball park really inhales sharply when Ruth connects. They greet the sound of his bat meeting the ball with indifference. But not its flight. If Joe Jackson caromed his shots off the walls like cannon fire, Ruth's majestic home run is a rain-maker. It arches higher than the upper deck, rising in slow motion, before it settles down in the last row of the right field bleachers. There a dozen young boys scramble as if one, diving their arms and heads beneath the unoccupied bench where the ball has bounded.

By the time the ball lands Ruth has reached second. His tight-legged trot propels him smoothly, head down, around the base-paths. But as he rounds second on his way to third, something catches his attention, maybe just a handkerchief waving behind third, or the sound of someone calling his name, and he looks up, his face open and bright and takes in the game, the park, the moment.

Foster stands in his seat and watches as Ruth coasts around sec-ond. He takes off his own hat and reaches his hand up to scratch the top of his head. "I'll be damned. Well, I'll be goddamned. Will you look at that, Miss," and Foster points at Ruth, his hat still in his hand, "look at that mister's face. He's a black man. I jus' know it."

Kid can barely peer over the head of the men standing in front of her and by the time she manages to crane her neck for a good look, Ruth has passed third, his back to their perch in the bleachers, and is trotting home. "I just don't know, Mr. Foster. Too hard to see him from here."

But by the time she finishes her sentence Foster is no longer stand-ing next to her.

A moment later the White Sox amble off the field into the home dugout. Williams has retired the next batter on two pitches and slams his glove onto the bench. "He ain't human. I tell you. He's as big and strong as a gorilla."

The game players follow shaking their heads. Ruth's shot has unnerved them — at least temporarily. It surprises them even more to find their owner deep in the shadows of the dugout staring at them. Brim pulled down over his eyes, the remnant of a cigar in the bite of his jaws, Charles Comiskey glares at his team. Gleason, as shocked as anyone, moseys over but the owner waves him away.

"Listen up," Comiskey begins. "I got news for yuz. We was gonna bring in a new player today. But you ruined that. He's gone." And he fixes Risberg right in the eye. "He's gone because you forgot whose team this is. Now you are gonna remember."

Comiskey looks from one player to the next, from Risberg to Jackson, to Williams, to Cicotte, to Gandil, to Freddy McMullen, to Happy Felsch, and finally to Buck Weaver. "Cause I'm gonna remember. I'm gonna remember who crossed me in there and you will pay, believe me. If we don't win the pennant and the Series this season, if that big guy Ruth beats us even one more time, you'll be gone before Christmas. And if you are lucky enough to win, you might get a contract next year. But you can bet your collective asses, the eight of you, you can bet your asses that it won't be the same as the one you weaseled out of me this year.

"That's right. I ain't gonna fine you for insubordination. Nah. That's too easy. I'm gonna make you remember every day next year who owns this team. I'm gonna dock you. And if you don't like it, tough fucking shit."

As Comiskey turns to disappear into the bowels of his ball park he looks down the bench at Eddie Collins and right next to him Ray Schalk still unbuckling his catcher's gear, and smiles.

❧ ❧

Rube Foster finds Pop where he knew he would — back at their old park, taking off his uniform. Pop tells Foster, "Hey. It don' matter, not at all. They like this, these white folks. Promise you stuff. Don't deliver. Happen all the time."

But Foster won't sit still for that. "Damn it Pop, this time they really promised. Signed a fucking contract, didn't they? We was gonna make history, Pop, don't you know. We was gonna change the world."

"Yeah. An' it done change us, didn't it. Can't make no one do what they don't want to do, can you. Not you, not me, not no one. Maybe if this here riot didn't take place, then we'd a had a chance. But I don' think so, not anyhow. I seen it comin'. Move a black man in and the white man gonna squawk. That's just how it is."

Foster sits on the bench next to Lloyd. He holds his head in his hands. It hurts all over again. The headache's mean enough to break his spirit. Sometimes it just won't let him go. When he looks up Pop sees the pain deep in Foster's red eyes.

"Well," Pop speaks softly, "we always got the American Giants, don't we? Maybe its time for taking care of that business. No more foolishness with these white folk. Stay with what we know."

Foster shakes his head as much in sadness as in agreement. "Time to work right here in Bronzeville."

For a moment he and Lloyd face each other silently. The clubhouse sweats deeply from inside its unpainted concrete walls, trickles of water bead down its rough surface, puddling on the floor. Never did have any electric in the room, just a couple of small rectangular windows at eye level that look out on the diamond's worn sod. The heat roasts the two men sitting there in the semi-darkness.

"Tell you what, Pop. You come back with me and we'll make some changes. Got friends in Detroit, Kansas City, Indianapolis. Time we made us up a league of Negro teams. Now the War's over I believe its time to make some real money."

Lloyd looks amused. "Yeah, Rube. An' you can be the commissioner."

In spite of the heat Kid hugs herself, wraps her arms around her shoulders, and shivers. She feels more alone, in the midst of the crowd, than she has ever felt before. It's as if they have all turned into ghosts. Or, perhaps she has become a spirit.

No reason to remain at the game, she realizes suddenly, Foster's gone to find that Pop Lloyd, and Sam, well, Sam just isn't going to return. And even if he does, then what?

Making her way across the bleachers and then up the aisle, Kid finds her way out of the ball park and suddenly onto the street where, in the distance, she sees the elevated train station on 35th Street, its grey-green siding blackened with the remnants of smoke and fire. Back to the lake, she thinks, all I have to do is walk back to the lake...

Sam can't believe that Lloyd has simply run off. In his bones he knows Comiskey has done something. And in his bones he also knows he'll never work for old TA again. He turns on his heels, ready to go back into the ball park, when he sees her strolling down 35th between Indiana and State. Unmistakable, he thinks, unmistakable, in that print dress of hers and that walk. Like she has just gotten off the train from Mississippi. He laughs to himself until he realizes that Kid really has just gotten off the train from Mississippi.

Sam wonders what her life was down there. Wonders what she thought about, where she was going. And remembers that her hand felt like a butterfly when she had touched him. Despite the heat Sam feels cool. Then thinking only about her eyes, he glances at the writer still leaning against Comiskey's concrete wall and begins walking quickly toward the lake.

Out of one eye, his left one, Errol watches Sam take off down the street. Don't want him to think he's being spied on, do I? Good thing — he and his brother Robert had played white so many times that they were regular detectives. Woulda made that Palmer, the head cop in D.C., proud.

Errol can't help this feeling, a gut-wrencher his pop would have called it, a hunch, that the real story lies with this lanky white man amblin' down the street after that gal, like someone filled with a dose of some lovin' spoonful.

One of the things Kid relies on, ever since that old fellow in the Delta had taught her how to play, is her intuition. Doesn't matter where or when, she can feel things before she knows 'em. Walking over on 35th Street she senses that something is about to happen. No matter that her heart already has Sam peeking out, she just feels his presence.

By the time she reaches Michigan Avenue Kid is winded. Must be past 6 o'clock, there ain't a soul on the street. Not a one.

Errol draws almost even with the white man. He hears him breathing with every step. Up ahead the girl slows, as if she senses them approaching. She's swinging her arms sweetly now as she slows. Errol is sure that the two of them know each other, that the story of the Negro ball player is wrapped up in their story.

He takes several hard paces forward and catches Sam just outside his left shoulder, drawing even, finding Sam's face a study in concentration, eyes fixed firmly straight ahead.

"'Scuse me, Mister. You got the time?"

"Well, let me see. I believe its 6 P.M.," Sam says as politely as possible, not wanting to lose pace.

"Sure walks sweet, don't she?"

Sam pumps his arms slightly, moving ahead and turns his neck to the Negro man who has just spoken with him. "Sorry. I'm in a rush. Glad to help you."

"Not so fast, mister. I just wanted to ask you a couple of questions," Errol replies, trying to keep up.

The two are stride for stride now, closing the distance between them and Kid, who glances over her shoulder to discover them barely two paces behind her.

Sam, she thinks. But what is he doing here with that man? Kid cannot read their actions and the two men walk ever more rapidly in her direction. Finally she turns to face them, her slight frame at the apex of their late afternoon shadows.

Kid and Sam both startle, as if they haven't really expected to see each other even as they hoped for it. Instinctively Sam reaches his arm out to touch the girl and Kid raises her hand, palm up, to graze against him.

"Lookit! You can't touch her. Not you white man, not here."

Errol doesn't quite know where his emotion comes from. But he finds it impossible to understand the tableau before him. That they might be lovers is even more inconceivable than what he witnesses.

"You keep your hands off her, mister."

Then, with equal instinct Errol brings his fist up from below his knee and sends it straight up, powerfully up, into Sam's gut. He hears the man exhale, sees his face implode, the blood rising to Sam's eyes, then drawing a red stain down his face, catching on the corner of Sam's mouth and chin. As Sam bends over his attacker's fist, his head down, Errol snaps his knee into Sam's jaw, sending Sam reeling backward, hat flying, jacket open, his face a mixture of blood and shock.

Errol stands over Sam, hands on his hips, fists still clenched, and tries to catch his breath. He looks up to find that Kid is gone.

❧ ❧

"The last train to Clarksdale. Leaves in half an hour. One way or round trip?" Kid Douglas, dressed in green, hefts her guitar case and burlap bag off the floor. "One way, mister. One way."

❧ ❧

Comiskey waves Sam away.

"Just go tell Foster, tell him anything. Tell him that you looked over the contract and that it's no good. Void. You know. Kaput."

The door slams behind Sam, who grabs his gut, wincing in pain where the man had hit him earlier that day. Alone he begins his long walk home, a solitary figure in the moonlight.

❧ ❧

When the White Sox arrived in New York in September for a late season set with the Yankees, they told their cabbies only, "The Ansonia." Set in majesty overlooking Broadway at 77th Street, all the city's sportsmen favored the Ansonia Hotel.

Chick Gandil lowered himself into the leather chair in his room, tossed his shoes into the corner, and picked up the phone.

Even before he heard Gandil, Abe Atell, an ex-pugilist and sometime associate of gambler Sleepy Bill Burns, himself a bag man for none other than Arnold Rothstein, knew what the first baseman had to say.

"Tell your friends," he said, smiling, "the money will be in your room tomorrow night. Eight envelopes. One for each of you."

CODA

In 1925 Andrew Rube Foster, President and Treasurer of the Negro National League, resigned from the organization he had single-handedly founded. He was convinced that his rivals were out to get him, and his headaches and suspicion deepened. The next year, following a nervous breakdown, he entered Kankakee State Asylum where he died in 1930.

Memphis Minnie performed throughout the 1920s in the city where she took her name. She often recorded with Joe McCoy with whom she cut *Bumble Bee* for Columbia Records in 1929. She returned to Chicago in the 1930s and lived on the South Side. There she played and recorded for the next 30 years on a succession of "race" labels before moving back to Memphis, where she died in 1973.

Pop Lloyd, player manager for the Columbus Buckeyes in the Negro National League, eventually retired from baseball and settled in Atlantic City, New Jersey. He lived and worked there for the rest of his life, becoming the city's Little League commissioner. The community named a local ball park Pop Lloyd Field in his honor.

Charles August Risberg passed away at 3 P.M. on October 3, 1975, in Red Bluff, California. He had worked for the International Paper Company for the previous four years. The coroner, one C.R. Milford, entered "congestive heart failure" on Swede's certificate of death.